Pastoral of a Far Land

COPYRIGHT 2020 JOHN ZEPF

Pastoral of a Far Land

A NOVEL BY

JOHN ZEPF

CONTENTS ARE COPYRIGHTED 2020 BY THE AUTHOR.

DEDICATION

This book is dedicated to my parents,

Reinhard and Anna Zepf

and to my family.

PASTORAL OF A FAR LAND

CONTENTS

CHAPTER 1 - OVERTURE: ONE YEAR EARLIER   *1*

CHAPTER 2 - PROLOGUE: THE PRESENT,
AND EIGHTEEN YEARS EARLIER   *22*

CHAPTER 3 - WOMAN IN A CAGE   *30*

CHAPTER 4 - FLIGHT   *39*

CHAPTER 5 - ONE KIND FAVOR AND OTHERS   *53*

CHAPTER 6 - ALMOST HEAVEN   *68*

CHAPTER 7 - THE LONESOME PALACE OF
MEMORY: PART I   *76*

CHAPTER 8 - A CONCERT, AND BEDLAM   *88*

CHAPTER 9 - A WELCOME OF SORTS   *100*

CHAPTER 10 - THE LONESOME PALACE OF
   MEMORY: PART II   *116*

CHAPTER 11 - THE FIGHTER   *125*

CHAPTER 12 - AT A SPRING   *136*

CHAPTER 13 - A CASUALTY OF THE TEKERIN   *142*

CHAPTER 14 - TOWARD THE COLDER
   REGIONS   *156*

CHAPTER 15 - THE LONESOME PALACE OF
   MEMORY: PART III   *160*

CHAPTER 16 - AT AN ARMY CAMP   *168*

CHAPTER 17 - GEMAAL BE WITH YOU   *176*

CHAPTER 18 - THE MOUNTAIN PASS   *188*

CHAPTER 19 - FINALE: APOTHEOSIS   *196*

AUTHOR'S AFTERWORD   *216*

CHAPTER 1 - OVERTURE: ONE YEAR EARLIER

The female had sought concealment near a gnarled and twisted fruit tree, down the slope from a dirt road that passed overhead. There was also, hidden from the road, a large round rock, and the female had stretched out against it and drew warmth from the rays of the sun that was now setting behind a grove of trees. The sound of some approaching wagons on the road above gradually roused her from sleep. There was the sound of the metal-trimmed wooden wheels passing over the uneven and rocky soil, and a primitive instrument that someone was playing among the lumbering wagons, that was local to this region. Without turning, she recalled how the player turned a crank, and pressed on or opened stops to release sounds that were pitched, but which were all more or less guttural in nature, and hardly anything that could be called musical to uninitiated listeners.

This sound, and the tuned bells that were heard everywhere on Ben-Ora, roused the female to a state of alertness, and she turned and peered around the large rock. A small open wagon drawn by a pair of water buffalo approached, followed by a larger covered one with a full team of four or more animals in front. From the rude music that accompanied the travelers, she did not imagine that they were army, or local security forces, either, but from long-ingrained habit she turned and looked into the brush and forest down the slope for any likely pathway should she have need of an escape. But there was no clear prospect of an opening, and hoping that one would not be necessary, she turned and studied the troop of approaching wagons again.

There was a third and final wagon of middle size, a covered one drawn by a pair of draft animals. The female struggled to see what had been painted on the canvas covering the largest central wagon, but the irregular motion of the vehicle upon the road, and the billowing of the canvas from the gentle late afternoon breezes made this difficult. To the sound of creaking wagon wheels, the groaning music-box, and the striking of one or more tuned bells, or metal triangles, resonating from inside the wagons on the road above, the female watched and listened and hoped that the strangers would not stop.

When they had drawn closer she could see, on the canvas of the central wagon, some images and advertisements of a traveling carnival or magic show: the featured performers, and commentary written in the peculiar hieroglyphic used by the Ben-Orans. There was an image of an attractive female whose head only was visible, which rested on a platform, and the legend encouraged the viewer to believe that she had neither torso or limbs. The female knew this to be an old trick played upon a very impressionable race, and she smiled inwardly at the simplicity of it. And there was, nearby, the image of a male whose expression and accompanying legend told that he was a wizard or mystic, or some such thing, but a fraud more than likely.

The caravan of wagons had most definitely come to a stop above her, on a level cutout from the dirt road. Great Gemaal, must they stop just here to make camp? But on reflection, from her redoubt behind the rock and small tree, she was not sure that the strangers' presence was unwelcome, for she sometimes found providence in unexpected circumstances. Perhaps they were not a threat, but her benefactors, rather.

The afternoon was quiet except for the tinkling bells, the

sympathetic murmurs of the music box, and a young woman's voice declaiming and rehearsing a sort of fairground tune.

Very distinctly now, she heard from the open end of a small wagon the voice of the young female ask, "Shall we really play, now it seems we have stopped moving?" The other female studied the roadway, crouched behind her rock and shrubbery.

Inside the wagon was a trio of musicians, who sat upon stools or wooden boxes in a circle. The young female, and a veteran musician who gripped the springy music box between his hands, and a younger male, a percussionist who held at this time a palette of hanging metal bars and a striker in his other hand.

"Play now?" the older musician asked. For answer he made with the groaning music box a kind of braying sound, then looked at the female noncommittally.

"Yes? Shall we play the new song?"

"Alright with me, Miss." He nodded to the other male and swung the music box between his hands, and started a long introduction of a sort while the female listened intently. The percussionist created his bell-like sounds. But somehow the female lost the thread of the music and missed her entry, and the music box bleated uncertainly for a moment and stopped.

"Do you not remember your cue, Miss?"

"And how am I to tell, when you are making noises like a stuck animal?"

"You are not serious, Miss?"

"You know I am not serious. Pray let us start again."

"Alright, then." And he nodded all around and began his introduction again, and the female sang in a clear and crystalline voice.

"The road is long, pray leave your cares behind,
Peace and light will calm the fretful mind.

Our tunes are held but cheap, oh, won't you buy?
Here among the land, the sea and sky."

The female behind the rock was taken by a lilting quality of the melody and listened very closely. She would have liked to approach these buskers, but she dared not. In fact her life on the road in recent months had become one of concealment, flight and loneliness. The musicians had paused. She peered as the wagons were moved forward slightly, and stopped. Only a light breeze billowed slightly the painted images upon the largest wagon-canvas. The female's eyes rested on a third principal image there on the cloth, of a male with a substantial facial scar, a nearly hand-sized patch of burned and darkened flesh that covered most of one side of his face. The subject had a baleful and malevolent look, the face cast down but staring up at the observer, and appearing as though he were plotting some act of evil at the very moment when the painter captured his image. The female's gaze lingered on the face, and then upon the metal shackles that joined the subject's hands, and she lowered her eyes as if she had been stung by a painful memory.

Turning from the crude portrait, and closing her eyes, she flattened her back against the rock. A patch of light from the setting sun through the trees fell upon her face, and it was then, as she turned, that one observed the similarly sized disk of roiled and reddened flesh, nearly as wide as her hand, below her left eye. Here it appeared that the skin had burned or boiled, and then darkened. Although the scarring was very old - she had suffered it while she was yet a girl - it still appeared raw and painful. The female's face appeared intelligent, and attractive except for this deformity, and she appeared to be several years short of what would be reckoned mid-life on her planet.

Feeling somewhat assured of Gemaal's providence - the strangers were clearly not vigilantes, at least, but perhaps only a harmless band of charlatans, rather - and feeling tired from the irregular sleep that she obtained living in the out of doors, she began to doze slightly. She could hear as yet no preparations for cooking or other sounds from the carnival troupe up the hill. Not far from her foot, a mashed piece of fruit lay on the ground, encircled by some buzzing, flying insects. Their appearance and seeming boldness were another sign of the waning of the short temperate season, and a harbinger of the long and blustery cold season to follow. The pale green of the sky had deepened with the appearance of evening, and the sky had a cold and metallic cast, like the green that some metals got with long exposure to the elements. There were strings of dark, purplish clouds, back-lit by the late afternoon light, which obscured at times two of the planet's moons that were already rising. Looking about her, she felt that the loneliness of the waning temperate season was crystallized in the scene.

She had helped herself earlier from the branches of this tree, but thought she could do with something more substantial to eat now - some bit of game, if she had the means of catching it, or else some grains, if she had not recently gone through her supply. It was growing colder in the dusk, and she pulled a dark and rustic cape around her and dozed for a time again.

Then she was pressed against the rock, and trying to see if any had stirred from the wagons. They must, at least, go looking for drinking water at some point. She was not sure if it was the male's voice which she heard first, or the snap of some sticks underfoot, or if it was just his unexpected and improbable presence so very near behind her that caused her to start, and caused the sudden shiver upon her back. But she turned instantly and charged the intruder, tripping up his legs, and then he was flat on his back upon the ground and the point of the knife she had drawn from her cape was pressed against the front of his neck.

"I mean no harm, Miss," the male said, his eyes fixed upon her face and remaining very still with the point of the dagger pressed under his chin.

It was several moments before she acknowledged his remark, withdrawing the knife and standing a small distance apart.

"Then why do you accost me like this? And how come you to be so close to me, and I not hearing you?"

The male rose and brushed some vegetation away from his clothes, seeming not at all put out. "I am sorry if I startled you, Miss."

"I did not see your approach down this hill. You seemed to appear from out of nowhere. Are you a member of that circus or carnival troupe?"

"I am."

"And what do you do?" Brushing some bits of dried leaves from her own clothes.

"Well, I am something of a wizard, Miss, if I may say."

"Indeed. You?"

"Yes, and by reputation too, as you see." He took a couple of steps until he had a clear view, and then held up his arm and pointed to one of the portraits on the wagon. "Can you see me - there, about the center of the canvas? I have a glass you may use, if it is not broken now."

She watched and saw that he withdrew only a short telescope from his coat pocket. "I can see it well enough," she said curtly. "But I am sorry that I threw you down. I did not know your intentions, and you appeared - well, so very suddenly. I would not wonder you are a wizard."

"It is forgotten, Miss. It is I who am sorry, for disturbing you."

She looked at the male, and at his portrait, and back, and said, because he seemed rather proud of it, "It is rather a good likeness, at that." His portrait did not appear central, or quite so prominent, to her, for that honor seemed to belong to others.

"It has faded somewhat over the years. I never thought that it quite did justice to my appearance, in fact."

"No, perhaps not." The female wondered if he were at all likely to offer her any food, and tried her best to be ingratiating after the rough treatment that she had afforded him. In fact she thought that this was the most feral and cunning-looking individual that she had seen in many seasons. But she said nothing to that point.

"Are you friends with the female who seems to lack a body?"

"Oh, I know her, of course. It is not real magic but trickery, frankly."

"So I thought." She pointed. "And that male there, with the shackles about his wrist--"

"He represents one of the Elohin."

"I can see that. Is he also a member of your troupe?"

"Oh, Gemaal no, Miss. That is to say, it is just an actor, with his features, ah, altered. It was a stage play that we performed, you see."

"I have heard that such productions are very popular. I have no doubt it is a very fair-minded and uplifting pageant."

"I could not say that it was, Miss. Particularly. For as I remember he was rather the villain of the piece. But we do not do that anymore."

"Truly?"

He nodded. "May I say, it is a pleasure to speak with one such as you. I hope you do not mind my tarrying?"

"Not at all. I had not spoken to anyone today, or day before either, unless it was to some brute animal. Tell me, if you are a wizard as you say, are you able to cast spells?"

"Spells, Miss? Some say that I can." He looked at her mysteriously. "I might say so."

"Good ones, as well as evil ones?" she continued.

"Perhaps."

"Then would you cast me a spell of good luck? That I might have food in my stomach, and that I might not perish in this cold, now the mild season is passing."

"Yes, it is trouble indeed," the stranger said, eyeing the patch of scar upon her cheek. He thought for a moment. "I will do more for you, Miss. I will treat you to a meal right now."

She considered.

"There" - pointing with his thumb - "in our camp. Why, it is dinnertime, there is a stew of some kind cooking now. Do you not smell it?"

"I - had," she admitted.

"Then nothing could be simpler. You shall be my guest." He strode a couple of steps up the incline of the grassy hill, avoiding the small boulders that were embedded there from among the stony Ben-Oran soil. Reaching his arm back from under a multi-colored cape, he paused and extended his hand to her.

She took his hand willingly, but paused. "I have little doubt about your intentions, friend" - in fact she had many, still - "but, just now, it is dangerous to one like me to be seen-_"

"If you mean because you have been marked, that is not any concern of ours."

Was it possible, she wondered, that he was unaware of the growing hostility of the majority population toward her and her kind? She had even heard that bounties were being offered for their apprehension, and that camps, or prisons, were even now being constructed for the purpose of isolating them. Some said that it was a government objective of many years' standing. Did these rootless individuals not hear and learn as much, in speaking to villagers during their constant travels?

"We do not believe," he continued, "such ninny's tales as that you and your kind have been marked by Gemaal for your transgressions."

"That is well. And yet I daresay you cannot speak for all of your performing artists. Even among such an exalted group--"

"Who? That rabble, do you mean?"

"I mean, it is likely that some others are not as large-minded as you are." And she stared at him, trying to gauge his sincerity.

"Let them go hang! But if you are loathe to meet them - and I could not say that I would blame you, really - you may sup in my wagon - that last one, there."

"That is truly your own space?" she asked, admiration appearing in her eyes.

"It is - mostly. If any are there now they will clear out soon enough. I scare 'em away when I receive guests. They are afraid of me, you see, because they know that I can cast a spell upon them. Or at least," he added modestly, "they believe that I can."

"Your offer is very kind, for I could very much do with a meal."

"Then, please, join me," he said again, starting up the slope and extending his hand back for her to grasp - which she did, but only briefly. Dusk had already fallen. He watched as she unwound a dark shawl from out of her travel satchel and covered the sides of her face with it.

The female heard him rousting someone or other from out of the smaller covered wagon, and she stood off to the side and turned her face partly away. When the wagon was emptied, except for the wizard, she looked about and, taking his hand that was extended to her she then climbed a crude attached ladder and stepped into the cabin.

A thrill seemed to pass through her as she looked about the commodious room on wheels, with its neat and simple furniture, and some artifacts, including colorful theatrical masks, hanging upon the vertical wooden supports of the walls.

"How very comfortable is your dwelling-place!" she exclaimed. "May I?" And she sat comfortably on a settee that was wide enough for two, and looked around her with a happy expression. "Oh, I should never want to leave it!"

The wizard looked pleased. "It is a humble abode, Miss. Perhaps it is only your recent experiences that may make it appear grand."

Her enthusiasm only slightly dimmed, "Nevertheless, if I were you I should cast any number of spells, every day if necessary, in order to keep the others away."

"Gemaal knows, you have spirit, Miss." The wizard pronounced the name of their planet's ruling deity with the usual hard "g." He pulled a cloth canvas across the rear of the cabin, against the evening breeze. "May I ask, are circumstances so dire at home, that you are compelled to tramp about in this fashion?"

"I do not have a home as such, that I might return to."

"Really, now. Well. Relax, and I will return very shortly with your meal," he said. He arranged a small table with a cloth over it next to the settee. Gesturing, "This serves as my dining table, ordinarily. Do you like spirits, Miss?"

"I should prefer some plain water or tea."

He pulled open the canvas and clambered down the few steps, and the female returned his smile. But when he had left, her expression grew serious, and she preferred to stand at the edge of the wagon and look about her discreetly.

"It is very lonely traveling like this," he said, after he had returned with a beaten metal tray holding the stew and drink. He set these before her on the small wooden table.

"You - lonely?" she said. "I doubt it is true. Since you are a wizard, I have no doubt that you are able to conjure any number of local females here for your companionship, in your dwelling-place on wheels. Am I right?"

"From your pretty mouth straight to Gemaal's ear, Miss."

She nodded at his gallantry. "Would that it were so easy."

"If it is sympathy you want--"

"No, Miss."

He had pulled a rickety chair up opposite her. "But it is a pleasure to hear you, Miss. When one is surrounded by roustabouts such as I am, it is indeed pleasant to enjoy some polite society. I have not had a deal of schooling myself. But you seem rather well educated, if I may say."

"I am not so very educated," she said. "There are circumstances that I cannot explain quickly."

"Well, I can rather imagine them," he sighed. "How did you come to be so close to the danger, if you do not mind my asking about it?" The female continued eating, and he added, "If you do not wish to answer, I meant no offense. It is just that I meet really very few of your kind."

She found that he was staring at the patch of scar upon her face. For his part, he was thinking that the scar, which was nearly half the size of her hand, appeared as raw and painful-looking as if the injury had been received only the day before.

"It was not my parents' wish that I found myself so close to the danger, as you say. I believe that I was trying to find them, and I was rather sure that they were at the scene of the conflict. But it was not only to find them, that I went. I remember feeling with joy, as young as I was, that the invaders might soon be ousted, after causing so much suffering. I managed to escape from my caretakers, and made my way--"

"And what do you remember of the scene?"

"I remember a fiery red and yellow ball of flame in the sky. That, most distinctly. And then the mass of individuals fleeing."

"It is so long ago now."

"Yes." Her eyes had gone out of focus at the memory, and then she came to herself.

"Is our poor country fare adequate?" he asked.

"It is more than adequate, wizard. It is all in all the best meal that I have enjoyed in weeks."

"And the company, Miss?"

"Again, quite wonderful."

The wizard moved and sat next to her on the settee, to her left, while she continued to eat, and to drink from the battered metal cup filled with warm tea. He kept up a steady stream of talk, and at first she did not mind the hand that rested familiarly, in a sort of friendly fashion, upon her shoulder.

"We ourselves live in a kind of continuous persecution from the law, you know." The female did not say anything, only seemed to eat and drink with quicker purpose, and he added, "I don't say that it is anything like what one like yourself must endure. But whenever some calumny is spoken against our troupe - say, that our games of chance are less than fair--"

"Do some say that?" she asked , mock innocently.

"Of course they do," he said emphatically. "If just one complain that our entertainments are not as advertised, or that we have rather deceived the public, then there is such a to-do, and the manager must offer restitution, or a bribe, or we must pack our tents and leave, just as we have become comfortable in a place."

"It really does not seem fair," the female said, trying to ignore the hand that strayed from the tunic on her shoulder, to rest rather warmly and insinuatingly upon her neck.

"Do you know, sir" - shaking her upper body and freeing herself, temporarily from his restless hands - "I am really most grateful for this meal you have provided me." The meal was nearly finished now, and she felt rather full. "You have been very kind. I do not wish for any unpleasantness to spoil our meeting. I should like to remain your friend, as I am not unaware of the kindness you have shown me. If it is payment that you would like, I have a small quantity of silver - how very little, you may judge."

"I do not want your silver, Miss. I want to be your friend, too." And she could feel his hand now clutching at her leg under the small table. She pushed the table slightly away from her and her hand closed over his. The wizard's expression changed as she began to bend his fingers back and to lift the offending hand well above the table. He turned his body and with his other hand he attempted ineffectually to reach for her neck, but she clasped that hand as well and bent the fingers of his other hand still more sharply.

"O-ww-ww," he complained.

"Will you stop now, please?"

"Yes, yes." Tears had sprung to his eyes.

In another moment she released his hands and said, "May I finish my meal now?" He nodded. "And let us remain friends."

"That we shall," he said contritely, moving a bit away from her on the settee.

When she had finished her meal he offered to bring her more, but she told him that she was quite full.

"Not even some berries?" The dish that he referred to, some local red berries with a somewhat acrid dressing, were a common dessert among the entire population. "Will you not stay here and rest, then?"

"I cannot. I have already placed myself at considerably more risk than is prudent. Oh, I do not mean from you, wizard - do not think so - but possibly from your fellow-artists, if they are really the scurvy lot that you say."

"Then perhaps you would like to wash, before you leave. There is a washroom, just there." And he pointed to a small curtained room to the side.

"You mean you would not mind? For I should really love to, before I go."

"Then you shall, Miss. It is no trouble at all."

In the little room, above a hammered metal wash basin, there was a small metal tank or reservoir, of a type the female remembered from other homes, years ago, with a sliding valve to let out the coolish water. And there was soap, and a towel and washcloth. She hung her cape on a peg on the wall, and her rough short tunic on another one. She could have wished that the room offered more privacy than the beaded curtain that swung to and fro when she had entered - especially as the wizard sat only five feet from the doorway, speaking to her convivially but in a chattering fashion.

She held her hands in front of her modestly and said, "You might sit in a different chair."

"I might," he said, "but I would not be so comfortable."

"Well, it is your house." The washcloth felt slightly cold under her arms. The wizard's expression was a mixture of lust and kindliness. She thought, on balance, that if the washroom had had a door, she would worry that at any moment the wizard might bolt from the trailer and hatch some scheme with his confederates (no more than that did she trust him), and that it was preferable to have a clear view of the rascal. Even if his stare was a bit familiar and insolent, she did not greatly mind. She loosened the strings of her breeches and lowered them, but was reluctant in the circumstances to step quite out of them.

"You are right fit, Miss. I suppose that you do a great deal of walking in the country." She did not say anything to his remarks, which seemed to flow out of the not unpleasant agitation of his mind at the female's presence here.

"You might, at least, turn your chair," she said. He did so in a moment, grudgingly, but continued to steal glances at her from time to time when she did not notice, or appeared not to.

"I don't mean to pry. But was there some difficulty at home, Miss - and was it really so much worse than living out in the open like this?"

When she had tied up the breeches again, she looked at his back from her side of the beaded curtain, rubbing the washcloth, which smelled pleasantly of citrus, about her neck. "It is not quite like that. I really do not have any home just at present, but wander as I like, and as I must."

"And do you really have no fixed home?" He pondered. "My, you are a vagabond like me. And such spirit! Do you know, Miss" - rising from his chair, and then swiftly averting his eyes - "you shall have one of my short tunics. You are nearly my size, and it will fit you admirably." He searched in a trunk on the floor and brought out a white shirt of a coarse fabric. "You see?"

"It is most kind of you."

He stood close to the curtain. The female extended one arm, the other being across her chest, and when she accepted the shirt the wizard's hand pressed upon hers warmly until she pulled her hand away.

When she had dressed and put on the shirt she emerged from the washroom, and did a turn about the cabin so that the wizard could see the fit of the shirt. She fastened the cape loosely about her shoulders.

"Must you really leave tonight?"

"I am doubly and now triply grateful to you, wizard, but I must."

"I wish you could stay."

"There is nothing for me here."

"Will you return to your little shelter by the fruit tree?"

"No, do not even look for me there, wizard. I must be away."

"Bring some food with you." And he reached into a burlap bag and removed some nuts which he placed on a shelf, and placed the remainder and the satchel in her hand.

"Are you certain?"

"Oh, these are very plentiful in the hills hereabout. We have plenty."

"Thank you for all your kindness. And do remember to cast one of your best spells of good luck for me - for I shall need it."

As little as she believed in spells - she trusted, rather, in the providence of Gemaal - her expression of confidence in the wizard's powers were part of the meager store of thanks that she could offer him. Wary of his embrace, she only clasped his hands and bowed slightly from the waist in the ordinary formal manner, and climbing out of the wagon she turned and waved, and made her way along the road.

The night sky was clear and filled with stars, and the two of Ben-Ora's moons that were visible cast a pretty yellow ribbon of light upon the wagon-road ahead. She preferred to walk upon the public road, rather than any forest path where she might disturb the lair of some wild animal. No one passed on foot or in animal-drawn cart, either, and she imagined herself in a rather desolate area.

With little to divert her except the moons and the myriad stars, the female began to think back to the first small school that she had attended so long ago. It was only a couple of short cycles of the seasons following the catastrophe, when it had become apparent that the scars upon her face - rather like those on her parents' faces, and her brother's - were not going to go away. In fact they had hardly faded at all, since her first shocked discovery of her injuries, when she and thousands of others had raced with their burning skin to the water of the nearby shores or inlet. The waters became a chaotic city of refuge which would soothe, but not, however, undo the lesions which the night's explosion had caused. This would be apparent to her, and the others, when the morning came, and she saw with shock her reflection in the water.

But her mind passed quickly from the scene of chaos to one particular school day, which was notable for a trip which the instructor had planned for her small class. She was the only one of her "kind" - this was the common expression, which she had also learned to adopt - in the class. Against her kind, who were so conspicuously marked, there was an implacable hostility exerted by nearly all of the majority population. The causes of this hostility were complex. It was altogether a confusing time for her, especially as, until the catastrophe, she had counted some of the same Ben-Orans who now shunned her among her friends. In time she would begin to associate almost only with her kind who were marked in more or less the same way.

On the day that she was thinking of, the small class of ten or twelve female students were transported in a wagon. It must have been seeing the procession of carnival wagons that brought the scene to her mind, in fact. But the weather was warmer then, the passing fields and trees were verdant with the beginning of the short growing season, and the wagon had no canvas cover that day. On the wagon were sufficient metal seats for the passengers, fastened to the wooden floor, and two and two across, separated by an aisle, with a driver in a separate box at the front, and a team of four or more draft animals (she forgot how many) drawing them slowly along the dirt road. The day was clear and the sky was the clement pale green of good weather on Ben-Ora.

The students, with their female teacher, were to visit a candy-maker in the adjacent town. The woman, or girl as she was then, was nearly late arriving at the schoolhouse, owing to some confusion at home, and the teacher directed her immediately to the wagon. The seats were nearly filled. The babel of voices from her schoolmates ceased when she appeared at the front in the central aisle. She saw that there was no row that was not at least partly occupied. When she had moved forward a few feet she found that any heretofore empty seat would be abruptly covered with a school satchel, or that one of the seated students would turn in her seat, ostensibly to speak with some classmate, and effectively taking up the other seat with an elbow or a knee.

The girl stood there in some confusion, and turned back and saw that that the instructor herself had climbed the few wooden steps and stood at the front and looked over the students with a stern expression. She walked toward the girl, who could see how the students next the empty seats now shifted their positions, or made tentative moves to lift their satchels to their laps. But the girl stood frozen as these spaces were however grudgingly and tentatively offered. Then the teacher put her hand on the girl's shoulder, and calling her by name, asked, "Will you sit with me?" And wordlessly, gratefully, the girl slid into the inside seat in front, and the teacher, with another look at the students, and an admonition for them to remain in their seats during the trip, took the aisle seat next to the girl.

The candy maker was a plain-spoken and jolly-seeming female who demonstrated her craft very cheerfully: the cabinet of sweeteners, and dried fruits for flavoring, and gums that made licorice-like strings of candy. Some work was in progress then, which she told the students they would sample if they remained patient.

"It is a splendid day to be out," the woman said to the teacher. "I did not see you all of the cold season. Is all well?"

"Very well. It is so difficult getting about, you know, the snows being severe as usual."

"And do you have a bright crop of students this year?"

"Tolerably so," the instructor said shortly. The attention of the students turned from the teacher to the smells of the warm candy that was being fashioned in a kind of mold within an oven. The proprietress brought the trays out and let them cool.

"Come forward then," she announced in a moment. "There is plenty for everyone."

The students all went up in turn. The proprietress would pull a length of the confection from off of the counter, and form a loop of the string candy that she cinched at the middle, and wrap it adroitly in a sheet of crackling paper, and hand it to the student. The first to receive the candy remembered to thank her, and the others followed, so that, a surprise for the teacher, she did not have to admonish her students on this point.

When the girl got up to the shop owner, the latter spoke rather more volubly than she had before. She held the girl's chin between thumb and forefinger, turning her face this way and that, and turning her head to change her own perspective. "Have you any brothers or sisters?" she asked her.

"One brother, Ma'am."

Turning her face again. "And does your brother look like you?" she asked artlessly.

A faint snicker was heard from among the crowd of girls, which was quickly suppressed when it was not seconded by any of the other students. The sound discomfited the blunt-speaking shop-owner, who meant no harm. The instructor's eyes searched the silent group to find who had made the sound.

The girl felt a warm flush in her face. In the silence, she asked in a small voice, "How do you mean, Ma'am?"

"Why, only" - turning the small face again with her thumb and finger - "is he handsome like you are?"

"Well, then, I suppose that he is, Ma'am."

"Splendid! And you shall have - two strings!" she announced magisterially. She formed the candies in loops cinched at the middle, as deftly as before, and wrapped them in the crisp paper and handed them in one package to the girl, who thanked her and smiled.

"And will you be sure to save one of the pieces for your brother?"

"I shall try to, Ma'am."

"Splendid indeed! We may only try."

The eyes of the other girls had widened at the unexpected display of generosity, and then narrowed resentfully because they had not received any extra candy themselves.

It was after they had filed back to the wagon, some of them already eating their candy, and the girl was seated as before, that one of the other students stood, as the instructor entered the wagon. She asked if she could speak.

"Alright."

"Ma'am, we have discussed, and we do not think it is fair that she has been given two strings."

"I see. This is the considered opinion of all of you?"

"Y-yes," the spokesperson said, seeming a little confused by the instructor's choice of words.

"But why not fair?" the instructor asked. The girl on her seat in front turned and stared at the girl who had spoken, an anger rising in her.

"Well," the girl answered, "we have traveled just as far as her. And some of us have as many and more brothers and sisters."

"H'm'm. I shall have to consider." The instructor stared up into the sky with a deliberating expression. The girl's gaze shifted from the one who had spoken, to what she could see of the teacher. She clutched the package of candy on her lap, and was on the point of shouting that the suggestion was not right, when the teacher spoke.

"I have given the matter careful thought, and my decision is - I cannot agree with you." When she heard this, a small thrill of triumph passed through the girl, and she relaxed her grip upon the package in her lap.

"Because, most importantly, it was our host's wish and expectation that the extra string be distributed according to her wishes. Therefore it would be wrong to do otherwise. Let us start, then." And she gestured to the few standing students to take their seats.

The woman remembered how, during the slow and bumpy ride, some tears fell upon the crisp parchment-like paper that wrapped the candies, which - perhaps alone among her schoolmates - she did not open until she arrived at home. Her tears were not so much due to the cruelty of her fellow students - hardly at all, really, because she had become nearly inured to their manner toward her - as they were to gratitude for the acts of kindness that were shown to her that day. And on balance she remembered feeling an unusual degree of happiness, as the wagon bumped along the dirt road back to their village. There were instances of kindness on Ben-Ora, even if they were rare, and had perhaps become increasingly so.

Daylight was beginning to form, and the female thought it wise to be off the road and away from passersby. She followed a path into the forest, and coming upon a clearing, she spread her bedroll and, exhausted, fell down to sleep for a long while.

CHAPTER 2 - PROLOGUE: THE PRESENT, AND EIGHTEEN YEARS EARLIER

When the spaceships began appearing in the skies above Ben-Ora again, after so many years, it revived painful memories among the inhabitants of the recent colonization of their planet. The invaders had arrived only about eighteen cycles of the seasons ago, hardly more than a quarter of a lifetime. They were representatives of what were clearly a very advanced species, who were intent upon exploiting the planet's mineral resources. They also required the inhabitants to work at forced labor in mines deep in the soil, and in processing centers and conveyor systems which were established on Ben-Ora's vast and pristine seashores, where the coveted minerals were extracted from out of the sea water.
The Ben-Orans were not nearly so advanced technologically. They had as yet no means of exploring the skies, but knew of their universe only what was visible to them, and lived a mostly agrarian existence. Here and there, a few small cities had sprung up. The rudiments of industrial production were in place on Ben-Ora, and the inhabitants had crafted, among other things, some crude firearms in their own fashion. There was no rail transportation in place; movement was primarily by cart or carriage pulled along by a strong, sluggish farm animal. The Ben-Orans drew a harsh existence from the planet's stony soil and rigorous climate. They defined only two seasons: a shorter, temperate growing season, and one that was cold and often blustery. Cloth or

leather capes, long or short, and of a heft appropriate to the season, and caps or bonnets were the usual dress.

The deadly force of the invading species was something unprecedented to the Ben-Orans, and of a different order than anything they had experienced. The invaders had on many occasions demonstrated their destructive powers by their obliteration of a small tree by fire, as an example, or of some innocent animal. And Ben-Orans themselves had been killed, when on rare occasions their discontent under the occupiers flared into anything like revolt. While the invaders remained, there was in fact little interaction between them and the planet's inhabitants. This was so because the invaders had somehow turned the minds of a sufficient group of Ben-Orans, who displayed, afterwards, no kind of fellow-feeling for their own species, and serving as guards and caretakers of the invaders' enterprise, would ruthlessly crush any show of disobedience. The unfortunate individuals who were selected as guards, following the eventual liberation, were thought to suffer from a long term mental debility, from whatever the invaders had done to their minds; an inability to adapt to changed circumstances, which would prove fatal to their long term survival.

Communication between the inhabitants and invaders was limited for another reason. When there was any interaction between the two species, the Ben-Orans seemed to recall it but dimly, as through a fog - unsure, very often, if any words in their own language had been exchanged. What they knew for certain is that the will of the invaders had been conveyed, and this was sufficient. Although the invaders were frailer, and unlike the Ben-Orans, hardly human in appearance, the Ben-Orans' fear of them was very real, and was based upon something more than the small, deadly side-arms which the invaders carried. The pain which these weapons caused was likened by the Ben-Orans to the rays from their sun, but many times magnified.

The invaders' forces, which were never very large after their initial appearance, were rotated on and off the planet at intervals, and this would be announced by the fearsome and mysterious arrival of a ship, a troop transport, from out of the skies. The ore, or refined materials that were being extracted from Ben-Ora's soil or seas were conveyed to another kind of transport ship, and these were regularly borne up into the skies. The Ben-Orans would watch in wonder.

Sometimes, the glint of an approaching spacecraft could be seen high up in the sky, if the weather was clear. Or before this, or after, the inhabitants would hear the propulsive rattling of a craft as it hurtled into the Ben-Oran atmosphere, as though in continuous collision with the surrounding air, and setting off booms that rattled the wits of the inhabitants who heard them. Sometimes, what appeared to the inhabitants to be a large and trailing plume of steam escaped from the crafts, slowly diffusing into the air as the outline of the ships themselves grew more distinct.

Some of the Ben-Orans - entire families, or perhaps only the relatively young and able-bodied - fled to the deeply forested woods at these times, if there was opportunity; for the invaders had also begun to conscript numbers of the inhabitants, forcing some aboard the ships and bringing them to their home planet. And whether they were to become prisoner-hostages, or slave laborers as they were on Ben-Ora, was little difference, for few had any hope of their return, or for their safety. This tribute of living citizens, now added to the other indignities suffered by the Ben-Orans, was, the Governor said, the price of peace with the ruthless invaders. Thus, the arrival of a ship invariably brought new terror and consternation to the Ben-Orans, and so many of them fled, if there was sufficient warning.

While the invaders were small in number, in the circumstances the Ben-Orans had little choice but to submit to the wholesale disruption of their former lives, to work without pay or public complaint, while they waited and hoped that the obscure, flinty minerals that were coveted by the invaders would soon be depleted, or that, satisfied with their plunder, the invaders would depart and leave the Ben-Orans at peace again. They would have their wish. The occupation in fact lasted for a span of a few years, and it ended explosively in circumstances that were variously remembered by the witnesses, or else were subject to the wildest conjectures by those who did not witness the conflagration.

The true circumstances of the arrival of the strangers, their occupation of one corner of the planet, and their eventual expulsion, were all shrouded in misunderstandings, rote thinking, and outright falsehoods. The natives of Ben-Ora were not a highly sophisticated race. They held to some notions of history, and of destiny, but were weak in comparative analysis, and in the present time had produced little recorded history, either of their own or any previous era. What most of the inhabitants agreed upon was that a group of the Ben-Orans, driven beyond endurance by their forced labor deep in the soil, or among the industrial plants and conveyor tracks on the seashore - where in happier times they swam or relaxed during the brief temperate seasons - carried out a violent revolt against their persecutors. That this group so harried the invaders, with spears and other such primitive weaponry, that the invaders repaired to their vast mother ship, and that when the Ben-Orans began harassing the underside of the great grounded ship itself with javelins, the commander of the invaders attempted a precipitate, and as it happened ill-advised departure until such time as some order could be restored, or a counter-attack devised.

The lift-off in these circumstances proved catastrophic. The Ben-Orans fled when with a burst of noise and heat the great ship suddenly and slowly lifted into the air. The ship seemed to totter slightly and rose to a height of about a hundred feet. Some of the Ben-Orans, forgetting momentarily that some of their burned and wounded lay on the ground, began to cheer spontaneously. And then the unthinkable happened: the great, impregnable mother ship of the invaders suddenly exploded in a fireball, and then the Ben-Orans began to run in all directions, as a firestorm of fuel and molten metal, and they knew not what, fell out of the skies. The Ben-Orans who had exulted a moment earlier now cast backward, astonished glances into the burning skies, and fled for their lives.

The terrible effects of the explosion began to be apparent, in the burning skin which caused most of the victims to rush to the nearby shore to splash water on their faces, or their arms or other exposed skin, but they would be revealed more completely in the peaceful light of day. And after the burns had healed, many of these Ben-Orans saw the characteristic marks, usually on the face, but sometimes on exposed arms or shoulders as well, where the skin appeared to have melted and re-formed itself, and where the flesh, in certain lights, appeared to glow red as if from within, as though from the embers of the mixed irritants that had rained down from the explosion that night.

And then something even more astonishing happened to these souls who were in the forefront of the revolt. Soon a harsh and very critical light was shined upon this minority of Ben-Orans whom destiny had so conspicuously marked. The mistrust, which in the course of time would often flare into openly expressed hatred, grew amid the recriminations and resentments which followed the ouster of the invaders; this feeling often seemed to grip the majority of Ben-Orans more than that of joy or relief at their release from bondage, for in fact the feeling of euphoria that at first followed their liberation was short-lived. It was a development which could only have its origin in the psychology of this alien race. And the scapegoating of the wounded and afflicted group of Ben-Orans, which followed so swiftly after the initial exulting at their restored freedom, may have been artificially encouraged by some of the nominal rulers of the region. There was a persistent rumor, for example, that at the time of the invaders' arrival many thousands of pieces of silver were secretly conveyed to the acting Governor of the region, in exchange for his facilitating their designs, and that as a diversion the Governor had helped to instigate the calumny upon a group which had already suffered disproportionately.

So it happened that in time, the popular perception became that all of the individuals who were so marked by their proximity to the fireball, far from being in the vanguard of a popular revolt, were in fact guilty of the vilest treachery, being collaborators with the hated enemy. Support for this popular belief seem to stem from only one piece of conjecture, namely that the proximity of these individuals to the enemy at this decisive time was proof of their perfidy. This circumstance, and the machinations of local authorities, were responsible for impressing this harmful chimera upon the perhaps overly impressionable minds of the Ben-Orans at this stage in their development.

But the true origin of these suppositions, which had become all but fact, were difficult to unravel after the span of many seasons and yearly cycles on the planet. Some did try to sort out the truth, in speech, or in the nascent leaflets or newspapers which were then starting to be printed. But it was perilous to suggest that the persecution of these souls was not something ordained by common sense, by government, and by nothing less than the great Gemaal himself, the deity who reigned sovereign in the minds of almost all Ben-Orans. After repetition, and habits of familiarity, had ascertained the guilt of this aggrieved minority in the popular mind, thereafter very little questioning occurred. The practical results of these opinions and perceptions were unprovoked and sometimes brutal attacks upon a group which could not hide its differentness, and who found few supporters among the populace or the organs of public policy, such as they were then constituted. The harmful impression had been formed, and it was unshakeable.

Verbal slights, and signs of subtle prejudice evolved over time into more or less systematic persecution of these individuals, whose faces, many said, were marked with the judgment of Gemaal himself. Provincial leaders found a ready audience when their speeches turned to invective against the minority whom the Ben-Orans called, in their own tongue, the Elohin. The term may be translated as "the marked ones," or perhaps more literally, the "hated of Gemaal," as it denoted both of these things among the majority population. Periodically, after the expulsion of the invaders from Ben-Ora, there were calls for the rounding up of the Elohin, and for their incarceration in what were little more than prisons. And it was at this time, about eighteen short years after the decisive event, eighteen cycles of seasons on Ben-Ora, that some claimed to see the spaceships - only infrequently at first - in the skies which by the light of day normally appeared a vast, pale green desert.

There was for example the young boy who climbed a small hill outside of his village, having gone there to dream away an afternoon and play with his small armies of crudely fashioned metal soldiers. The story that he tried to tell to his incredulous family, in his own fashion, was that a vast shadow of a hovering, circular spaceship moved over the hill, and that when the shadow passed over it caused the small toy warriors that he moved with his fingers to suddenly stand still and fall, while he turned and stared up at the sky. In a short time, similar stories were told, sometimes by witnesses who were considered more reliable and less imaginative than a small boy. Many Ben-Orans were fearful that the ships heralded a return of their former persecutors. They became proportionately more distrustful of the minority, and many were filled with rage, certain that the Elohin, their supposed collaborators, were once again in league with the hateful invaders. The drive to identify and incarcerate the marked ones loomed as a dire necessity in the minds of the majority of Ben-Orans.

It was a season of change. Something new was in the air, a strange spirit had overtaken the minds of the inhabitants.

CHAPTER 3 - WOMAN IN A CAGE

Two females were being led in chains along a dirt road that was lined by tall trees. A half-dozen males accompanied them, some carrying firearms. The younger one looked more girl than grown woman, and the other appeared several years older. The group stopped at a small stone building and waited, and then the women were led to an attached outbuilding, or rather cell, for it was a substantial metal cage which was exposed to the elements. The male who had entered the stone building used a key to open the door to the cell. The hands of both of the women were joined together in front of them by links of chain.

The man who seemed to be in charge grabbed the more mature woman roughly by her collar, so that she, and the younger woman behind her paused at the entrance to the cell. The younger woman averted her eyes and was plainly frightened, but the other one was stone-faced, showing no fear. She saw no means of escape, not now, and only wished the minutes to pass without incident. One of the men held a candle lantern up to the younger woman's face, and she struggled to turn her head away until one of the men grabbed her hair. There was a large red patch upon her cheek. In the light of the raised lantern it looked almost as if the girl's mottled skin glowed there from within, as though enclosing hot embers.

The man brought the lantern still closer to her face,

while the girl whimpered soundlessly. "That's a pretty one," he mocked, and turned and looked at the other males.

The other female, who had remained silent, looking on coldly, said, "Leave her alone." A male behind her immediately struck her on the shoulder with the base of a weapon which looked like a primitive rifle, and she staggered and turned. The villager only leered, and feinted another blow with the rifle, but the woman didn't flinch.

There was an ugly blue-ink tattoo about his greasy fat neck, which identified him as a member of some wretched clan, or group of ruffians; obviously an inveterate hater of all who were different from his kind, where his kind was identified in the narrowest possible way.

"That's enough," the male who appeared to be in charge said. Then he drew up to the older female and said, "Here you will stay and make no trouble." He pointed to the cell door, but as the woman turned, he landed a blow with his fist to the woman's lower back. It happened so quickly that the younger woman would not even have had time to shout a warning.

The woman gasped, and fell forward, then turned to look into the face of the man who had just struck her. So help me I will remember this, she thought, and spit on the ground.

The men only whooped, with an odd, animalistic sound, the younger girl was pushed roughly into the cell, and the door was slammed behind them.

When they had gone, the woman looked at the girl briefly and said, "Try to get some rest." Then she reached and pulled the short black cape that she wore more firmly about her shoulders, and curled up on the ground on the side of her body that didn't hurt.

When she awoke in the chilly early morning, she heard the sound of the jailer walking across the yard, and she rose to a sitting position. At a glance, it was the old gallant who'd punched her in the back on her arrival at his prison farm. It was the jaunty, jangling sound of the crude skeleton keys on his belt that first woke her; she made a mental note of their location. The jailer was bringing food and drink, and she stood up and stretched.

"Be your most charming," she said to the other female, who only continued to stare ahead apprehensively. Her own face she made into a blank mask, in spite of the contempt that she felt, which was very like hatred.

The jailer drew up and placed the tray of food on a small table, which seemed to have been left out there for the purpose.

"I have brought food and drink," he announced, "but first there is something I should like to know." He addressed his comments to the older woman, who stood at the door with its central, rectangular slot and small ledge. The other woman stood to the side deferentially.

"Miss - I will come right out with it - what do you know about the ships?"

"The ships."

"Yes - up there." He gestured with his thumb. Two of Ben-Ora's seven moons could be seen faintly in the early morning sky.

"I don't know anything about them."

"Really, Miss."

"I only hear rumors, like some others."

"Do you believe them?"

"I have no idea."

The woman could see the disappointment in the jailer's face, and she looked longingly at the food outside on the table.

"They say that they are coming back again. And that they will force us to work in their mines again, like before. Do you know if it is true, Miss? The people are very worried I'm sure."

"I am sorry if the people are worried," she said. She

hadn't quite managed to keep the sarcasm out of her voice, and she chided herself for her recklessness, staring rather obviously again at the food outside.

"If it is true, won't you tell me?"

"I tell you I know nothing about it." His obtuseness was maddening.

"Are you a leader of your kind? Some have said you are."

"A leader of my kind? Oh, hardly. You give me too much credit."

"H'm'm. I am not convinced, however. When word is out, there will be gawkers here in my yard tomorrow."

"How distressful for you."

"Yes." Failing to see any irony in her remark. She did not say how much she herself detested the idea of villagers gawking at her.

"Well," the jailer continued. "These are very uncertain times. No one knows what to think. Do you know, you are safer in my jail than you would be out there, just now."

She thought a moment. "Still, I think I would prefer to take my chances out there."

"I am sure you would, Miss. And would you harm me, to win your freedom?"

The woman only looked at him. A slight smile appeared on her face. "I only say, I know how to look out for myself. I have learned to."

"I am sure you have, Miss. And I believe it is a shame, I'm sure. But I have my orders to hold you here until the Governor arrives."

The jailer turned and started walking away. The female was about to say something, and then he turned back as though remembering. "Oh, yes. The food," he said, standing off from the cell and placing the tray on the ledge in the slot. "You - he nodded to the younger female - you will be moved this morning."

The older female spent a long afternoon alone in her cell, trying to think of nothing at all. The temperate season was passing, falling leaves drifted into the open bower of her jail cell, and for warmth she paced up and down the length of the enclosure. She rather missed the other woman, or girl, though she had been frightened and not very articulate. She was probably bound for an internment camp, and who knew if she might be safe there. The woman hoped so.

For herself there was an outside chance for escape. If an opportunity arose she could only hope to improvise a solution, based upon a few scenarios that had played out in her mind. Just as she had on other occasions. She never understood, until she experienced these recent years of hiding and resistance, how resourceful she could be. But escape had to happen soon, or there was no chance. The Governor and his force would arrive within days, most likely. And after that, for her, prison - or execution, if the authorities thought that she was important enough, or dangerous enough.

It was dusk when the jailer arrived bringing the evening meal, of some baked grains and a kind of tea. She accepted the tray but immediately placed it on the floor of the cell.

"Why don't you stay and talk to me," she said. "Do you know what they will do to me?"

"I am sure I do not know, Miss."

"But you know a great many things, jailer." How simple he is, she thought.

"That is doubtless, true, Miss. But I cannot tell them all to you."

"No, I suppose you cannot. It is very lonely out here by myself."

"I have no doubt, Miss, and I am sorry for you. But we are all responsible for our actions. And you - you are no ordinary marked one, from what I have heard."

"Who do they say that I am, jailer? And what do they think that I have done, that I must be treated like one outcast, and kept here like an animal in a cage?"

"Oh, I am sure I do not know, Miss. But you know what they say about - well, all of your kind."

"No - what do they say?" she asked, an innocent expression on her face.

"I am sure I do not have to tell you, Miss. It is that you are guilty of a very great betrayal. And that you have been marked by Gemaal--"

"I?"

"There, upon your face."

"This, do you mean?" And she pointed to the roiled, reddened disk of flesh below her left eye, which was the width of a few fingers in diameter. As she pointed, the manacles around her wrists jangled with a sound that was strangely beguiling to the jailer, like a plaintive and solemn music that she fashioned from her captivity.

The Ben-Oran moons were rising, and cast a glow upon her face, which was pale except for the area of the wound. "Then if this displeases you," she said, "I am certain that I made a mistake in acquiring it as I did. I should certainly have chosen differently. Do you want to know how I gained this mark, which so prejudices you and others against me?"

"I am sure I can imagine it, Miss. But now I think you are playing with me," said the jailer, unaware for the moment that he was standing dangerously close to the bars of the jail cell.....

"And do they say as well, that I am cursed by the great Gemaal?"

"Indeed they do, Miss. I am sorry for you. Do you know, Miss, if it were not for the mark, I should say you are a very pretty female."

"Truly? You really are a gallant, aren't you?"

"Well, I--" He stopped, trying to search her meaning. "If you are referring to how I acted when you first arrived here--"

"But surely it is not sporting to strike someone whose back is turned to you?"

"No. I did not mean an offense."

"I am sure you did not," she said warmly.

"Call it a danger of my occupation as jailer."

"That I shall do. It is forgotten."

"You are most understanding, Miss."

"Do you know, it is very cold outside."

"I am sorry for the weather. The mild season was so short."

"I am sure it is warm in your jail."

"Just so, Miss. But that is only my office. There is no cell there for you."

"That is too bad. I shall freeze outside. And do you have games there, in your office?"

"Games, Miss?" The jailer drew fractionally closer to her cell. The woman's voice seemed to have softened in volume, and he was drawn closer to her without realizing it. Without looking, she sensed where the keys hung down from his belt.

"Do you not have any games that you like to play?"

One of the jailer's hands had strayed recklessly into her cell as though he meant to touch her. She followed the movement of his hand without taking her eyes from his face.

"Well, as far as that--"

She saw her moment, and pressed down with all her force upon the jailer's upturned hand, pinioning it fast upon one of the horizontal cell bars.

"Ow-- Blast you!" The jailer rose up on his toes and tottered, trying to improve upon the angle of his smarting hand. His other hand shot through an opening and nearly clipped her chin, then tried ineffectually to reach for her hair, or find some other purchase upon her. She drew her upper body away, while drawing all her strength to constrain and ratchet the force on his hand.

With the fingers of her joined hands she grasped one of the jailer's fingers and bent it down almost double over the bar. Immediately the jailer's free hand stopped its restless movement. He was a strong devil. If she could hold on only a few moments more, she thought.

Gemaal save me from this ruffian.

He gasped. "I am not going to scream, Miss, for I would not give you the satisfaction. But you cannot escape my jail."

"Open the cell - now."

"Oh, Miss, you are making a great deal of trouble for me."

She increased the downward pressure upon his finger. "If you don't open the cell I am going to break it off, I swear."

"Miss, I can't - ow! Alright. As you say."

Carefully he reached for the chain of keys with his free hand, and unlocked the cell door. "Now throw them inside," she said. There would be no easy path past the jailer. She pushed hard on the cell door, but the force barely moved him. He wrenched his finger from out of her grasp. "Now you shall pay, Miss," he said. He opened the door carefully and she retreated a few steps into the cell.

"You did not think I could just let you go. You know I am obliged to stop you, Miss."

"Are you sure that you want to try?"

"Oh, I do. And I shall not be so kind to you, either." Advancing, he lunged for her but she stepped agilely under his arms, and stepped away from him. Maddened, he charged at her like a large bear, and this time she side-stepped and threw her foot out in a practiced way. As he went hurtling by her she clubbed the back of his head with her joined wrists, and, propelled by his own force, he fell forward and struck the metal bars of the cell with his head, and lay there.

The woman caught her breath and was on the point of striking him again for good measure. But he seemed a defenseless heap, with his mouth hanging open and some blood trickling down his forehead. She patted his pockets for some sign of the keys for the manacles, eyeing him warily, but could find nothing. There was no time. She thought she heard voices, and crouched, waiting, as the sounds drifted out of range. She picked up the keys to the cell, exited, pulled the door closed and locked it, and tossed the ring of keys in the yard, some feet away. She looked around to get her bearings, and then ran swiftly along the dirt road alongside some woods. Pausing only to conceal herself at the sound of voices, or a shadowy glimpse of someone passing along the road, she did not stop running for a good while.

CHAPTER 4 - FLIGHT

She slowed to a walk and continued for a couple of hours along the dirt road without stopping. Sometimes she would hear the creak of carriage wheels approaching from either direction, and the snorting of the water buffaloes that pulled the carriages. Then she would find an opening into the woods, either a narrow path, or if there wasn't time, stepping through the brush and briars. The moons cast a yellow light over the narrow ribbon of road on which she walked. There did not seem to be any militias out looking for her. Either no one knew of her escape, or at least she had gotten a substantial head start.

Her only object was to get as far from the town as possible. In no direction was there safety. No one region where her kind predominated, and where she might find some welcome. How to make contact with any of them now, without putting herself at risk? And travel to what remained of her family was unthinkable, as the authorities would certainly be watching the area. There was a small minority, or so she had heard, of Ben-Orans whose minds had not been completely turned against her kind - but what was her "kind," exactly? A small minority whom fate, or bad luck, had distinguished in a cruel and obvious way, who were almost universally viewed as physically repulsive and morally treacherous. They had not even chosen the name that denoted them among the majority population, rather it has been imposed on them: the Elohin. The "marked ones." The "cursed of Gemaal," and so forth. As though it was by the great Gemaal's decree that her kind should wander their world as outcasts; when it was fairer to say that a misunderstanding, and a cruel and sweeping calumny, were responsible for so much hardship.

For a good while she had not observed anyone. Thoughts of the past ranged through the woman's mind - randomly, like the glimpses of Ben-Ora's moons among the clouds, and between the almost leafless trees.

Not many years after the expulsion of the invaders, the Elohin began increasingly to be imprisoned in detention camps. It was alleged, at first, that these measures were for their protection. The term of the confinement was indefinite. From what they could learn, administration of the camps had seemed benign at first. Then came reports that those incarcerated lacked sufficient food and basic comforts. The woman, while still young, had seethed at the injustice of it, as more of the minority population faced imprisonment - either for their outspokenness, or for no particular reason that she could discern. If the camps had been models of clemency - which they were not - probably she still would have rebelled, because her spirit was offended.

When she herself was first incarcerated, she observed how a group of Elohin children of her age, those who had not been physically marked by the conflagration (who in any case stood in an ambiguous relation to everyone else) began to accede to many of the most harmful prejudices against their group. As a result, the relations of the unmarked ones with both peers and parents had subtly deteriorated. At first she was rather astonished at their behavior, and the obvious disloyalty of it. Some children were in fact moved to denounce their parents before the authorities, in the conscious or unconscious hope of living a more normal sort of life. The children, being viewed as somewhat redeemed by these actions, were in some cases released and accepted into majority families which lacked children, or which wanted or needed more of them.

At that moment she heard the welcome sound of a stream or river off in the woods, and sought a path off of the road. She thought she would drink and perhaps rest, for she was very tired. She kneeled at the water's edge and scooped water into her mouth. The metal manacles joining her wrists jangled, and she thought again that she would be well to be rid of them. Along the river bed were round stones of various sizes. She thought, if she could flatten the circular ring of the manacles and make them more nearly oval, they might slip over her hands. She set to work, placing one of the manacles on a large stone and pounding it with a smaller rock held in her other hand. There was no progress at first, and she stopped periodically to listen for any activity along the road. Everything seemed quiet. The brook murmured gently, small salamanders stopped on the smooth stones and craned their necks upward in her direction, only to scurry off at the next blow of stone upon metal.

She found that after a good while there was some flattening of the circular shape of the manacle, and then progress came more swiftly. The opening was still small, however, and in attempting to withdraw her hand her flesh caught and the abraded skin began to bleed. With a final great effort, and moaning softly in pain, conscious that she must not make too great a noise, the ring of metal slid over her hand with a further tearing of flesh. She gasped, and got up to soak her hand in the cool running water of the stream.

It would be easy, she thought, to go to sleep there and then, for she felt exhausted. But she knew that she should cover more ground before daybreak, after which travel on open roads would be very doubtful. As far as she knew, the authorities were rounding up all of her kind, and she herself would be a particular target, as one of their nominal leaders. Reflections of one of the Ben-Oran moons rippled in the water, a salamander smaller than her little finger floated onto the small stones in the river bed and paused to crane upwards at her. It was a peaceful scene, in which she recognized that nature is seldom truly quiet. A wind sighed through the trees, the stream gurgled, and insects thrummed in the night, a drowsing, droning sound as though many fingers were moving over a zither's strings; as though the insects were grateful for one more day of life, toward the end of the short temperate season.

She found she was grateful for this singing chorus of nature. For one thing, her hearing had simply never been the same, since the explosion. And it might have been that the rugged life she had led for ten years, frequently in the out of doors, had exposed her to too many severe colds and general hardships. The fact was that she never seemed to enjoy any true silence any more, but rather assorted rumblings, and ringings, which were not without her but within. And so she found that for her the varied sounds of the temperate season, when nature was most alive, were very kind and soothing, and the most favorable.

The salamander flipped out its tongue to spear some small moving thing she could not see. Since nature had provided so abundantly for all living creatures, why, she wondered, was there this protracted strife among those who were, by common conception, the most advanced species on the planet of Ben Ora? And why did this strife often have to do with abstractions, with nonessential things, which individuals rarely paused to examine rationally? And why (among the majority population, primarily, since riches were not a reasonable expectation for members of her caste) the desire to amass more and more riches, which to her thinking was tantamount to snatching a bit of bread from out of the mouths of the most wretched, the neediest, and most desperate inhabitants of the planet? This seemed to her one of the eternal laws of life, but her view was very far from the general one. If others had any knowledge of this law of life, it did not stop many from wanting to acquire more and more riches. Even though it was well known that all the wealth in the world would not prolong the most cosseted kind of existence by even one day, if it were not Gemaal's will; nor could silver in any amount buy its owner one sincere friend, or win back a love when it has turned cold, or insure happiness, or the blessing of good health, either.

In her society it seemed that wisdom was held cheap but acquired very dearly, like the precious powders that the apothecary measured out to cure a sickness. And she wondered, if she herself could be said to possess any kind of wisdom, what portion of it had been hard won from out of the many struggles of her existence.

She found herself almost on the point of sleep, and roused herself after a final drink from the stream. With a strip of cloth, she bound up the one remaining manacle high up on her forearm, under the sleeve of her cape. At least that would keep it silent. She walked out cautiously to the road again and proceeded. Before the day grew light, she would retreat to some densely wooded spot well off of the road.

She had no clear destination except to add, each day, some distance between herself and her pursuers - if they were in fact still pursuing her at all. Perhaps there was now a state of general war between the majority and all of her kind. It seemed that none were safe from detention now, that all were equally in peril. She knew that with the short temperate season now waning, she could not for much longer remain living in the out of doors as she had been. Her mind sought for a solution but could not find one.

She lived by eating some stray tubers found in the wild, which she had learned to identify upon the ground by the red shade of their tops. And sometimes she made reckless forays to the edges of farmers' fields or orchards, finding some pieces of fruit left on a tree, or vegetable left on its stalk. She knew that these depredations put her at increased risk of apprehension, but there seemed no alternative. If a better solution did not reveal itself to her soon, she could see herself falling on the mercy of some farm family, but this she regarded as a desperate gamble with unknown odds. The mistrust, and open hostility of the Ben-Orans toward her kind seemed almost universal. The Ben-Orans, she repeated to herself - but she was also a Ben-Oran. It was her planet too, and she refused to stop believing that it was.

It was in this extremity of increasing cold and hunger, and her increasingly bold forays in search of food, and of walking when she might better remain concealed in these woods which had become her place of hiding, that she seemed to hear a subtle music above the forest floor. Music, among the Ben-Orans, referred almost always to the chiming rhythms of bells being struck, or of wooden blocks shaped or hollowed to certain pitches. The sounds were faint and rather unexpected on this early afternoon in this place, and she wondered suddenly if they contained more of menace than music. For the sounds, as she strained to listen, suggested not so much the striking of bells as the rattling of lengths of chain, or perhaps of manacles striking upon each other. Then, crouched and watching, she heard the unmistakable sound of voices, not yet close. At first, she thought they might only be hunters, or some youths out exploring. Yet in her circumstances, even such locals as these might present nearly as great a threat as the Government's forces. She found a narrow path and walked quietly away from the presumed direction of the voices. But then other voices joined these, but from different directions, and with these, the striking of sticks or clubs against the trees. She retreated to some deeper brush, her heart now racing, and waited. She could see males moving among the leaves and brush through the forest, not very far from her.

She thought that the band of searchers might have

passed her. From her vantage point near some thickets, she sensed that there was a dirt road not far from her. The few people who passed along the road looked like farmers, and were mostly female. Some carried hemp bags of produce, possibly bound for a market in a nearby town, or else leaving it. She heard male voices again, now between her and the road, which she saw was the width of a couple of wagons. But she could not see anyone moving there, and it seemed that none had seen her, either. But her position here was perilous, and rapidly, as quietly as possible, she made her way to near the edge of the road. She was fairly certain that no one had seen her. From behind a tree she had a fairly clear view of the road, on which a few females continued to pass. Some were in pairs, and others walked alone. From behind her she heard voices, and the sound of a stick crushed under someone's footsteps, and urgently, sensing that the end of the file of walkers had passed, she stepped swiftly and resolutely out onto the road.

She carried with her a dark bolt of cloth, and this she instantly wrapped about her head, somewhat like the other females who were forward of her, except that her scarf more nearly covered her face. Staring straight ahead of her, she hoped to blend into the sparse file of villagers moving along. There was a female walking about twenty feet in front of her, and the woman kept her steps as slow and soundless as possible. After a moment she cast about to see if her arrival had been noticed by anyone. Pulling her scarf up to her eyes, she risked a backward glance: there were no villagers immediately behind her who could have seen her enter the road. Then she discerned, back at some further distance, someone who might have been a militiaman. That was what he looked like. But she didn't dare risk another backward glance, but continued ahead with the same stolid gait with which the other females walked.

She thought she heard a man's shout behind her, but she

continued moving. The female in front of her turned and looked, and seemed to register mild surprise at seeing someone behind her. Then the village female's eyes seemed to take in a broader canvas, some scene on the road behind both of them. The remaining manacle was tucked inside the sleeve of the woman's black cape; with a tug, she could bring the circle of hard metal into the palm of her hand. With her other hand she clutched the scarf almost up to her eyes, and tried to appear old, and harmless, and all but invisible, if she could have willed it. Then the militaman's voice was unmistakable behind her, and she heard his running steps.

"You. Halt!"

The woman in front of her stopped and turned.

She stopped, too, and turned and clutched at the scarf with which she hoped to hide the crimson mark below her eye. But the militiaman drew up and grabbed at her shoulder and yanked the cloth away.

A triumphant and recklessly joyful expression appeared, but very briefly, on the militaman's face. The woman let the manacle fall down to her wrist and she swung a roundhouse blow that landed with dead metal certainty square on the militiaman's chin. With a brief look of surprise on his face, the man went down in a heap on the side of the road. She dragged his body a few feet into the woods behind some brush.

"I have paid dearly for this scarf," she murmured softly, "and would prefer to keep it." She drew it from out of the male's inert hand. When she joined the road again it seemed clear of any other militamen. She felt hopeful until she saw the village female standing in front of her with a foolish expression, her mouth gaping open in fear, or silent reproach.

"You!" she hissed.

"Yes, me. One of them, or whatever you say. What are you going to do?"

"Your kind are evil."

The female had heard this and a hundred other variants of such speech by these foolish and impressionable Ben-Orans. She felt the dense metal ring heavy at her wrist. The old woman saw this too, and haughty dislike became abject fear in an instant. She began edging to the other side of the road. I ought to club her like I did the militiaman, she thought. But she couldn't - the female could have been her mother.

"What are you going to do to me?"

She placed the scarf over her head again, letting it hang about the sides of her face as before. As though some things could be hidden, she thought. She looked intently at the village female. "Nothing, ma'am. Only please, do not draw attention to me, but only be quiet for awhile. It is nothing to you."

The woman picked up her pace, and then behind her she saw that the village female was walking hurriedly in the other direction, and she heard her voice keening in alarm, and then screeching, the sound blending with the vigilantes' whistles. She was disappointed but not particularly surprised at the villager's action, and picked up her own pace. There was nothing for it but to run now, as fast as she could. She passed a number of villagers, who for the most part only stopped and stared at her in wonder. The road opened to a small square, with houses and small shops to the left: the village center. The road led directly to a stone and metal bridge that crossed a broad river.

The scarf flew from her head and she caught it and slowed, pressing it into her waistband and breathing deeply. Some of the townspeople looked into her face with a shock of recognition, and the onlookers quickly grasped the meaning of the chase.

A female ran up to the knot of townspeople, paused for breath and cried, "Stop her!" Adding, somewhat needlessly at this point, "She is one of the Elohin."

While the woman looked about, pondering, a burly male villager nearly twice her size made a reckless charge in her direction. When he closed to within about six feet, with both arms raised like a bear's, he seemed suddenly to register the fiercely determined look in the woman's eyes. At the same moment he saw the unfamiliar object, the grey metal manacle with its length of chain, coiled about her right fist which was drawn and ready to strike. His legs failed him, and as though he had encountered a very demon, he not so much stopped as sagged abjectly to the ground, and lying on his back he slowly began inching himself away from her, his feet and hands seeking some purchase in the dirt.

A sigh of disappointment seemed to escape from the ragtag crowd of about twenty individuals. The woman looked around her for any similar charges, but the circle of villagers, all bravado seemingly vanished for the time being, closed no further around her. More pressing to her was to find a means of escape. The bridge itself seemed the only promising route: perhaps it gave on to the open countryside, and as tired as she was, she felt fairly confident if all came down to a footrace. There was no time to lose; in the distance, from the road on which she had passed, came the shrill alarms of crudely fashioned whistles. Just as she made her resolve to cross the bridge, however, another of the male villagers emerged from the crowd with a shriek, and ran straight for her pointing a spear-like wooden pole which he brandished at chest level. He was smaller and clearly more agile than the other villager. The woman didn't move until he was nearly upon her, and then she adroitly side-stepped him, grabbing the pole as he passed and clubbing the back of his head with it. He remained on the ground. The crowd was stilled, also, seething with a sullen anger at the ineffectualness of their attacks thus far, and murmuring like maddened animals. In their consternation they seemed to ask themselves what sort of extraordinary being this was, whose thwarting of their every attack seemed a mockery of them.

The woman took off at a run, and none of them followed. The bridge was quite wide, and she could see at a glance over its stone parapet that it crossed a deep and fast-moving river. She passed a young male villager, a raggedly dressed boy, at about the middle of the span. He was one of just a couple of vendors standing on the bridge. Next to him was a battered wooden table, or what might have been a small door, set up on some folding legs. There were a few assorted vegetables lying for sale on the table, but at the moment there were very few who had come to buy. The boy appeared thunderstruck to see the woman running toward him, and he looked to see if she were being pursued. He heard the militamen's whistles drifting shrilly from the other side of the bridge.

When she was quite close and he saw the raw patch of scar upon the woman's face, some of the mystery of the scene was revealed to him. He did not feel any animosity, though, but rather a spasm of sympathy, and he drew the ragged sleeve of his coat across his runny nose, pondering. The woman in her turn saw at a glance that one of his eyes was missing, from disease or from an accident she didn't know.

The boy felt rather sorry for her. He thought of how, when he had been able to attend school, others had seemed uncomfortable around him, and had drawn attention to his disfigured face. The woman passed, but in the next instant she watched as a band of villagers on the opposite side of the bridge appeared to coalesce, and press as a unit in her direction. It must have been another band of militamen aroused by the clarion call of the whistles. She slowed, and then she was moving backwards with light steps. But the other group had closed at the end of the bridge from which she had come. Her pursuers' movements were slow but inexorable.

She looked over the bridge parapet. There were some

boats tied up along the banks on either side. Some of the boats were of a good size, and evidently a deep draft. There seemed only one chance of escape now: her hands on the parapet, she tried to further judge the depth of the rushing river below. She thought there was an even chance of its being deep enough, but the water was a thirty foot drop from the bridge. If she could survive the shock, the cold might be manageable. She was not sure about either, but in this extremity there were no better choices.

The whistles were not sounding any more, only the unarticulated shouts of the male villagers. From both sides they formed a grim and slowly moving wall of flesh - militamen, hangers-on, and the idly adventurous. While the woman deliberated, a rifle shot rang out. The boy ducked at his crude table, looking out anxiously with his good eye. They could not see or hear clearly, but the firing of the rifle seemed to draw immediate shouts among the nearer crowd to hold fire. The woman felt a piercing pain in her shoulder, and winced, and then with an instant resolve she stepped toward the young peddler and grabbed the corner of his display table and lifted, with obvious pain on her face. The boy resisted, clutching determinedly at his corner of the table. "No," he cried.

"I am sorry."

He saw then the crazily swinging manacle that hung from her wrist, and the angry-looking patch of scar below one of the woman's eyes, so raw that it looked like a wound that she had just now sustained; and then he saw that there was actual blood coursing down her wrist, running in rivulets from her arm or shoulder and collecting on the small battered door, which for some years had been a tool of his trade, and companion to his itinerant peddling. His heart was turned in an instant. He thought that he could find, or steal, another board, one that was better suited to his small stores of merchandise, and which would travel better.

"It's alright, ma'am. I'll help you." And he lifted his end of the table, and they got it up to the ledge, and then he helped her heave it over the edge and into the river.

The converging crowds gasped and shouted their disappointment at the boldness of this escape in the making. The woman swung one leg over the ledge, then the other. Multiple shots now rang out, and the boy dropped instantly to the ground, covering his face and not daring to look up, despite his curiosity. Instantly from her sitting position, the woman pushed with one arm and with her heels away from the bridge. The mob roared their astonishment, and their disappointment at being deprived, for the moment, of the capture - even if, to many, the woman's chance of surviving the fall was negligible.

The woman watched as the door floated slowly below her. She kept her upright position, and plunged deeply into the cold water. The shock and cold caused her to lose consciousness momentarily, and to drift in what seemed to her unconscious mind a welcome and longed-for sleep, a restfulness that seemed to offer a relief from cares. The small sector of her mind that still clung to consciousness told her that there was only death in this peculiar peacefulness, and she roused herself and kicked savagely for the surface. She winced at the pain in her shoulder.

When she swung her head above the water she could hear the gunfire again, and ducked and kicked with her legs to bring her farther away from danger. When she lifted her head out of the water next and glanced backward she saw that some villagers were running toward the bank of the river on both sides, while a much larger group remained staring over the bridge's parapet, as if they were spectators in a gallery. But the water was moving more quickly than the running men. Soon, she hoped, the current would bring her out of range of their gunfire. The door had moved some twenty feet in front of her during her plunge, and its movement, moreover, was fleeter than her own. With her arm that was not injured she could not so much swim as paddle in order simply to keep her head above water. The effort was exhausting her. When shots rang out she would duck under the water again, and when she raised her head and turned to glance backward she still saw the angry villagers scurrying along the river bank, and pausing to fire weapons; but they were thankfully falling further behind her.

The door, her raft, skimmed and bobbed along the surface of the water even further in front of her, now perhaps thirty feet downriver. Her legs kicked harder, and eventually she began to close on it, and her hand clasped on an edge. She barely had the strength to pull herself onto it, and then slowly to draw her upper body to the forward end. With an effort she turned her head for another look behind, and was satisfied that she was out of their range for now. She was aware of sporadic, ineffectual weapons fire, and what sounded in her ears like a tumult of furious voices, if they were not an echo that had already passed. But growing more distant in any case; then, quite exhausted, she passed out and was borne along the swiftly moving river.

CHAPTER 5 - ONE KIND FAVOR AND OTHERS

The woman awoke once during the night, and attempting to raise her head slightly, a sudden pain shot through her injured shoulder, and she fell back. Her raft was still drifting, though perhaps not as swiftly as before. The night was dark except for the light of one of Ben-Ora's moons, though it was partially eclipsed. Now turning her head slightly, in the moonlight that shimmered upon the rippling waters, she guessed that the river was about half as wide as when she last saw it. She attempted to lift up on her elbow, and the single manacle on her wrist and its links of chain jangled next to her ear. She remembered that she was lying upon the peddler's door that was her improvised raft. There came back to her inner ear, in imagination, the furious shouts of the villagers of the nearby town. She remembered how the mob closed inexorably upon her.

Looking up into the night sky, she felt curiously empty and weakened, and tried to imagine how much blood she had lost since yesterday afternoon. But out here, on the narrowing river, there was little to be done for it, anyway. Before she could think any further about her situation she fell asleep again. Her raft went on drifting.

The scene was quite different a few hours later, and several more miles downriver. The river's flow grew sluggish, as its banks contracted. The woman had no idea of the river's course, nor that her improvised raft had drifted nearly to a stop. The day was nearly beginning. The raft came to a gentle rest on a shore of sand and clay, screened partly by some tall dried grass, and within view of a country farmhouse. Grey smoke curled from the main house's chimney. The woman lay sprawled on the raft of wood, which rested undisturbed by any currents. Her damp clothes seemed plastered to her, the black cape thrown across her torso, and her dark hair clung to the sides of her face.

In a little while a young female ventured out of the back of the house with a pail which seemed heavy for her, carrying it with both hands in front of her and loping in this fashion towards the detached barn which stood between the main house and the river. It was only on her way back to the house, after scattering some feed in a pen that attached to the barn, that she saw the strange apparition on the river shore. The girl set the pail down on the scrubby grass where she stood, and walked slowly and soundlessly toward the water. Her circumspection was exaggerated: the woman showed no movement at all. When the girl was almost close enough to reach down and touch the woman, she began backing away, and then turned and ran directly for the main house, forgetting the pail where it lay on the ground.

In just a few moments the girl emerged from the main house again, pointing, and followed by the farmer couple, and the girl's brother who appeared to be a few years younger than her. She and her brother raced ahead of the two adults, who approached the scene unhurriedly and with apprehensive looks; as though afraid of what was unfolding. A strange woman washed up on the shore was about as unexpected a thing as either of them could imagine. The female told the children to hush, and pushed them behind them, and stood and looked down at the strange woman. The female looked doubtfully at the male farmer, who stood there looking about the river for some moments. He ventured closer, walking on the soft soil of the stream bed, and turned and crouched slightly to better see the woman. With her dark and disturbed clothing, and black hair lying across much of her face, there was not much of her to be seen.

"You stand over there," he said to the children, and the surprise of his voice made them jump. Reluctantly, they moved off several paces. With the toe of his shoe he nudged the woman's foot, without any response.

The woman who had come out of the house with him chided him, saying, "That's no way." So he crouched near the woman, but contrived to remain outside of striking distance, touching with his hand and moving one of her ankles from side to side. But there was no response.

He clutched a corner of her raft and attempted to pull it out of the muck, studying her appearance as he did so. The woman's head moved very slightly, and some hair fell away from her face. Then he observed the disk of roiled and reddened flesh, nearly as wide as her hand, below her left eye. The other woman now saw as well, and the farmer nodded silently to her.

The expression of the farmer had changed abruptly from curiosity about her to plain apprehension.

"Oh, Gemaal, no," the farmer said. "She is one of the Elohin."

"Are you sure?" the female said, still standing some distance apart.

"You have eyes to see. You may come closer," he added soberly.

"How in the devil did she get here," he added. But it was obvious to him, looking up to where the little stream broadened placidly, that she must have been borne upon the great river, and her improvised raft joined a small tributary, until she came to rest here. He rose to his feet. "I wonder if anyone has seen her." He looked up and down the river.

"Not likely anyone has seen her," the woman said. "The day is just breaking. Aleph - is she even alive?"

The man drew closer and with his hand he gripped one

of her legs below the knee and exerted a subtle and then increasing pressure.

"Do you know, there is blood upon this-- What *is* this?" He felt and tapped on the improvised raft. "A board of some kind."

"Be careful," the wife said.

He kept his eyes upon the woman's face and then he was sure that she winced slightly, but without coming to consciousness. He backed away carefully and then simply nodded to his wife.

"A fugitive from the law. Like about all of her kind, I guess."

"If I were her, I know I should do all I could to be shut of the authorities, too."

The man frowned. "It will go very hard with us if she is ever discovered here."

"Aleph, what is that on her wrist? Is it a chain of some kind?"

"Why, I believe it is a chain and manacle. You know what this means. That she is doubly a fugitive - a recent escapee, too. Great Gemaal, why here?"

"You know I believe she is hurt. We have to help her. Aleph?"

"I heard you," the man said.

The children had moved to just behind their parents. "What does it mean?" the female one asked.

"Don't you worry about it now. Stand back like I told you."

"What are we going to do?" the boy asked.

"I don't know."

"We must do what we can for her," the woman said. When the farmer did not reply. she added, "We cannot send her out again on her skiff, and hope that she does not drift back to us."

"No... " he said. "Of course not."

"Should I go for the doctor?" the girl asked.

"No. We can't call the doctor," the man said. "Help me," he said to the boy, and they pulled and dragged the raft several feet out of the water, where it rested on sand and near some small rocks.

"Aleph," the woman said. "Can we remove that chain?"

The man looked at her, and back at the woman. "In my view, that is hardly her biggest problem just now."

"I just believe it is bad luck somehow."

"Bad luck? Well, I suppose we can try." He said to the boy, "Go and see what your lazy brother is doing. Wake him up if he is sleeping and tell him to come out here quick. You go help them," the man said to the girl.

When they had run off the man said, "We'll take her to the barn." The day was lightening. He looked around apprehensively again.

"This could bring us trouble. But I suppose we do not have a lot of choice, but to help her somehow. If you agree."

"She's a living creature," the woman said. "Maybe not very different from you or me."

The older son was handsome and well built and stood a head taller than the father. Brown hair fell over his eyes as he approached and looked appraisingly at the female, his boots sinking in the clay. He looked with interest into her face. His eyes were drawn to the patch of red scar on the woman's cheek, and he stared before averting his eyes. There was some brackish discoloration of the board below the woman's shoulder, which he took to be from dried blood, and when he rubbed the fabric of her clothing there he could see on his fingers a similar discoloration and dark specks. It was not possible to see any wound, yet.

"Run up to the road, will you, and see if any are passing," the farmer said.

The son jogged up the road, and back, and reported that all was clear.

He looked at his father and asked, "What shall we do then?"

"Why, take her to the barn, before it gets any lighter."

The son seemed comfortable with whatever his father proposed. "Then let us move her door and all, if we can. Her shoulder looks badly hurt."

The adults each lifted a corner of the board, and the two youngest took another corner, and they moved toward the large barn and set the door and woman down at the first clear space. She did not stir at all.

The daylight did not extend very far into the barn, and the father had the boy light an oil lamp, with a metal clicker, and set it nearby. Then he asked the boy to bring into the barn the largest flat rock that he could carry from the river bank.

"And don't be all morning. Will you bring the great hammer," he said to the older son, and himself looked into a wooden cabinet on the wall and brought from it a couple of large chisels. When everything was in place he selected the great hammer for himself.

The son carefully moved the woman's manacled hand until it rested on the flat stone, and with his other hand he grasped the largest of the chisels. He carefully threaded it next to the woman's wrist and pressed the sharp edge upon the metal. He looked up and nodded once to his father. But his hands shook, and he tried to concentrate only on maintaining his hold.

"Try not to let her arm move," the farmer said to the woman. She pressed her hands on the woman's forearm and looked away. "Hold that lantern over here," he said to the boy.

The boy held the lantern in front of his chest and looked about at the chisel which his brother held in place, and his mother who held the woman's arm down and looked away. Most of all he looked fascinatedly at the red raw mark on the woman's face, the mark that seemed to glisten wetly in the yellow light of the lantern. I wonder does that hurt, he thought to himself, and then he saw his father spit on his hands and lift the great hammer up to his chest and then above his head, his eyes fixed on the blunt edge of the chisel which he would strike momentarily.

The woman on the ground was stirring back to consciousness. In her mind lingered the restful travel over the river, the play of the moonlight on the water, and finally a picture of the morning fog that hovered over the water dissolving, borne up into the air. The strange cabal of voices had drifted into her consciousness, and the light of the lantern played over her closed eyes. Then she was aware that she was being held down on one side, and when she opened one eye slightly she saw in the yellow light of the oil lamp the outlines of the great hammer swim into view, poised directly over her body and being propelled downward.

She flinched then and attempted to swing her upper body to the side, and was aware of the sudden raised voices of alarm, and the sound of the chisel falling on the rock. A man who crouched near her upper body lifted his arms into the air above her, and then the man holding the great hammer tried to arrest its downward progress, nearly falling forward. The younger man succeeded in grasping the hammer as the other man strove to hold it back. She looked up at all of the faces above and around her and waited to see what would happen next.

"Great Gemaal preserve us!" the man holding the great hammer cried. In a quieter voice he said, "Why I could have crushed you, Miss."

The woman went on looking as before, without moving her head.

The mother brought her face closer to the woman's. "We don't mean you any harm, Miss. The thing on your wrist, we would remove it. But I am afraid we have startled you."

"I should say so," the older son said, coming around and looking down at her equably. "We will try again, if that is your wish."

The woman looked at him. "Please. I will be grateful."

"Just don't move, Miss, and it will be alright."

The family all took up their former places, and the father essayed a tentative strike at first.

"Have you got it, son?" he asked.

"Go ahead."

After several whacks of the great hammer the manacle split open. The woman rubbed her wrist, but it was from the pain in her shoulder that she winced.

"What has happened to your shoulder?" the man asked.

"I was ... struck there."

"With shot?"

The woman nodded very slightly, taking some notice for the first time of the two youngest children who crowded around, their mouths agape.

"We will do what we can for that," the man said. "Perhaps you would like some food and drink first."

"I cannot repay you."

"It isn't necessary. We will bring it here."

The family walked toward the wide doors and into the yard. The older son lingered. "Is there anything else I can do for you, Ma'am?"

The woman shook her head no.

In a little while the daughter brought refreshments out to the barn on a tray and shyly set them on a rough-hewn table. "Can I bring anything else for you, Ma'am?"

"I am sure this will be fine, thank you."

"Do you have pain, Ma'am?"

"Some. Do you not have school?"

"There is no school today, Ma'am. It is not a working day."

"You are probably a few years from graduating."

"That is right, Ma'am." The girl lingered and spoke again. "Did you come here in one of the space ships?"

"I? You saw how I arrived, in that little bark." She seemed a serious child.

"But they say that your kind travel in great ships." The female looked at her. "I mean--" and the girl stopped, abashed.

"Believe me, if I could have chosen a more comfortable vessel, I certainly would have."

"Why didn't you?"

"You are very inquisitive. I did not have time to select a better one."

"Oh. I don't mean to be inq-- what you said."

"It is alright, and thank you."

"I will go back to the house now and let you eat."

When the woman had eaten and drank, the farming couple entered the barn and lingered, collecting the dishes and glass which were emptied. "Can I help you," she asked.

"You just remain and rest," the farm woman said.

"I cannot repay you for your help. I will leave when I am able."

"You are in no condition to go anywhere. Your shoulder, is it badly hurt?"

"It pains me, yes."

"Miss, it really ought to be treated," the man said.

"I know," the woman frowned.

"Let us help you. Do you feel strong enough to tend to it now?"

"I would be most grateful."

The man returned in a little while carrying a pail of heated water, and the woman with what looked the same tray, but resting on it now were a small basin with a powdery liquid in it, and a cloth folded over some metal objects, pincers and the like.

"We have some little experience of these things - of

tending to the animals, mostly. But we will not harm you. I will ask my son - he is young, but I believe his hand is surer than mine."

"If you could clean the area--"

"Of course, Miss. And remove any shot, if we see any. And here are some spirits you may have, if they will help with the pain."

They left. When the son entered the barn she was struck anew at his youthfulness - although, she supposed, there were only several short cycles of the seasons separating her from the young man. He used a bit of straw to fire a second oil lamp, and set both on metal crooks which he pressed into the ground. He moved the small table to the side.

"It is a deal of trouble I am putting you all to," the woman said.

The young man shook his head dismissively, whistling a few jaunty notes of melody in answer.

"You could not know how someone like me is forced to live."

"I find it hard to imagine, Miss. You have not done any wrong to me."

"I wonder you are all so understanding."

"I think it is our belief that it is a duty to help our fellow mortals, if we can."

"Well, I am very grateful to have found you."

"Now - the wound, is it on the back, mainly?"

"Just so." Pointing to her back shoulder.

"Then you shall sit here on the bench, between the lamps, like this."

The woman was facing out to the barnyard. The man went and closed the pair of wide swinging doors.

"For privacy, Ma'am. And if you should feel compelled to yell, why, go ahead." He brought a chair up behind her. "Alright, then."

The woman began removing her cape. He eased it over

the injured shoulder, and she folded it and laid it on the bench next to her. Her shirt was of a rough fabric. She removed and held it in front of her, her back straight.

"I'm going to clean the area. This may hurt a bit." He ran a dampened cloth over her upper back. The wounds were still fresh and continued to bleed. When he pushed at the flesh around some of them, randomly shaped bits of metal, small and grey, pushed to the surface. The woman gasped slightly. "I'm sorry, Ma'am. The wounds are not healing because there is some shot here. Bear with me and I will get them out." He picked up a small metal probe from its cloth blanket.

"You have had some experience of this?"

"Of weapons fire, I cannot say that I have, Ma'am. I will do my best."

There was a larger wound near the top of her shoulder, about the diameter of his little finger. If I may look, Ma'am. And he got up and studied the front of her shoulder in the lamplight, where there was a wound opposite of about the same size. He touched her back shoulder with a finger. "This was the largest one, Ma'am. But I believe it has exited here, from the front." He could see a bit of her face. But she was staring forward, fists clenched, and in obvious pain. "Does that sound correct?" he asked.

"I thought that it went through, and out. I was turned away, you see."

"Then it is very fortunate, if it has gone out."

"Do what you must, farmer. I will hold up."

"I am sure you will, Ma'am."

"May I ask, why do you call me Ma'am?"

"Ma'am? I mean--"

"Do you think, compared to you, that I have lived for so many more blessed seasons on this planet?"

"I was not really thinking of that. Shall I call you Miss, then?"

"Yes. For now."

"You haven't told me your name, Miss."

She didn't answer. In a little while she heard the *ping!* of a piece of shot land in a metal dish.

"Do you see many more?"

He pressed the cloth into the warm soapy water and wrung it out. "It is a little hard to see, Miss - you are very brave." He wiped more blood away from her shoulder and then peered more closely in the lamplight. Minutes passed, and soon the dish held a palmful of misshapen bits of metal that he had extracted.

The pain had subsided to a dull, generalized ache. One of the farmer's hands was on top of her right shoulder, the uninjured one, and with his other hand he daubed and ran the wet cloth over her shoulders and neck. She felt a strange sensation, a sort of thrill to his touch, in spite of her discomfort. She heard the washcloth drop into the pail, and was aware of his hands resting atop her shoulders. She could feel his breath warm against her neck, and she enjoyed the sensation of it. The young man ran his hands over her shoulders, gently over the injured one, and then she was surprised to feel his lips press against the back of her neck. The barn was very still and quiet.

She spoke into the silence. "Do you know what you are doing, my friend?"

"Doing, Miss? Well, I have had generally good results," he said briskly, and then she could sense the play of his fingers over the metal instruments on the tray, more than upon her flesh. "In treating the farm animals, mostly," he continued.

"Yes, the farm animals."

"Yes, Miss."

"But I was not referring to your technical skills - for which I am very grateful, to be sure."

"Then what, Miss?"

"Well, I believe you are trying to make love to me."

"Why--"

Without turning, she could tell that he was somewhat abashed. There was a pause in that tireless kneading of her shoulders - a caressing, almost - in which his ardor was very obvious. The woman felt a twinge of disappointment at the brief spell that had been broken - necessary though it was.

"If I have caused any offense, I am sorry. Miss?"

"There is nothing to be sorry about. You are doing rather well at it." Then he only heard a hiss and a low moan of pain escape from between her teeth. "I am not scolding you, farmer. I rather like you. But we must keep our wits about us."

"I understand, Miss. I think I am awfully fond of you." Still turned away from him, she could feel the urgent press of his hands upon her shoulders. "I will try not to act the fool."

She reached back and patted his hand that rested lightly on her injured shoulder, and a thrill went through him.

"For the first time, Miss, I begin to question the things that I have been told about - your kind, I mean. The things I have been told since I was a boy."

"We are not so very different, except as we have been forced to be."

"And do you know," he said, "from this side all that I see is a beautiful female creature."

"Indeed." The woman laughed briefly. Her smile was wistful, concealing as it did a heartache that the young man could not guess at, or begin to imagine. But her tone, when she spoke, was light and almost bantering. "And from the other side?" she asked. But she turned only fractionally toward him, on her bench, so that the scar remained concealed from him. She did not see the nonplussed look on his face, and after a pause, added, "Well, there is nothing that I can do about the rest of my face, farmer."

"Oh, I did not mean to give offense. I am such a

clumsy--"

"Well, at least there is nothing clumsy about your hands, farmer. They have served me well today, and I am grateful for it. Indeed, you have very sure hands. Do not hold back, but do what you must. I can hold up."

But she gasped as he probed and removed more of the shot. Partly to put him at his ease, she spoke with an effort.

"But, in either case, beauty does not last. You must not place too great store by it. Of all qualities, it is the one whose possessor should take least pride in, for it was given to one rather than worked for. Not that *I* am beautiful--"

"Oh, but you are!"

"You do not have to say it. We are not youngsters courting."

"But I am very sincere."

"Very well - I believe that you are sincere. Now let us have an end to it."

"You must think me an awful fool, Miss."

"No - do not think that. And do not be cross with me, for my direct way of speaking." She turned a little further toward him, and reached and touched his cheek affectionately. He moved closer to her and they embraced. The man fell to his knees and clasped her to him. The tunic that she held in her hand covered her nakedness. With her other hand she kept him at a certain distance.

With a sudden determination, the woman held his head between her hands and looked searchingly into his eyes, kissed him, and said, "Let us leave it like this, farmer."

"Miss?"

"I mean, let us not begin something that we cannot finish."

"I will do whatever you say, Miss."

"It isn't that you are not an attractive male, farmer. You are - very. You revive feelings in me which have been dead for many years."

"Let them live, then!"

"I have much to think about, farmer. Do not worry that I shall leave soon. I cannot, yet, if your family will allow me to stay. But I worry about putting you all at risk."

"We all feel the same."

"You are very good."

"You must remain here, I think, in the barn. There is some heat, from the hearth."

"Yes, it will be best if I remain here. Should any come searching for me."

"I hate to think of it."

"Do not worry, farmer. Continue, and when you have quite finished, help me to put my clothes back on."

CHAPTER 6 - ALMOST HEAVEN

When the farmer's son next visited the barn to look in on her, the woman was struck by the brisk and businesslike tone that he assumed, and she imagined that he felt chastened by his bold behavior of the previous time. This was exactly what was in his mind. He felt regret at the moments of intimacy which, for him, ended much too soon, and abashed by her confident and gently mocking manner with him, in which she was so different from any other female that he had met. This time he would be more sensible, or so he hoped.

"I am glad to see you, farmer," she said, as he opened the great door and strode over to where she sat, near the metal stove and hanging lantern.

"How are you feeling?" he asked.

"I am pretty well. Have you come to look at me?"

"Of course."

"Your family is well?" He nodded silently. "I think the shoulder is feeling better, but I will await your professional judgment about it."

She turned slightly away from him, unbuttoning her shirt. He helped her injured arm out of the sleeve and then kneeled behind her, looking at her shoulder in the lamplight.

"I want you to know, Miss, I will not take the liberty of touching you."

"Except in a professional manner, farmer?"

"Exactly so."

"But why are you being so formal? If I have hurt your feelings somehow, I am sorry."

"If I may, Miss." He peered closely at the mottled flesh of her upper shoulder

"You may be serious, then, if that is how you feel. How do I look?"

"The wounds are dry, and they appear to be healing. I am pleased. I will rub a bit of spirits, to clean. And a bit of salve. I believe they are still here. He got up and walked toward a wooden cabinet. Do you know, Miss, sometimes our water buffalo fight, and one will give the other an awful bite, sometimes just on the shoulder, like this."

"Not really?"

"Yes, Miss. And it is I usually attend to them. Believe me, the salve we are using, it is just the thing for it."

"I don't doubt that it is very effective."

"Do you know, sometimes, I give names to some of the animals."

"That is extraordinary. Is life so lonesome here?"

"It - was."

"Am I anything like your water buffaloes, farmer?"

"You, Miss? Oh, no. You are nothing like them." In fact her skin felt like polished stone to his hands, except for the raised flesh near her wounds.

"Nothing like them? I think I am sorry to hear it, for you seem very fond of your water buffaloes."

"Not nearly so fond as I am of you, Miss."

"Since you have said it, I will believe you."

"It seems you must always joke with me."

"I will stop, if it bothers you. Oh, do not worry about it." She reached back and patted one of his hands on her shoulder. "Let us be serious, then. For my life is in your hands, farmer."

She turned fully around. "Oh, do not mind me." She reached behind his neck, and pulled him forward and kissed him on the lips. Then she brought his hand to her lips, saying, "These hands pulled a handful of shot metal from out of my flesh. You must know how truly grateful I am. Please continue, and I will sit here quietly. I think it is an excess of happiness that causes me to talk so, that others show such extraordinary kindness to - one like me."

When he had patted her shoulder dry and helped her on with her shirt, he said, "Come, I want to show you something."

"It sounds like a secret. Is it?"

"If you will."

She followed him up some narrow stairs to a sort of loft, with straw-covered floor and, to the side, a raised platform with a narrow cloth mattress. "And out this door," he said, "the back barnyard, and the hay wagon that is kept just below."

She could see the stream that brought her here not far in the distance. "Yes, I have explored here the first night."

"You probably have not seen this." His fingers pried into a recess in the plank walls, and he pulled a hinged section of wall, the height of a person, into the loft area. "It is a false wall, you see. I don't know why it is here. But in an extremity - I mean--"

"I see." She stepped into the opening and pulled the panel to, and found herself in a recess which she could stand in with a little room to spare. Through what small cracks existed in the planks, she could see dimly into the loft.

"I see," she said. "It is very good to know."

"So long as there were no belongings left out here, you might be safe, if any come and search."

The woman paused at one of the small windows, which was covered by a moveable wooden panel. She shifted the panel slightly and looked out on the main house. Some white smoke curled from its chimney. "I think I shall stay here," she said. "There are views on two sides, and I can hear anyone enter below before being seen."

She closed the panel and turned to him again. She put her arms around him and rested her head against his chest, surprising him. "I am grateful to you."

The woman had thought him to be quite younger than her, but when she thought about him now, she supposed that only a few short cycles of the seasons separated them. Perhaps he had seemed younger to her owing to the simplicity of his outlook, as things seemed to her. But if there was a simplicity to this individual, it was a simplicity tempered by both logic and fairness. And she supposed, too, that being one of the favored majority, his mind had not received as many shocks as hers. It seemed that to some was given a life of simple happiness, while the portion given to others was misunderstanding and loneliness, and a never-ending flight away from danger. How could she compare the two of them? If life were different, she thought, the happiness that she might enjoy!

"Your mind seems to have gone far away, Miss."

"No, I am still here. Do you know, farmer, we live in different worlds."

"I wish it could be otherwise."

"Life is not always what we wish it to be. And anyway" - she turned, facing him - "you would not want to live like me."

"I will do anything, to be with you."

"Soon I will have to leave. And you will stay here with your family, where you are needed. That is how it must be. Let us not look too far beyond this little time that we have together."

"As you say, Miss."

When only a couple of more days had passed, their relationship was very much changed. It was as though both recognized that there was no opposing the force of nature which drew them together. All resistance, and restraint, seemed futile. This was especially so to her, whose future appeared so much more uncertain. Only great Gemaal knew how many more chances of happiness remained to her in such a turbulent existence. If the farmer's son seemed very innocent to her, he was intelligent, and good company for all that. It was a long time since a male had paid her this kind of attention.

She was sitting on the cloth and straw mattress in the small barn loft. The family had given her a shirt to keep, of a plain white fabric, and it was only this shirt, and some underclothes, that she wore now. The heavy breeches were cleaned and drying on the wall nearby. Her legs were tucked under her. Her short leather boots were arranged neatly just under the cot.

"AN-nota," she said, essaying the man's name for only the second or third time since he had told it to her. "Annota, aside from this hideous scar, what do you really think about me?"

"Think about you?" The farmer's son was dressed in his work clothes. He got up from the small chair on which he was sitting and took some steps toward her. He kneeled next to the bed and took her hand. The nearness of her, the sight of her body, made the heart of the farmer's son leap in his chest.

"Think about you," he repeated. He grasped her knees, ran his hands over her smooth and taut legs, clasping her to him. "Why, I am falling in love with you, Miss."

His words took her by surprise. "In love! Oh, no, no, no, you mustn't say that."

"But why not? It is what I feel."

"No, it won't do at all, farmer. In such a mad world as this, it is folly to speak about love."

"I do not believe that."

"But it is true. For us, anyway. I did not create this

world, but I have learned enough about it to know."

He was silent.

"Did I say something wrong?" she asked.

Drawing away, "It seems that my feelings must always be made fun of."

"What!" It took her a few moments for her to realize that he was quite serious. The simplicity of this young man, how he surprised her!

"Oh, I did not mean to make fun. Here, take my hand." She extended her hand and held it there for a few moments, until she could catch his eye. He took her hand, crouching back on his heels.

"I am only trying to be realistic," she said. "Enjoy me, be kind to me if you care for me, but there is nothing to be gained in this world by speaking of love."

"I do care for you. But I will mind what I say. You know," he added in a moment, "to answer you, you should not concern yourself about the scar, when there is so much of you that is perfect." His fingers touched lightly upon her skin

She saw how his gaze rested upon her body. His face had taken on an avid and hungry expression whose meaning was unmistakable. But when she spoke, it was in a bantering voice.

"Do you mean to say that my character is perfect? Because I don't think it can be so."

"Your character is very admirable, Miss. But I confess it was not your character I was thinking of just then."

"No?" A small smile had formed on his face. "Oh, you!" she said. And she pushed at his forehead with her palm, lightly she thought, and was surprised to see him totter backward, and sprawl upon his back with a thud.

"Are you alright?" Bringing her feet to the floor. "Oh, I am such a clumsy..."

"Nothing damaged, Miss." Brushing himself off. "And I daresay I deserved the rough treatment."

"No, you know I did not mean it - now I think it is you who are joking with me. I don't mind you at all, and you have very skillful hands, as I think I have told you."

"Several times, thank you. Are you happy, Miss?"

"Of course. Within a short time past I have been beaten by a gang of ruffians, and thrown into a dirty jail, and escaped, and was chased, and lived in the woods, and lately I had the privilege of leaping from a bridge whose height I thought had a fair chance of killing me, into that great river that winds to a little stream past your family's property--"

"That can't be so. Do you mean from the Natharu bridge, that is a day's walk upstream from here?"

"Oh, it sounds the right distance, but I did not walk it. It was more than six times my height, to the water."

"It is not possible," he repeated.

"Possible or impossible, it is what I did, and what I have lived to tell you."

"The Natharu bridge--"

"If that is the name for it. But I have no desire to know its name, for I have no wish to see it ever again."

"You dear--"

"I do not say these things to distress you. I only say that, being now out of the cold, and due to your family's kindness, not having to live on what roots I can find from the ground, or leftover fruit on the trees, and being in good company, and having my wits to deal with whatever adversity may come my way - for all that is good at present, I can truly say that I am content."

He appeared to think for a moment. "With all that has happened to you, are you never sad at times?"

"Of course there are times. I wish that life could be different, and more simple. For me there is no proper home to go back to now, even if it were safe to travel. There is no golden hour of childhood that I can think back to, when I was ever very free from worry for my family. Rarely a time when

I was not misunderstood and misjudged by others, who read my character not as I am but according to what they believe is written upon this face, and knew no different. Hold my hand? Now I can feel how truly unhappy I was until this moment. Being here, now, it is almost a heaven. Except, I do not have my liberty, of course. And I do not know when it may end - though it must end, I know."

"You are not eager to be away?"

"Indeed, I am not. If this heaven is wrong, I am heartily sorry for it. And may Gemaal forgive my selfishness."

"I do not think that you should be sorry. You have a right to some happiness, Miss."

She still had not told him her name.

CHAPTER 7 - THE LONESOME PALACE OF MEMORY: PART I

Lifting the wooden window panel from her upstairs room, the woman saw woodsmoke curling from the chimney of the main house. There were no neighboring farms within her view. The dirt road that led off (so she was told) to a small town at a couple of hours' distance was empty of any travelers, as usual, and seemed somehow desolate to her this morning. Whether the chimney smoke was from a hearth or a cooking stove the woman was not sure, for she had not yet been inside the main house. For a couple of weeks now the barn had been her refuge. It was as though, without speaking of it, the woman and her hosts were aware of the particular danger of her being found inside the family home, should any search party arrive at the property. And anyway she preferred her chances of escape from here in the barn, if things should come to that; or more likely, she would make use of the hidden recess that Annota had showed her in her loft room.

Flight was not a true option with the onset of the Ben-Oran winter, which would undoubtedly prove deadly to any unsheltered traveler. Also it seemed to be understood, without anyone's speaking of it, that if the woman should be found in the barn, the family might plausibly deny any knowledge of her having stowed over there for a night, like any wild creature as it were. And if she should be found out, even behind the false wall, she was resigned to the impossibility of standing and fighting. That would certainly reflect very badly on her protectors should any of a search party be injured or even killed in the fray. Her hosts already risked their safety every day that she remained here, and she would not place them in further danger if she could help it.

She only allowed herself, for a bit of exercise, some brisk walks up and down the dark interior of the closed barn. And she trained herself to look regularly out through windows with their movable wooden panes, for she supposed that the different views, in total, allowed her some warning of any who were approaching; but that, too, was problematical. Nothing said that pursuers could not arrive by night, or silently along the river, or by some approach other than the main road.

The farmer's son continued to visit, but less often and more briefly. Mostly they talked, or they exchanged furtive embraces at most, which the woman had decided was the only sensible course for them. The time hung heavy for her. Lying on her cot this morning, she became aware of a sound of small ringing bells that seemed to be drawing closer. She got up, and sliding one of the window panels to the side, she could see through brief clearings in the trees along the roadway the approach of a wagon and team of water buffalo. She saw, too, that the dampness of the early morning air had yielded to a light snow.

There where the road was not lined with trees, she could see clearly the cart and team approaching from right to left. The water buffaloes were caparisoned with bright multi-colored cloths that fell nearly to their flanks, and the small bells that first announced the approach of the vehicle were evidently attached to the yoke or to the wagon itself. The vehicle passed out of her view, and she closed the panel and quickly ran to the window to the left, on the right-angle wall, and from here her view was once again unimpeded. Kneeling on a wooden chair which was just below the window, she peered out avidly. There was just the driver on the front seat of the wagon, snapping the reins lightly.

She looked on almost wistfully as the team pressed on with a jangling noise past the farmer's property. The dry, windblown snow fell on the yard and the road and the fields beyond. From the way that her shoulders sagged, an observer might have thought that she was almost disappointed that the team and traveler had passed by, leaving only the silence behind. When the scene was quite empty, with only the falling flakes of snow, and the curling trail of woodsmoke from the house, she turned her body on the chair and allowed the back of her head to rest against the barn wall. Something about the scene, or perhaps the enforced idleness of her sojourn in the barn, caused a kind of nostalgic feeling to overtake her.

She began to think back to the day-school that she had attended, over a span of perhaps nine years in her native village. The old stone building, made of a peculiarly vivid sort of red-purple stonework, used to burn a soft coal that was native to the region, and on some school days, at recesses perhaps, she would see the black flakes, by-products of the basement furnace, float in the air and sometimes fall onto the snow on the ground. She was grateful now for whatever she had learned there, but on balance she had hated the school experience.

It was not that as a child she was either lacking in intelligence, or disinclined to learn. But it was fair to say that her true worth as a citizen, as a thinking and creative being, were simply never appreciated within the caste system which in Ben-Oran society relegated all Elohin to pariah status. The laws which governed the society were arcane but inviolable. A basic injustice was the cornerstone of popular beliefs. Outside of family, and a few friendships among her "kind," she could remember nothing of fellowship, and very little of kindness.

On Ben-Ora very little of the complex of received wisdom was ever challenged. Even if much of this received wisdom was no more than a skein of superstition, conjectures, and familiar habits of mind. Where a spark of individuality did thrive, it was gradually extinguished by a spirit of creeping conformity. Of literature, per se, Ben-Oran society had as yet produced no true examples. In almost all of the penny-dreadfuls that passed for topical reportage or entertainment, the one constant, whether fiction or nominally factual, were stories which told of the nefarious ways of the Elohin. It was typically only work of this kind and style which would receive a sympathetic reading from the makers of public opinion, editors and such. And what literary work which was not actually harmful, was nevertheless equally formulaic.

It was also true that any sorts of efforts that defied conventional wisdom, or did not appear to relate directly in spirit to the example of some recent success, would elicit no enthusiasm at all. Stories of Elohin perfidy were as wildly popular as they were harmful to the public welfare. Such dreadful screeds as were circulated among the Ben-Orans, a substitute, almost, for any literature worthy of the name, helped to fan the flames of hostility and resentment, and over time would make of the calumnies against the Elohin almost ingrained articles of faith among most of the citizens.

So it was that the woman, or girl as she was then, at the age of about ten cycles of Ben-Ora's seasons, made her way in an environment of danger and degradation. But the girl exuded a youthful confidence that was all at odds with the real situation of the Elohin on Ben-Ora. She suffered as yet from no mental complex from being denoted as different by the majority. She exhibited, instead, a spirit of confidence and a defiant belief in herself, however disheartening her actual circumstances were.

In this environment, taunts against the Elohin were an everyday occurrence, to be expected like the flakes of soot that drifted over the schoolyard in the cold season. The young Elohin tended to congregate in small groups for safety, although, at recess for example, their mingling with others was not expressly forbidden. The woman, alone at that time among her kind, exercised nearly undiminished freedom in the schoolyard, and would for example, challenge any of her co-students to footraces - among the females, at any rate, for an invisible line ran the length of the schoolyard and separated the males - and she would usually win them. Already she showed a physical athleticism.

Her confidence was a goad to the majority students, who saw an unacceptable cheekiness in her manner. And one day, standing apart and catching her breath after a successful race the length of the schoolyard and back, a few of the majority students crowded sullenly near her, and were soon followed by others. The girl noticed that a couple of burly female matrons stood talking not very far away, but by experience she knew that they preferred to stay clear of conflict. The biggest girl, her face empty and malicious, stared at her and spoke.

"The Governor says that your people were all in league with the invaders."

"It isn't true."

"Your people are liars."

"We are not."

"Then why do you think that we none of us like you?" the big girl asked, a foolishly triumphant grin on her face, which set the other girls around her to sniggling.

She answered, "If you think such things about us it is because you are an impressionable and stupid person." Part of this expression the girl had heard from her father. What the larger girl could understand of the remark drove her to a cold fury. The girl saw this and was already thinking ahead. The matrons heard the raised voices but seemed indifferent to whether a fight was looming. The big girl lifted her hands and seemed intent on throttling her, but before her grip was quite set the girl threw a short punch straight out from her chest which caught the big girl on the chin and caused her head to snap back. Then what sounded like a cry of injustice escaped from the big girl. She was too shocked to move, but her confederates began throwing punches wildly at the girl, who responded with some more well-aimed punches that sent some of the girls back on their heels. Someone caught the girl with a punch - there seemed so many hands flying - and she was chagrined to find herself bleeding from the nose. Her mother would certainly discipline her if she dirtied her school-clothes.

She landed a couple of more hard punches, and the crowd seemed to be somewhat in retreat. It was only at that point, when a full blown melee had erupted, that one of the burly school matrons waded in to the disorderly group, and pushed some aside, and caught the girl by the scruff of her winter coat, and began dragging her out. The girl aimed a swift kick at someone who'd just kicked at her from behind, and the matron pulled her along roughly.

"None of that, now!"

"I didn't start any of it!"

"Sure you didn't. Come along now!" Pulling her forward. The matron made a move to box her ears, but the girl feinted, and then the matron was shocked at the girl's defiant expression, and her fist that was cocked to defend herself.

"You bold thing! Your father is a jailbird and that is how you will end up."

The girl looked at her contemptuously.

"She looked about to kill me!" the matron would complain to sympathetic listeners later. For the moment the matron thought it best to keep her free hand at her side rather than attempt any more blows.

A small knot of Elohin girls crowded near to their path toward the schoolhouse. Even while watching the scene, their faces seemed somehow averted; fearful looking, their faces darkened by the painful-looking patches of scar on their faces. The girl nodded very subtly in their direction, and when the matron's grip on her collar became too insistent, almost costing the girl her balance, she threw off the matron's restraining hand forcefully and continued walking, but a half step further away from her. She gave a small wink to one of the girls, and one or two of them smiled to her in a very shy and discreet manner as the girl and matron made their way, no doubt, to some punishment in the school principal's office.

She was brought first to the office of the school nurse, who washed the girl's face roughly, and then to a study room used by the instructors. The principal had seen enough of the girl this school year and she did not wish to see her.

The matron knocked on the door and then brought the girl inside in tow.

In the study room was only a middle-aged male instructor who was grading papers. He sat at one of a few large desks in the room. There were some small chairs with writing boards about the middle of the room. A fire was burning in the grate, and oil lamps cast a faint light. The winter morning was overcast, and not much light came through the windows.

"I'm sorry, sir. This girl has been fighting--"

He stared at the girl. "It's alright," the schoolteacher broke in. "Do you know why she was fighting?"

"I'm sure I have no idea, sir. Except that she is just naturally evil."

"I don't think that can be true, matron." The girl looked up at him briefly, from the small uncomfortable chair to which the matron had directed her. "Leave her here and I will see that she commits no further mayhem. Good day."

The teacher ignored the girl for a while. She sat sullenly and heard the scrape of his pencil across paper, and the papers being rustled and moved about. Then he drew them all into a pile and studied the girl who was sitting there rather morosely.

"You are here again, child?" he said. She didn't respond, only worried a fingernail between her teeth, fidgeting. "If you would like to look out the window, or walk around a bit, you may do so." The girl remained where she was. "No? You know you must stay here for a time."

The girl got up then, and without speaking, nodded low toward the schoolteacher for his consideration. The round patch of scar on the girl's cheek, which was a dull satin in the gloom of the study room, seemed to cast her face into deeper shadow. The teacher thought, as he often had, of the strange destiny of Ben-Ora and its inhabitants. Of the intertwined destinies of the majority and of - this *race*, was closest to the word that was in his mind. This race, he thought again - but that was very unsatisfactory, for they were Ben-Orans like him, nothing more. It was circumstances, and wild suppositions about their supposedly inimical qualities, that set the Elohin apart. Did other people see it? he wondered. He felt quite alone in his opinion.

The girl walked toward the window. The schoolyard had emptied of students, and so she had no opportunity of making a face at any of them who should look up.

"I hate them!" she said.

"Hatred is a very strong drink, child. I think that too many of the inhabitants of our planet are mad with it. Why don't you be different?"

She turned and faced him. "I *am* different."

"Well, so you are. In many different ways, if I can judge. You must be careful of the things you say. As a public official I am obliged to report attitudes which are harmful to the greater good of Ben-Ora."

This was a rote speech to the schoolteacher, and his voice sounded hollow to him.

"It is your beliefs which are harmful. Are you as false as the rest of them?"

"I do not mean you any harm. Just be careful of what

you say, especially to those you do not know. The times are very dangerous."

The girl looked at him, trying to understand his meaning. He walked to the window where she was standing. He placed a hand on her shoulder and brushed some hair from her forehead. The girl could see, on the wall opposite, a switch from a tree hanging by its strap. In other circumstances she might well have been whipped today. She thought that his counsel was good, but was very unsure if she could resist being goaded into more fights.

"Now," he said, "I have some more work to do, and then I will take you back to class when I leave here. If you like, take a story from the shelf to read, or paper to draw."

She would often be sent home with a sheet of paper with some biased description of the disruption which the girl had supposedly caused. These would have to be signed by her parents and returned. She always dreaded handing one of these reports to her parents. For one thing, she was very aware that they had their own problems to contend with. The years of occupation had created hardships for many; and in the aftermath too, the girl's parents were having difficulty maintaining a hold in Ben-Oran society.

On these occasions her mother would be all for beating her, but her father admired the girl's spirit and would seldom allow it; except for those few times when the offense seemed genuine and not merely embellished. The mother would read aloud the report of the school-teacher or matron in a piteous and outraged voice as though she actually believed it (though such impressionability seemed unthinkable to the girl).

On this occasion, the mother read aloud from the school report.

"I have already heard it," the father said.

The girl's mother spoke the matron's name in sympathy and mortification. The girl said of the matron, "She is a born liar who has improved with practice."

"Is that any way to speak about your elders?"

"As far as I'm concerned, she can go to Dorah-el."

"Shame on you!"

Dorah-el was in fact a place in the underworld for liars, or at least that was the popular belief.

"You must apologize to her for creating a disturbance," her mother insisted.

"I will not."

"Then you shall get the switch!"

While her mother went off for the dreaded switch the girl wondered what she ought to do. She thought she was now old enough, and developed enough, to defend herself, even against her own mother. She studiously avoided looking at her father. He got up from his kitchen chair and stood rubbing his hands agitatedly on his work coveralls. She fought down the urge to plead with him, for it didn't seem fair to the girl to pit parent against parent.

When her mother returned to the kitchen in a fury and made to strike the girl on the legs, the girl stepped aside dexterously, and before she could contemplate her next move her father's voice boomed.

"Stop it! I am going to talk to the girl."

"You stand aside!"

The father wrenched the switch out of her hands and crushed it in a fury, throwing it on the floor. "Enough!"

"Oh!"

"Daughter, come outside." He removed coats from a rack near the kitchen door, and pushed her before him. Standing outside their mud-and-brick house, with the smell of burning wood and soft coal in the dark, early evening air, she went with her father along the narrow walk that bisected his summertime gardens and the small, roofed-over patio to one side.

He stopped and then placed a hand on the girl's shoulder. "Why were you fighting, then? Were you defending yourself, child?"

He seemed to understand the situation exactly, before she had to speak.

"Of course I was," she said. "Nothing else but defending myself."

He pulled her to him and said, "Then I can ask no differently of you. I will settle this with your mother. Do not be worried about it."

Her father's voice drifted into the sooty night air, and returned just as vividly now in the quiet barn loft.

In these challenging circumstances, while still at school, but many years later, young males took an interest in her. There was one, a non-Elohin who had seemed kind, who was even from one of the better families, and whose attention to her seemed a sort of balm in a mostly friendless existence. He kept her company, usually in the fields or forests, and often outside of the village gates. At the school they were strangers - he must think of his parents' feelings, for now, he said.

She did not consider, at first, that the attentions that he paid her were all furtive and secret. It flattered her feminine ego that this very presentable young male wanted to make love to her. As a result she discouraged the attentions of the young males of her caste. There must have been some who were of decent character, whatever their physical deformities. (It was an unsatisfactory term, but it was how the majority felt, and for the moment she herself could not think of a better characterization.)

Because of her family's reduced social standing as members of the Elohin, she was deprived of any public displays of courtship with this admirer, who she would have considered a worthy trophy, indeed. For this reason, the feelings of triumph that she might have enjoyed, from the gratification of her youthful vanity, were impeded and compromised. Her feminine triumph could not be consummated. When young, she seemed to believe, instinctively, that goodness must always display itself outwardly, and that a plain exterior must enclose an inferior character. She learned too late that a charming appearance sometimes concealed a false nature, while the appearance of many individuals of exemplary character held no obvious novelty or attraction. Strength of character, had, too often, outwardly nothing especially to commend it. When she thought about these things now she grew furious with herself. It disturbed her that she had not proven smarter, at that time at any rate, than the common run of Ben-Orans. She hated the person she was then for her superficiality, and chided herself because, with her qualities of intelligence and discernment, she could not have seen the truth more clearly, even then. It seemed rather that her mind, then, was controlled by some instinctive and biological view of existence.

When she told the young man that she was pregnant with their child, he said that there was not anything that he could do except to provide what money he could for her. She was surprised and crestfallen at his coldness.

"If you really loved me," she said, "we would be together. You wouldn't care what others think."

"You cannot expect me to do that. I would stand to lose my inheritance. I cannot live like a vagabond among your people."

Later, she had to leave school. Her mother said that she would raise the child, or find a decent home for it. She only asked the daughter never to return to their village.

"You have brought shame upon our family," were the last words that she heard her mother speak.

CHAPTER 8 - A CONCERT, AND BEDLAM

"I shall have to leave soon, I think." The woman was speaking to Annota on the ground floor of the loft. She had been helping him to carry feed to the animals' stalls.

The man didn't say anything, but stopped and held her in his arms. "Isn't the air rather cold yet?"

"No, I can see it is changing for the better." She chafed his forehead with her hand. "Why, even *I* can see it, shuttered up in this barn for, what, nearly half the year?"

"Not quite so long."

"Where were you yesterday? I was rather lonely all day."

"Did I not tell you? There was fencing to be repaired near the hills, and I brought one of the wagons out."

"Yes, I think you did mention it."

"I am sorry life is so slow here. For you."

"Do not worry about me," she said. It was a fact that she saw little of the rest of the farmer's family, and had almost never seen any of the family's neighbors from her windows. After a while, "Do you not think it surprising that in this time none have come searching for me?"

"None have come here, it is true. But I believe there are standing orders to arrest all of you. They mean to place you all in detention camps."

"Yes, they had already begun when I escaped. I am not sure what the authorities thought my crime was. They seem to believe that I am a leader of the Elohin, although I have never tried to be. We are too scattered now, anyway, those of us who are not in prison."

"And would you be safe there? If you were to turn yourself in, perhaps?"

She turned her head and put a finger to his lips. "Do not think of that. No, I must be free, if I can manage it. You can hardly imagine the constraints under which I have had to live my life. I will not willingly give up what freedom I still possess. I am not the dangerous undesirable which your society is determined to make of me."

"I understand. Pardon me. I was only thinking of your safety."

"So do I think of it, farmer."

"What you were asking before, it is possible none have come here to search because my father is a rather important person in the town."

"You said that he runs an advertising-sheet?"

"Yes, it is that, and a little more. My father expresses, well, I should call them opinions, and he invites readers to send in their opinions, too."

"Opinions about what?"

"Our society here. My father feels that we are in many ways a backward-looking society. I agree with him in some ways."

"Well, it can be dangerous to express such opinions on Ben-Ora."

"Indeed. Just tonight he and my mother are attending an event in town. The governor of the district will be there, and an orchestra, and I don't know what else."

"It sounds very festive. Are you going as well?"

"No, I shall stay here."

"Is it that you do not wish to leave me alone?"

"It is not only that, but my siblings are young and must not be left to themselves."

At that moment the latch of the great doors was heard to lift. The woman pulled away from him, and instinctively drew behind a wooden beam nearby. It was just the father, with the youngest daughter trailing behind him and carrying a tray with breakfast.

"I was just telling our guest that you are attending an event in town tonight."

"Yes, I see you are. Good morning, Miss. Well, it is necessary to my business, and I am rather fond of music. The orchestra is coming from Taphaia to play. Good day. I shall be home for supper," he said to Annota. "There is breakfast inside. Do not be long." The father and the girl left the barn.

Over breakfast the mother said, "My friend Natael tells me that you have not been to call on her daughter in a great while. Do we keep you too busy with work?"

The father stared at him. "She is of a good family, and seems pleasant enough."

"Perhaps I am a little bored by her."

"Bored!" the father said. "Great Gemaal, what is that supposed to mean? She's young, and I should say fairly good-looking. I see no reason to be bored."

He did not say anything. The daughter said, "I think you are making Annota feel uncomfortable."

"Well I don't care if he is uncomfortable. I am only asking him frankly-- Or is that you have taken more interest in a certain stowaway, to whom we have given refuge? The blazes. Son, that female is not for you. You do see that, don't you?"

"I am rather fond of her." He reached into a basket and took one of the small rolls, filled with sweet currants, that the Ben-Orans favored. "I know you are right."

"Children," the father said, "You must continue to tell no one that that woman is here. Not even your closest friends. Swear?" Following the father's cue, Annota's two siblings all raised a hand from the table, with thumbs tucked into the palm, which was a kind of local pledge of fealty to a cause. He lowered his hand and said, "Bah! of course I am right. Nothing to be done about it."

After breakfast the father readied the wagon and drove into town to his office. He had fashioned his own sort of printing press, from the available models which then existed on Ben-Ora. In this he had shown a good deal of ingenuity, as well as dogged persistence in personally crafting the types which he used, which represented the principal hieroglyphs of their language, sufficient to allow some basic communication in writing. For some days he had been composing his own definitive thoughts about the situation of the Elohin. He felt pride as he set the type-blocks in place, with their large heading, A HARMFUL LIE. His exposition of the problem, which followed, was both revolutionary and unheard of at the time.

His views had been, if not transformed, than at least sharpened, by the woman who had lodged in his barn in the recent period. Her stories had made a deep impression upon him, revealing as they did her evident courage, and the paramount importance which freedom held for her, which caused her to endure so many hardships when others might have surrendered to fate, or at any rate to custom, which on Ben-Ora seemed equally inescapable. To the editor it seemed past time to speak out. He had long ago ceased printing the sorry and scurrilous fictions which attacked the Elohin as harmful and malevolent creatures. Such pieces he rejected as pure trash, which had first offended him aesthetically, and secondly injured his sense of fair play.

When the proof-sheet was rolled off and the assistant saw the title and what to him seemed the incendiary words which followed, he looked doubtfully at the editor. But the editor looked determined as they both proof-read the article which would appear in that morning's edition. He went home in the late afternoon, leaving the assistant to transcribe some merchant advertisements which had been received recently.

The evening's concert was a rather formal dress affair with the usual two or more lengthy intermissions. Music, insofar as it existed on Ben-Ora at this time, brought out a spirit of conversational ease among the concert-goers, which could only be satisfied with milling of groups of various sizes, in the large lobby of the village concert hall and spilling to the broad walk in front of the building. There were also meeting rooms within the building, one being virtually a private club for the district's elite, which included local and regional leaders and the editor. And there were other such rooms, not as well appointed, for laborers, some for females and others for males, for Ben-Oran society was rather stratified along class and gender lines. Spirits were very freely drunk on these occasions, either at the long bar near the street entrance, or more commonly from bottles brought by the concert-goers.

The provincial orchestra which was visiting had about twenty players and singers. Their instruments consisted entirely of bells and gongs, which was normal for Ben-Ora at this time. The tumult that was created by the beating of gongs with sticks, and of variously sized bells with metal or wooden mallets - all to single, double and even treble meters simultaneously - was a joy to most hearers. A dense and lush sort of jungle rhythm was created by the confluence of so many hands in syncopation; the feeling of repose only came when the music stopped, or during rare muted interludes when the players wrapped their mallets in cloth satchels and struck at the bells delicately, without their customary vigor. From the expressions of the concert-goers, they entered a kind of elysium at these times, which was augmented as well by the potent liquors that they drank on the occasion.

Sometimes a male singer would take center stage and sing a romantic ballad, or pious hymn to great Gemaal, generally in a high tenor voice which was very stylized. And sometimes a female sang in a relatively lower contralto voice, and once a trio of females, all with songs which carried similar themes.

During the first lengthy intermission, the editor with his wife sought out the visiting Governor in the great lobby and engaged him in conversation. The Governor's wife - the Ben-Oran term was closer to "life partner," and was not gender specific - stood next to him. The males wore long jackets, the females, gowns.

The editor suavely asked the Governor's wife, "Are you enjoying the concert so far?"

"Oh, it is very pleasant," bringing a glass of spirits to her lips. She and the Governor appeared some years older than the editor and his wife.

"And how about you?" The Governor nodded politely toward the editor's wife.

"Well" - and the editor began biting his lip at her first word - "I don't understand why all our so-called modern orchestras play nothing but bells."

"But - that is music, Inna," the editor interjected.

"Indeed, the very finest," the Governor agreed.

The editor's wife sipped her drink, and said, "Oh, bells, bells, mallets and balls!"

"Really, Inna."

"Yes, clanging away in an absolute frenzy. It's - indecent. I don't doubt the musicians wouldn't have a bit of energy left for doing - well, anything else."

When she spoke, her husband frequently had a worried expression at what she'd said or might be about to say. Years ago he had found her irreverence refreshing, but she could be very impolitic. To someone observing the editor's nettled expression, he might have looked like a weary traveler arrived on the morning coach and in need of rest, who finds that his lodging is located across the lane from a noisy and bustling cooper's workshop.

"And that male singer, with the very high voice--"

"He sounds just as he is supposed to, Inna," the editor interjected. "The result of years of training."

"Maybe so, but he sounded just as if his underclothes were in a bunch. Looked like it, too!"

"No doubt you speak as an expert on such things, Inna--"

"And why do the women sing in bass voices?"

"Oh, this is rich," the Governor's wife said. Only the Governor was looking very dignified and not smiling.

"The Governor helped to bring the orchestra here tonight, you know." The editor twisted up the side of his face visible only to his wife, in a signal.

"Did I not also say they are wonderful? And that the concert is really tremendously diverting?"

"Yes, I believe you did say that." Although the editor was definitely unclear on the matter.

"It is only that my friend Nimma says that in the capitol they have formed groups of musicians who play on metal strings that they pluck, or - I don't know - scrape across, and that they perform publicly with excellent results."

"It takes time," the editor said in his suave voice, "for these modern trends to reach the provinces. And plucking and scraping strings may be only a fad, anyway. Give me bells anytime. With bells one can express anything."

"Oh, bells!" she snorted. She made to go toward the bar, along with the Governor's wife.

The Governor placed a hand on the editor's arm. I should like a word with you in private. Let us adjourn to the meeting room, if you would.

When they got there the editor said, "If it is about my wife, I have tried to reason with her."

"Oh, no, not at all. She is very charming I am sure. But let us talk. Here are drinks." A waiter came up to them.

At the same moment, at the other end of the town's main road, by prearrangement, some villagers carried a sheaf of money to the town's peacekeeper. He had arranged previously to look in on a ranching family out of town, which had complained of poaching, and also to dismiss his assistant for the night.

"No one is to be harmed," he said, closing his office and setting out on foot.

Not long after, at the newspaper office, the assistant saw the trouble forming immediately. The light inside was dim. He saw the men with hoods over their heads just outside the window and, suspecting the worst, told his young son to run out the back door to the opera house, and tell the editor that there was trouble here and to come at once. While he was peering out through the glass, uncertain whether any of the hooded men could see him, a rock crashed through the window, followed by a flaming torch, which the assistant stamped out with difficulty.

The door opened and the hooded figures walked in. They were armed.

"Stay out of our way, we don't want any trouble with you."

The assistant thought he recognized the voice. "Why don't you clear out of here?" He hoped only to buy a little time, until the peacekeeper should see something was amiss, or a group arrive from the opera house. "I won't let you damage this place."

"You don't have a choice. Now clear out of here and you won't be hurt."

"I will not."

"Suit yourself, then." At a signal, one of them struck the assistant on the head and he collapsed to the floor. They began turning over the press and the type trays and other devices, and grinding the metal types underfoot.

Some villagers looked out through windows at the scene. Others, passing near, saw the darkened office of the peacekeeper, and shrugged and walked on.

The Governor and editor were joined by the town mayor and other interested villagers in the assembly room. The Governor placed a hand on the editor's shoulder and spoke first. "Many citizens believe that you have crossed a line with your editorial."

"Is this a warning, Governor? I am speaking my conscience. I simply do not believe this calumny that is spoken against the Elohin."

Some of the others were moved to visible anger, but the Governor said, "You must watch yourself."

"Nevertheless I believe I am free to express my opinions."

"And societies are free to suppress them. I cannot say if I believe you are fortunate to have a forum for your rather strange ideas. For you place yourself in mortal danger in expressing such beliefs."

"But there is nothing strange about my ideas. For any who will listen without prejudice."

The Mayor broke in, "You have committed a blasphemy."

"A blasphemy! You cannot be serious, Mayor. Where is your proof that the Elohin are guilty of any crime?"

"Proof! Hasn't great Gemaal said it is so?"

"How did He say it?"

"Why, He has revealed it to seers and holy men. We are all of us in accord. And I cannot guarantee the protection of those who would subvert established opinion and the public order."

"Established opinion which is inimical to the lives of a people who have done no wrong? No, I cannot accept it, even if thousands of you insist I am mistaken. Governor, what do you say about this? You are an honorable man. And I do not believe that you are as simple as you make yourself out to be."

"I will take that as a compliment, my friend. I am only a provincial Governor. I did not create these policies but I am bound to enforce them. What would it matter if I say that I find no fault with these individuals? But mind you: Conscience is not something to be displayed too openly in our world. I do not say you are right, or wrong. But you must learn to temper your words--"

At that moment a young male scampered into the assembly room pursued by a pair of music hall employees. He ran straight up to the editor who, recognizing his assistant's son, raised a hand and said, "It is alright, I know him. What is it, son?" Bending down.

"Sir - your shop - my father -" catching his breath - "they are being attacked, sir."

"Attacked! "He turned and said, "It seems trouble has come sooner than you expected, Governor." Then he ran out the exit and turned up the main street.

The Governor said to his personal bodyguard, "Go, see that no harm comes to him. I am alright here."

When the editor arrived at his newspaper office he found the front window smashed and piles of rubble on the wooden sidewalk. The hooded men did not try to stop him, but two stepped from the shadows and disarmed the Governor's bodyguard, holding him at gunpoint.

The editor found a scene of chaos inside, of overturned furniture and tossed papers. His assistant was struggling with one of the hooded men. The editor managed to spin him around and tore at the pointed hood upon his head, recognizing a village idler. The villager clutched at the hood and tried to set it back over his head and align the eye holes. The editor in a rage swung hard and caught him on the side of the head with his fist, and the vandal fell with a thud to the floor. But as he scampered to his feet, a shot rang out from the street and the editor ducked and pressed his assistant to the floor. The assistant had some facial bruises but his eyes looked alert. The editor gestured to him to stay down.

He heard a few more shouts from the street, and then scampering footsteps, followed by an intense sort of quiet. Getting to his feet he ventured carefully to the wooden sidewalk. None of the vandals were visible, or any villagers either, and he noted that the town peacekeeper's office had no lamp burning. The last gunshot had splintered a high horizontal board above the storefront, and the sign proclaiming the name of the newspaper swung freely from only one fastener, almost striking the editor's head as he stepped to the dark sidewalk. The sign read, in the peculiar and for the moment unstable hieroglyphic that was used on Ben-Ora, TRUTH.

The woman could hear the yoke and harness bells of the water buffaloes pulling a cart, arriving in the farmers' yard, and she strained to see who had arrived in the darkness. Annota and his siblings were in the main house over supper, she knew. The new arrival was a stranger, and he nearly leaped from the slowly moving cart and pounded on the kitchen door. She remained where she was on the ground floor, peering through the slightly opened barn doors into the yard but making out little of the animated conversation at the back of the house. Soon the new arrival remounted his cart and made his way slowly back in the direction of the village center. Not long after, the farmer's son came out and told her what had been related to him.

"You must go and see that your father is alright."

"Yes, I am come to fetch the other wagon."

"And I am afraid I must go. Tonight."

"Must it be now?" The farmer's son seemed bereft. "I understand, if you must."

"I do not know just what yet, but there is something unpleasant happening here. I do hope that your father has no more trouble. Do thank everyone for me."

"Collect your things, then."

"Really I haven't much. Let us not be sad, farmer. Thanks to you and your family, you see me in much better condition than the day you found me. I cannot repay you."

"I will bring you some food very quickly, Miss."

He went into the house and returned shortly with a satchel of the day's bread, and a quantity of dry fruit which was something like figs.

"These will keep for a long time," he told her.

Near the barn door she drew him to her. Then with her finger she raised his downcast face to see him more clearly. Wiping tears from his face she said again, "Do not be sad, farmer. We always knew this day would come. Gemaal bless you. Who knows, maybe we will meet again in different circumstances."

"I shall always hope so, Miss."

She held her satchel of food and small bedroll in one hand, and with the other she drew the black cape closer about her shoulders, for the evenings were still cool.

"And by the way, farmer - my name is Amara."

He mouthed the word back to her, and then spoke it aloud. Amara. A smile came to his face.

She kissed him once more, and then with an effort she turned and went out the rear barn door. Once in the rear yard, she turned and followed the route which they had discussed many times. Ford the river at its shallow spot, and then follow alongside the other side of the river, which would widen after two days' walking. The route led to open country, at least, and there might be safety in that.

CHAPTER 9 - A WELCOME OF SORTS

She walked near the tree lines, seldom in open fields, and usually within view of the river. She traveled for several days without seeing anyone. Except, from a distance, a group of four individuals who she took to be a hunting or trapping party. They walked in an open field, but at first sight of them the woman moved in among the trees and continued walking in the same direction. She lived mostly on tubers that she found in the ground, left over from the growing season and preserved by the cold. These she would wash and peel with her knife, roasting them when it seemed safe at a fire that she made with a small metal clicker.

She arrived at a small town. The town did not look like anything special from where she stood. There were very few homes at this end, and before her, the broad main street of dust was empty of anyone. There were raised wooden sidewalks on either side of the street, but no carts to be seen, or anyone moving in or out of the small storefronts. The woman stood behind some shrubbery and waited.

She had been walking for several days since leaving the farmer's family. Mostly she walked during the day. The land here was sparsely populated. If she saw a stranger approaching in the distance she would try to disappear, wraithlike, into any surrounding trees, perhaps in some interval where a hill, or shrubbery, intervened between her and the stranger. She had become very good at concealment, and she imagined that with her disappearances she had perplexed more than one passing stranger. And when an encounter was unavoidable, she would generally only nod, averting her face if possible. If there was a lone individual who recognized her for an Elohin, he did not let on, and none had confronted her.

The woman's provisions were almost gone, except for some of the fig-like fruits that the farmer's son had given to her. She had a little silver currency, and thought she might buy a bit of food in the town, if some shopkeeper was not unsympathetic to her - or she might steal something, if necessary. It was mid-afternoon. The woman approached the main street and stepped lightly upon the wooden sidewalk. There was a private residence, then a shuttered millinery shop, and then what looked like a lodging house. But no individuals stirred, and she stepped out to the middle of the dusty street and continued walking. She could see, first on the other side of the street, and then very generally, strips of white cloth nailed to the doorposts of some residences and stores; on Ben-Ora the cloths were universal marks of illness and possibly death. The woman had happened upon a scene of epidemic, or plague. Instinctively, her breathing became more shallow.

With her mind concentrated upon the scene of desolation around her, rather late she could feel, and then see, the long shadow of a person from behind, and simultaneously she was startled to hear a footstep in the dust close behind. She whirled instantly, but remembered to keep the side of her face averted. The figure - an older female - did not advance upon her, but backed off a few steps with the palms of her hands raised in the air.

"Miss, I am sorry. Can you help us?"

"How?" Turned, by necessity, partly away from the woman.

"Sickness has carried off so many, Miss, there are hardly any able-bodied, to aid the deceased."

"I am sorry."

"Can you help, Miss?"

She did not see how, much as she would have wanted to. "You mean to aid them how?"

"Why, to bring them to a place of burning, Miss. It is all we can do for them now."

"It is dangerous, and I do not know any of you." Looking away.

"I am aware, Miss. I understand. I have cloths, here in my satchel, that may be wrapped around the face, and coverings that may be tied around the hands. And I have cleaned them myself. But if you will not..."

"No. I will help. Give me one of the scarves--"

"Gemaal bless you, Miss."

"Yes, yes." She took the scarf and wrapped it about her face, and tucked the ends under her cape, so that only her eyes and forehead showed above the cloth. Now she could look directly upon the village woman.

"You look right strong, if I may say, Miss."

"Let us start."

"Right away."

In a small alley between buildings, a broad cart but no animal to pull it, and a tarp that was weighted down with pieces of metal. One lifeless hand could be seen pointing downward below the tarp. The village woman stood nearby. "These passed overnight," she said.

"Right. Let us try to wheel it in the direction of your fire."

About an hour later the fire blazed very high. The village woman stood not very far away from it, and from a satchel she removed a small palm-sized triangle of metal, with some irregular metal rods attached to it. She raised the apparatus before her by an attached cord, and with a rather solemn expression she lifted a short metal rod and struck it against the triangle. After she struck it an echoing, second chime sounded, and after the same interval a third, nearly as loud and all of them in the same tone, and accompanied by a sort of ground pattern of other sympathetic chimes of varying pitches. Before the sounds had gone silent she would strike the triangle again, and the echoing and contrasting tones would follow so that a sustained rhythm was created. The wide dusty street was silent except for the delicate bell-like sounds, and the murmur and crackling of the blaze.

When the woman had struck the triangle a sufficient number of times, she waited until there was near silence, and carefully returned the instruments to the satchel. Then she removed from her pocket some short strips of paper, and standing rather close to the fire, a few at a time she flung them into the blaze. The strips of paper were marked, in the common Ben-Oran hieroglyphics, with the names of the deceased, or else were marked to represent some quantities of local currency. The pieces of paper floated above the heat of the flames, and singed and curled, darkening, and drifted upward and vanished.

During this time Amara stood off to the side, observing. It was not necessary for the woman to explain to her the significance of the ceremony, for these rites - the simulated currency, the printed names and the ritual, solemn music - were almost universally believed to provide comfort to the souls of the deceased, to allow them to move on into the afterworld with a minimum of confusion or hardship.

Later the two females sat a good distance away from the blaze, only close enough to see if it faltered, and if so to throw more brush upon the pile.

"May I have something to drink?" Amara asked.

The woman passed her a battered and rather heavy canteen of metal. In the growing dusk she turned slightly away and unwound the scarf from her face, which felt uncomfortably warm. She turned her head up and trickled an exploratory sip of water into her mouth. It tasted fine, and so, holding the canteen an inch from her mouth as before, she nearly drained it.

"Is this all that you wished to do today?"

"It is quite enough, thank you."

The woman sniffled and Amara thought she might ask her if she had lost anyone in the plague, but she kept silence. There was so much trouble in the world, she did not feel compelled to inquire into the particulars of this villager's experience. But something else struck her.

"Tell me," wiping some sweat from her forehead, "are there *no* able males in this town?" she complained.

"They are at service mostly, Miss."

"Do you mean they are pressed into service against the Elohin?"

"No, Miss. That is, many of them are. But most of the townspeople who remain here are now praying at the house of worship."

"Are they, indeed. You mean I have been working while they are praying?"

"Oh, do not think badly of them, Miss. These are desperate times and I'm sure many do not know what else to do." After a pause, "Have you any home, Miss?"

"I am traveling at present."

"Yes, times is very hard, lately. So many individuals have taken to the roads. For helping us, will you come and have supper with my family?"

"I could not impose upon your kindness." Turning incrementally aside, in proportion as the woman turned to see her more clearly.

"May I say, you keep very to yourself, Miss."

"It is just my way. I am very hungry, though."

"Then I shall prepare you something to bring with you, or you may consume it in my side-yard, if you are so scrupulous about not imposing on one."

"I should welcome that very much."

"Then let us start."

They began walking toward the village woman's house.

"Let me have your things," she said - meaning the scarf, and makeshift cloth mittens. Amara handed them to her. She found that by keeping consistently to one side of the woman, and holding her neck rather straight, or inclining her head away, she could conceal the patch of scar from the woman. The day was nearly dusk. She did not feel in any danger from her in any case, but dared not reveal herself if it could be helped.

"There is nothing more to be done about the fire?" Amara asked.

"It is nearly out now. It will be alright I am sure. Only it is turning cold again, after such pleasant weather. Have you somewhere to stay?"

"Oh, I am alright."

"But, Miss."

"Thank you, though. May I ask you, are there any Elohin here about?"

"Oh, they have all gone into captivity, Miss. Those who did not flee earlier."

Amara considered for a moment. "And has it eased the villagers' minds, that they have gone into captivity?"

"I am sure I could not say, Miss. I do not understand such things."

"Do you know where the others have fled to?"

"Many say, they are moving toward the less inhabited areas, where it is colder."

The woman led Amara toward the back of her house, and before entering by a kitchen door said, "I have something already prepared, and you may eat it here, if you prefer. There is a pump there, and water. Please, refresh yourself, you have worked hard."

"I will, thank you."

While she stood with a drying towel to her face, the woman brought out a kind of stew in a metal bowl and set it out with something to drink on a table in the door-yard.

When she had done eating, Amara stood holding the cup and emptied bowl and was about to knock on the kitchen door, before pausing. She placed them on the low wooden table nearby, and knocked briskly and quickly moved off several steps from the lighted windows, and further into the darkness. The door opened, and she only waved at the woman, thanked her, and turned to go. At this distance, her face was certainly concealed by the growing darkness.

"Miss--"

The woman walked toward her, and Amara remained with her face turned slightly away, as before.

"Miss." Pressing some silver coins into her hand.

"I cannot accept--"

"I am sorry for your kind," the woman said, "and I wish Gemaal's blessing upon you. Please do not think badly of us."

Amara could not think of anything to say, and was in fact too overcome by the woman's gesture to speak. She only raised her hand in a gesture of thanks and hurried off into the darkness.

The woman had remarked upon the change in weather, and when Amara had walked some distance she was very aware of the cold. The woman had pointed out the house of worship in passing, the place where several townspeople were said to have been praying earlier. So she went in that direction, through the emptied streets, straight up to the front double doors of the church, which she found were not locked. Stepping inside, she found a rear corridor or lobby lighted with some oil lanterns on the walls, and she looked carefully into the interior, past an opened set of doors, and found this place to be empty, too. The space felt a little warmer, and she could hear, but not feel the wind that swept over the town. She loosened from her shoulders the knapsack which she had fashioned, and standing at the inner entrance, she made her obeisance in the normal Ben-Oran way: a simple bow from the waist, hands brought together to the lips. The gestures were now a little strange to her, living as she did, and not having attended any services at all for many and many seasons. Even long ago, she found that she could not help feeling distinctly uncomfortable at the services, with all of the changes that had happened in her society since she was a child.

It was not that the Elohin were ever barred from religious services - or if it happened, it could only have been rarely - but rather that the everyday manner of the majority group, and sometimes even the off-handed words spoken by the officiating clerics, said plainly that in the sincere view of the majority, the Elohin were transgressors whose souls and appearance alike were repulsive. There was no pleasure, and no uplift, in participating in the services, often seated apart in their own sub-group, as it were - when Amara, in fact, recognized herself as the equal of any of the majority. But on this occasion, when she bowed at the back of this rather large church, she was moved by the hushed stillness of the place, and it was with sincerity that she thanked Gemaal for another day of life and safety, and for the night's shelter, and hoped for an interval of peaceful days to come.

The seating consisted of pews of smooth wooden benches with high backs. When she assured herself that there was no one else inside, she made her way to the right of the central nave, and toward the end of one of the benches she lay and rested her head upon the bedroll that she withdrew from her knapsack. Before very long she was sound asleep, being very tired from the day's exertions.

She woke before there was any light streaming through the high windows of the church, when the sounds of some object striking upon wood, or perhaps a bench groaning under the weight of some early parishioner echoed through the wide, quiet sanctuary of the church interior. Amara supposed that she ought to steal away immediately. But her body still felt stiff with sleep, and how could there be any danger in such a peaceful haven - especially in a town that was as decimated as this one by sickness? After another short interval of sleep she began to hear, not human voices raised up in harmony, but from a balcony at the back of the church (she was as yet too sleepy to know from just where the sounds came), a crystalline chiming of bells. The variously sized bells were tuned in such a way, and struck with such accomplished delicacy, that the sound was as peaceful as a river flowing over rocks, and inspiring as a gentle hymn.

It occurred to Amara that the musicians were only tuning up, as it were, and she fell off to sleep again. Then she became aware of voices nearby, and looking straight up from her bench she was aware of some townspeople - mostly older males, they appeared, with rather scraggly facial hair, and furtive expressions - staring straight down at her. One even held a rope in a lasso, as if he meant to tie her up like some farm animal. She quickly closed her eyes again, and felt for her knapsack on the floor, and then with a decisive movement she reached behind for her bedroll and slid away from them on the bench, and stood up. She looked about, brushing hair from her face. There were about a half-dozen of them, and a few more villagers at the back, and in the central aisle.

"Careful, she has woken up," one of the males said rather obviously.

"Surrender, Miss," the one with the lasso said. He lunged into the pew toward her, but she pushed him down and backed away a few steps.

"I don't want any trouble with you," she said. "I am leaving your town."

Silently, the group of males pursued, moving among the pews to the left and right. She was obliged to leap over the bench to her left, and so jump over several pews, in the direction of the altar, until she could run into the central nave.

More male villagers appeared at the back of the church and pressed toward her, attempting to bar her way. She dashed into another pew, on the opposite side of the church, and as others approached she was obliged again to leap over benches to find some means of escape.

For a town that had none able-bodied yesterday, they all showed a good deal of energy today, she thought. Perhaps the entire remaining village was now here. She was aware of the holy man, wearing a gaudily colored surplice, looking impassively on the scene from the front of the church.

Villagers pressed from all sides, as she stood on one of the forward benches very near the central aisle. She was obliged to strike the male closest to her as he lunged into the pew, and as he fell she leaped over him into the nave. But her foot caught on a collection box there and she landed with some pain in her ankle and fell, just as the slotted wooden lid of the strongbox opened and the box crashed on the floor next to her. The crash startled even her as a tumult of silver coins clattered to the floor. With the sudden and untimely pain in her foot, she quickly got to her feet, leaving bedroll and knapsack on the floor, and raised her hands in front of her, shoulder-high. Now she stood within the altar. The main cleric stood nearby with his hands folded, with a calm and mildly chiding expression on his face, at the damage to church decorum that, in his mind, the strange woman was wholly responsible for. But he did not say anything immediately.

The woman had no thought of escape just now, rather to gather her strength and to rest her ankle. She was winded from the exercise, but the village males who were gathered around, she noticed, drew their breaths even more noisily than her.

The cleric asked, "Are you quite finished with making a disturbance?"

"You are asking me?"

"Who else?"

"I came here for rest - and to offer a prayer." Prayer was, perhaps, a secondary reason for her visit, but on balance she thought she had made a true statement.

"Indeed."

"Strange, it is my understanding that in Gemaal's house all are welcome."

"In His house it may be true, Miss, but this is only a plain old country church."

She nodded with slight mockery, as though suddenly enlightened.

"It is not very often that we are visited by your kind."

"Does it surprise you?" she replied. "And anyway, from all I have heard, you have sent most of my kind, as you say, off to prisons."

The cleric's eyes turned venomous, and narrowed as if she had struck him. She counseled herself to be a little more conciliatory in her speech; at least, until the present danger was concluded in one way or another.

"The affairs of Government are not my concern. You will be held for the Governor." He nodded toward the village elders crowded around the altar, and backed off some steps. The one with the rope approached her.

"May I at least put on my backpack?"

One of the villagers retrieved her backpack and bedroll from the floor, and assuring himself that there was no weapon in the backpack he handed her things to her. None had thought to check the inner pockets of her cape. She folded her bedroll into the pack and slung it over her shoulders.

The one who held the lasso reconfigured the rope, and pulling one of her hands behind her, and then the other, brought the end of the rope around her wrists and started to make them fast together. The woman didn't resist, only looked coolly into the faces around her, or to the vaulted ceiling or toward the back of the church. Some congregants had come to pray but found themselves more absorbed by the drama that was playing out near the altar.

The cleric watched the congregants, too, with an impassive expression. But when the tying of the rope had already gone on for too long, and it appeared that the knot had slipped from the woman's wrists, and had to be started all over again - and when the curiosity of the parishioners (or could it, conceivably, be sympathy?) seemed almost palpable to the cleric, he thought it prudent to say something.

He placed a hand on the arm of the man with the rope, and close to the man's ear he hissed, impatiently, "Oh, not here, *fool*!"

The male paused, and all looked to the cleric, including Amara to the extent that she could turn her head.

"What's wrong?" the male asked, the rope limp in his hands.

In answer the cleric only looked piously up into the apse. The ceiling was painted a pretty pale green, with arcs of geometric, star-like designs in white. He looked meaningfully at the villagers, hands crossed over his ample stomach.

Understanding came gradually, and the group shambled several steps away, Amara guided by the man's hand on her arm, until all stood just outside of the altar area.

"Here, preacher?" the one with the rope asked artlessly.

Rushing toward them and fluttering his hands, "Fine, fine, just do it quickly!"

The woman did not resist, but she had learned, from experience, to hold her wrists behind her a little apart as the man tied them together. She even took the expedient of crooking one of her fingers between her hands, to insure a space there, which the villager did not notice.

After some moments the cleric asked him, "Are you finished?"

"Yes, preacher."

In a quieter voice, to the group at large, "Can we get into

the jail? The jailer had been one of the first to be carried off by disease."

The villagers asserted that they could, and the cleric himself decided to lead the procession from the church to the town jail. He calculated that he still had time to do it and return before his first morning service.

"Let us go."

He thought for a moment that it might be more politic to exit through a side door, and pass along the leafy church grounds, away from others, but reasoned that the congregants were already quite aware of what had happened, whether they quite approved of it or not. So the group passed straight down the nave and through the main church doors. They reached the dusty main street. Amara was at the back of the procession, with the rope either taut between her and the man leading her, or trailing on the ground, depending as she walked slow or quickly. She wondered if her ankle would be good for running, should it come to that, and she paused to test it; but the rope suddenly tightened, and her arms were pulled awkwardly to the side when the male yanked on it, and she nearly lost her balance. The male turned and smirked after this show of swagger, but she made no reaction; only wished that she might be able to twist the rope about his fat neck, if only briefly, before taking her leave of the town.

In the decimated town there seemed to be none out to watch the procession, nor any faces that she could see in windows or doors. She began to hang back until the rope would tauten again, and found that gradually the male let out more slack, so that in time the rope dragged in the dust before her, and she had to watch her feet to avoid stepping upon it. She tested her ankle, but more discreetly this time, and it did not feel especially sensitive.

She began prying her hands apart, and in a very little while she had freed herself of the rope and merely held it behind her. One of the men glanced back at her, but they were generally occupied in a discussion about she knew not what, and for long moments they seemed unaware of her. A female child with tousled, straw-colored hair stood on the raised wooden sidewalk and watched them, smiling slightly as though it were a game the adults were playing. The party was approaching the point where a narrow alleyway led off to the left between the small and mostly adjoined wooden buildings of the main street. She thought she remembered, from yesterday, that the alley led straight through to open land.

Just before they reached this spot she lightly dropped the rope onto the ground in front of her, and stepped quietly toward the alleyway, just where the child was. The child uttered a greeting, and the woman raised a finger to her lips and smiled, and hoped that she would remain quiet. When Amara entered the alleyway there was only daylight straight ahead. The child stepped carefully down from the raised sidewalk and made for the villagers. Amara could only hope for the best, and took off at a light run, and, clear of the buildings, she looked up at the Ben-Oran sun and turned and ran to her left. This would take her away from the posse, and it would take her in the direction that the woman had spoken of, toward the cooler weather, where the Elohin were tending. She did not enter the main road immediately, but walked parallel close to a long stand of trees.

It was also, she thought, precisely the direction in which she had been walking before she interrupted herself to explore the little town. She had experienced some kindness, and received some silver and one very decent meal - but no other provisions, unfortunately, and nothing to be done about it now. She supposed that stopping here had been a fair bargain overall.

She could not hear, or see, the posse trudging toward the town jail, or the child drawing up closer to them. The male who was holding the rope said to the cleric next to him, "Do you think this might earn me the sheriff's old position, since he was taken off with the sickness? Or at least a deputy? I would be glad to have something so regular."

"I would not fret too much about it. Ask for now that Gemaal preserve us from this plague, rather." The cleric himself then had a passing thought of an audience with the Governor, who might extend his personal thanks to him for apprehending the fugitive.

Smiling to himself, the other male turned and looked briefly behind him. He saw no person back there, only the length of rope trailing along in the dust behind them; but the fact did not immediately register with him, and it was only after a few more steps that the smile completely disappeared from his face. He stared resolutely forward. Alarm and consternation filled his mind, along with intense reluctance to inform the cleric of what had happened - necessary though it was.

The child had drawn up behind them, trying playfully to stamp her feet upon the trailing end of the rope, and stirring up a quantity of dust in the process. The male wondered: had the stranger simply vanished, like a magician? At the thought, the hair stood up uncomfortably upon the back of his neck. And was she even now taunting him with these tugs which he could feel upon the rope? He forced himself to turn again, and look. Seeing the young female with the tousled, sand-colored hair was a shock to him. He wondered if the prisoner had transformed herself simply to madden him, then he assured himself that from her appearance the girl was indeed one of the inhabitants of the town. But in his distracted state of mind he was not sure if that was conclusive, either.

The cleric, in his bright burgundy cloak, turned and said to him, "I say, what the devil is wrong with you?"

"With me?"

"You are looking here, and there, and back again--"

"Preacher--"

"And don't carry on about the sheriff's position. I will speak up for you when the time comes."

"No - preacher--" And here the male stopped and turned, forcing the cleric and the others to stop and turn and look behind them as well.

"But, where is your prisoner?"

They all studied the quiet main street.

"Is *that* your quarry?" the cleric asked sarcastically, nodding toward the girl.

"Indeed, I don't know, reverend."

The little girl, the rope now still, and hearing herself spoken of, began backing away as though she had been chastised, and ran off. The villager holding the rope looked abashed, and one of the others, with a frightened look in his eyes, said, "Why, she is a sorceress, or demon, escaped into thin air!"

"Oh, fool and double-fool!" the cleric thundered. He pressed his hands to his forehead in exasperation. Wringing his hands, "Oh, if the Governor learns of this, what might he accuse us of?"

CHAPTER 10 - THE LONESOME PALACE OF MEMORY: PART II

One day, when Amara was nearly a grown woman, she lingered in the town after her school day, and ventured rather far from the main road, over some sloping hills, on one of which the foundling hospital and home was set very high and well back from the dirt road. The building was of red-purple stone and featured a turreted tower to one side, a sort of campanile, and in this the building was more expressive than most that could be found in her region of Ben-Ora. The burnished colors of the stonework, in the last fading light of an early winter afternoon, created a somber picture. The sky, too, had a leaden quality which, blending with the deepening green, resembled the patina of the hammered and flattened metal-work of some of the building's roofs. It was too early yet for supper, and Amara had no mind as yet for doing schoolwork, and so she lingered over the scene before wending her way homeward.

The village houses, of both wood and brick, were expansive on the outskirts of the town. If she passed any villagers here, on the walkway in front of these grand houses, by habit she had learned to avert her eyes, at least most of the time. To look openly into the faces of any strangers would be to see the common range of emotions that registered there: the curiosity as their eyes ranged over her face and took in the particular marks of her disfigurement; and then the absurd look of, not quite revulsion, but of disapproval, certainly, and sometimes a muttered aside. A rote and mechanical "Gemaal forgive them," perhaps - about which there was generally an unmistakable air of smugness, however. From the manner of many of them, it was as though they believed that she had willfully marked herself in this way to show her differentness, to denote her deliberate sundering of herself from the privileged lives of the majority. At other times, when some members of the majority were not distinctly unfriendly, or when she thought their clothes were especially grand, or their features had some unusual quality, sometimes she would allow her gaze to linger upon them for a moment.

A brickwork portal, with an opening high enough for a team of pack animals and wagon or coach, and driver on top, and wide enough for two of them to pass through: in relief, large faces, which were nominally smiling, and a few faces with mouths turned down, were carved into the stonework, both directly above the road, and in the structural stone uprights to either side of the pass-through. The faces used to frighten her at one time; now, whether the faces were meant to be whimsical or diabolical Amara was not sure. Perhaps it depended on time of day, or one's mood. The faces looked decidedly gloomy this winter afternoon. A fortified wall extended from the large portal at either side, but these remnants of the settlement walls crumbled away within a short view from the road, and became overgrown with thick vines and roots which seemed to have eviscerated the historic stone ramparts. On the other side of the pass-through, there was a natural rise in the land extending to both sides, above the road, and stands of small windblown trees on the short slopes which Amara could see from where she stood, a distance of twenty or so feet in front of the stone portal.

After she passed through, the road opened out again, and a few little storefronts appeared. The road was dirt here, not even a wooden sidewalk. The housing which had been fairly grand on the village outskirts, now appeared more close and huddled as she approached her own neighborhood. Smoke of wood and the soft native coal hung in the air. She drew up to her parents' house by the back or kitchen entrance. The width of the small fenced-in backyard she could cross with fifteen steps. There was the central path, with the family vegetable garden to the left, now bare or cut back to sere stalks, and there was a gnarled fruit tree to the right of the path, only twice her height, and next to it a metalwork table and two chairs. The property was small, but with her father's income as a hand at the twine factory the family nearly owned it outright.

She entered the kitchen and found her mother at work there, a pot of soup on the wood stove.

"You are late," her mother observed, with that crossness of tone which had become second nature to Amara. "You have not been kept after school again?"

"No... Why do you always think that?"

Her mother, crossing to the stove, only shook her head vaguely. Amara walked into the small den where her father was sitting. He squinted at some sheets of paper in the light of an oil lamp.

"Hello, my treasure," he said.

She went up to him and bent forward and he kissed her on the forehead.

"You are becoming so tall! Are you as tall as me now?"

"Almost."

"That is a wonder. I cannot sit you on my lap anymore. Stay - where are you going?"

"Only to wash my face. I have schoolwork to do and would start it now."

"You shall have this chair. The light is best here."

"If you say," she smiled. She went to the kitchen for a kettle of hot water, and brought it upstairs.

Her father turned the small, tabloid style sheets of what constituted the local newspaper in the unsatisfactory yellow light. The light was especially so for him. For as he turned in his chair and craned his neck to better see the folded pages of the newspaper, one could see that the flesh next to his left eye had melted and that this eye did not move, nor did it see. The scar extended from the edge of this eye across to his hairline and halfway up his forehead.

"Are you very hungry, husband?" His wife stood wiping her hands on a small towel.

"I am fine. It smells like an excellent stew."

"I have got some sweet turnips from the market. Hataal has gone for some bread." The son in fact had gone for a type of sweetbread sold in loaves, which was especially popular at this time of the year, being a symbol of thanksgiving to Gemaal for, as Ben-Orans said, His mercy, and for the sweetness of life.

"Yes, it is the holiday again," the father said. He went back to his reading.

He turned the page and folded the paper so that he looked on just one sheet. On it was a crudely rendered drawing, or caricature, of a male Elohin, with a feral and cunning expression, and clutching a cloth satchel to his chest, which, in the familiar stories of this kind, must have held ill-gotten pieces of silver. The father cared nothing for the article, and tried for a time to turn his glance to other and less upsetting features on the page. He found, though, that the image seemed to mock him, until he could see or think of nothing else. He turned the sheet over and, finding nothing of interest there, either, in a cold fury he crumpled the page into a ball and stuffed it behind him.

When he looked up Amara was standing at the base of the stairs and watching him. As he looked at her some of his anger melted, but a feeling of cold rage remained; not for himself but for her, and for his son and so many others. He would say nothing about the article. But she was such a clever girl, she seemed to understand anyway.

"Please," he said. "Come and sit, and do your work." She demurred. "No, I insist. I must go to the kitchen anyway."

When she had worked at her school exercises for awhile, she heard her father, evidently seated at the kitchen table, ask, "Just where is Hataal gone to for all this time?"

Her mother did not answer immediately, and Amara instantly placed her schoolwork next to the chair and walked briskly into the kitchen.

"Why, he is at the market," as I told you, the mother said, sounding doubtful herself.

"I will go and find him," Amara said, yanking her cloth coat from near the door.

"Are you sure, daughter?" her father said.

But she was already opening the door. "Yes, I will see about him," she said in a steely and determined voice.

She already suspected some mishap, or some mischief. After she reached the street she began to quicken her steps.

She had not gone very far when she heard voices and turned into a lane. Here she found that a couple of male youths, older and taller than Hataal, had grabbed or knocked the wrapped loaf of sweetbread from his hands, and now held it aloft while Hataal attempted to retrieve it, and sailing it high in the air to the other whenever her brother's flailing arms got close to their object. Deciding that the case did not require any special pleading, she walked straight up to the nearest youth. He held the package aloft, and at her arrival he tossed it over her head toward the other youth and smirked. Amara slapped him hard across the face, and nimbly sidestepped as he lunged toward her. The youth began to circle her, but she kept him at bay with flicks of her hands.

She saw that the other youth, although much bigger than Hataal, nevertheless circled him warily. Worse, she was infuriated to find that the bread must have fallen or been thrown to the ground. Her brother turned in a circle, but otherwise seemed rooted in the spot.

"Hataal, come here!" she said. "Where I can see you."

Her opponent was large but clumsy. When he attempted to close on her she repelled him with her fists, but when he attempted a wild, straight-ahead tackle at her mid-section she boxed both of his ears, which sent him rolling to the ground in pain. Suddenly the other youth left off with her brother and charged for her, and when the other youth recovered the two of them had closed around her. Her arms pinned from behind, with difficulty she swung her head and fended off the worst of a blow. Hataal seemed to be frozen in place - was it fear, she wondered - and she yelled to him, over the shoulder of the youth who seemed about to level a blow at her--

Hataal, help me!

Hearing Amara's words startled him, and Hataal moved with quick steps to the back of the youth and boxed him on both ears as he had just seen Amara do. The youth howled and made for Hataal, and Amara managed to free herself. The circling game began again, now with Amara and Hataal at a common center, either side by side or back to back. The street was very quiet and had grown dark. There was not a passerby to be seen.

Amara's feints maddened the two youths, and when the clumsier one charged and quite lost his balance, she landed him more than a glancing blow to his head. But then the other seized Hataal around the neck, and squeezed, while Amara tried to loosen his grip or land a solid blow upon him. The other youth, nursing a cut on his mouth, scurried away and pulled a thick board, a few inches square it seemed, and half his height, from a bin in front of a nearby building in progress, and made for her from behind.

Hataal seeing his approach as he was being spun about, yelled, "Amara, look out!" She turned to find the heavy board in mid-swing and aimed at her head, but she averted it at the last instant. The youth was propelled forward as the board missed her and struck the ground, and him after. As he attempted to retrieve it she stamped hard on the board, hurting his fingers, and when he looked up from the ground she saw the opportunity to land him a hard kick to the head, which sent him reeling backward.

This tide was turning, she thought confidently.

Then she made for the other youth who was still holding Hataal, alternately trying to pry his arms away or strike with her fists against his head and body, until he succumbed, and fell, and started off toward the other youth.

"Amara, look out!"

Turning wearily, and almost spent, she saw that the other youth had retrieved the heavy post and meant to launch it at them from about eight feet away. When it left his hands she turned her back and ducked, shielding Hataal. The board sailed over their heads and did not stop until it sailed through a storefront window with a crash.

At this development the two youths started running away, but not quickly enough, for Amara was in a fury. She ran and caught up with the one who had thrown the post, leaping knees-first onto his back, and soon her weight and the blows that were being rained upon his head caused him to sink heavily onto the hard ground.

"Lousy shit-for-brains," she hollered, pummeling the youth while he lay prostate on his stomach and could only attempt to shield his head and howl. His partner had fled.

Her arms were very tired, and it struck her that for the smashing of the store window, if the authorities should arrive, she and her brother would certainly be blamed. That was just how things were on Ben-Ora.

She stood up. "Say nothing about this, or you will get worse," she threatened.

The youth got to his feet, and without turning around, silently except for his wheezing breaths, he ran off.

"We had better get out of here," she said to Hataal. "If

any saw the window smash, surer than Dorah-el they will blame us for it." There was still no one outside. If any looked out from windows she couldn't tell.

She moved a few paces and stopped. "Here is the bread." But Hataal made no move to retrieve the thing which his parents had sent him out to buy. So Amara bent and lifted it from the ground, and elaborately dusted the wrapping of any dirt that might have befallen the package

"I don't have any money," she said, "or else I would buy another. But it is wrapped, it is not really hurt. Here. Do you want me to carry it?" She pressed, and in a moment he agreed to hold the bread, securely under one arm.

"We need not say anything about this," she said.

They made off at a quick walk then, and only slowed down when they had made half the distance to their home.

The family had nearly finished supper when there was a knock on the door. It was a peacekeeper come to complain about the disturbance, and especially the matter of the smashed window. A young male, his uniform was a scarlet cloak. For weapons they were typically armed with a wooden club.

"It appears your children were involved," the peacekeeper said.

"Oh, Gemaal preserve us--" the wife began.

But Amara's father gestured with his hand, and asked his daughter, "What has happened?"

"We were there, but we did not break any window," Amara insisted. "There were two youths trying to steal our bread, and we stopped them--"

"Stopped them!" the peacekeeper repeated. "It appears they were beaten nearly senseless."

"They have not got any sense," Amara said.

"Please, Amara!" the mother said.

"But they haven't. They are both cousins and one is more stupid than the other. Whatever they got they deserved it."

"There, you see?" the father said peaceably.

But the peacekeeper only looked at her. "And you think I am to believe *her*, as simply as that?" the peacekeeper gestured.

"Why would you not? She is a truthful girl."

"She may be lying."

"I don't believe she would lie. And if you will not be respectful then I will ask you to leave here."

"Leave? But I am a peacekeeper--"

"My young friend, if you were the Governor himself, I will not tolerate a lack of respect. It appears to me that those two fools were looking for trouble and they found it. There is no reason for my daughter to have sought out their company. I believe her. I do not have any sympathy for them and I must insist upon my rights. We have not been convicted of any crimes."

The peacekeeper only looked at him coolly and then nodded slightly, drew himself up, and went out the door that the father opened.

For the father this was one of several similar brushes with Ben-Oran authorities, in the past and to come. It appeared to him that the spirit of intolerance toward the Elohin was growing daily.

But when Amara asked, later, "Have I made more trouble for you, as Mother said?" he told her not to worry.

"You have spirit. Perhaps she does not understand you. Always do what your conscience tells you and you will be alright."

CHAPTER 11 - THE FIGHTER

Sounds of the morning wafted over to the small clearing where the woman lay on the ground, wrapped in a dark cape. She began to hear the rustling breeze in the trees, the drone of some insects, the humming sounds made by small flying things, the murmur of the vast universe itself. The woman had begun to stir, but her limbs felt very stiff. She noticed that the animal sounds had quieted - that was strange. Then she could hear footsteps breaking small sticks on the ground, but no voices. She opened one eye. The two men were so close that there was no point in making a run for it. Not yet. Anyway, she didn't yet know what their purpose was, except that it was probably not favorable to her.

The woman had acquired a long metal blade in her travels, and had fashioned for it a crude wooden handle. (Proper knives were hard to come by, especially away from Ben-Ora's few cities.) She kept it in an inside pocket of her cape, which, partially raising herself, she now threw over her shoulders. The men were standing not twenty feet from her. One leveled a crude-looking rifle in her direction. She brought her legs under her and muttered a sort of greeting to the two men, nodding and trying to sound as calm as possible. The woman's hair covered part of her face, and she stood up and looked at them sidelong, as though shyly, to buy time until they should identify her by the mark on her face.

"Are you all hunting?" She glanced briefly at them and then looked down at the ground. If they thought she was simple they might leave quickly, she thought.

"You might say. Why do you sleep out here in the open?"

"Oh."

"Don't you have a home?" The one with the rifle was doing the talking. He raised the angle of the gun and motioned to the other one. "Go and have a look."

The woman tensed, and when the other male drew up to her she only looked vaguely to the side, watching both of the strangers peripherally and thinking hard. He stooped. One of her hands was just inches from the knife inside her cape.

"Well, look here." He pulled the hair away from her face. "It's one of them." He glanced back at the other stranger. When he placed a hand under her chin and forced her head up, shifting slightly so the other could see, the woman regarded them coldly for a moment and then quickly swung her fist and it landed hard between his eyes. He staggered away a few steps, and then, enraged, started for her. She quickly got to her feet.

"Stop," the other male said. "Think she's going to like you handling her, fool? Come away from her." Reluctantly, the other moved away and stood next to the other one who held the crudely fashioned rifle waist-high.

"Who are you?" he said.

"I am not anyone."

"I think you are one of the leaders of the Elohin. I think we have made a great catch."

"You are wrong. And I have not committed any crime."

"The authorities probably think differently."

The clearing was only about thirty feet across, and except for two narrow pathways on either side there were only woods and brush to be seen. In the direction she had come, the path led to a small dirt road; the other direction was unknown. There were only her and the two vigilantes, or should she call them bounty hunters. In fact, unknown to all there was one other individual on the scene, watching from behind a tree, and not daring either to intervene or to flee. He felt rather sorry for this female who was clearly overmatched.

The one vigilante said, malevolently, and fingering the welt that had formed on his forehead, "Let me pay her back."

"I am talking to her here. Don't you ever learn, you dumb thing? Alright, you hit her back, if you want. It's nothing to me."

Like a child given his liberty, the man lumbered over to where the woman stood. He attempted to make a circle around her but the woman turned and would not allow him out of her sight. Then suddenly he closed on her and spun her around, and his hands clasped over her chest. The woman remained still, eyeing the one with the rifle, and then the other man released his grip and clasped her by the shoulders, pressing against her back. Patience, she thought, thinking hard. She felt his clumsy hand feeling her leg.

"This is intolerable," she said. "Take me in if you are going to." The man with the rifle only looked on noncommittally. She felt the other one's hand clutch at her leg. "That is enough," she shouted. Choosing her moment, she bucked and freed herself from his grip, and then spun her elbow around and brought it sharply against the vigilante's jaw, and followed with a punch to the side of his face. He fell down to his knees and howled with anger.

"That's enough now," the other one interjected.

But the other got to his feet and made a clumsy charge at the woman, which she avoided. She drew the knife from out of her cape and held it in front of her, thrusting it toward the one who crouched in front of her.

"Stop," the one with the rifle said, but his associate ignored him. The woman moved in a circle and parried his charges. When he lunged for her she swung and caught his arm with the tip of her blade. He howled furiously and clutched at the wound on his arm.

The other man yelled at him sharply, "Stop now. You are going to ruin this thing."

The other retreated, still seething, and standing not far from the one with the rifle he said, "Just shoot her. Wing her, at least."

"You shut up. Let me think."

The woman took a step toward them, the knife held at her side.

"You stay right there," the one with the gun said. "I am going to take you in."

But she took another step toward them, and had closed to within about ten feet.

"Don't make me do it. It matters not to me if I bring you in alive or otherwise."

"Do it," the big one said, grinning ecstatically.

"You shut up now."

The woman drew a long breath and said, "Go ahead and shoot, you bastards." And she charged toward the one with the gun.

"Look out," the big one said vaguely.

The stranger who was standing behind the tree was astonished at this turn of events, and stepped out from his place of concealment. What kind of an individual was this, he wondered in amazement, who would risk life itself to be free?

The woman stared at the eyes of the man holding the rifle, charging, and at the critical moment she dived to the ground. A tremendous explosion tore through the clearing. Looking up, she saw that some pieces of metal, and a more substantial cloud of black soot, washed up into the face of the shooter. The woman's knife had dropped to the ground. The shooter clutched at his face to clear the soot from his eyes. Her fist struck him cleanly on the forehead and he groaned and reeled backward. The other one tackled her to the ground. Her knife was a foot out of reach. The big one clasped her in a bear hug and drew her to her feet.

The other one recovered himself, his face blackened with soot. He looked at the exploded and now deformed barrel of the rifle, and in a rage he brought the handle into the air and brought it down towards the woman's head. She shifted at the last moment, but the end of the rifle caught the side of her face and opened a gash. He threw the rifle down and struck her with his fist.

It was at this moment that the stranger lumbered out of the brush and charged into the melee.

"Strike a female, will you!" he cried out.

All appeared surprised, and none more so than the woman.

The one whose fist was raised in front of him appeared to freeze, and the stranger clasped his hand and spun him around, and landed a blow to his head that sent the other instantly to the ground, where he stayed.

The other released the woman and began backing away, but the stranger caught him by the collar.

"You - devils!" he shouted. He landed a blow against the astonished bounty hunter's face that caused him to remain motionless for a long moment, and then fall abruptly to the ground.

The stranger, recalling a common expression from his days as a professional fighter, thought to himself with satisfaction: the rascal went down like a sackful of tubers. I have still got it, he thought, making a fist in front of his chest. But he needed to minister to the woman. She was lying on the ground and bleeding profusely from the face. It's a wonder they haven't murdered her, he thought, walking towards her.

At this moment the one who had been the shooter began to come to himself. The game was not up yet, he thought, as his mind turned again to the reward money. The gun had been home-made, or anyway at least half of it was. He was still shocked that it had simply exploded like that. But obviously the woman had simply gambled on the gun misfiring, and she had won, he had to give her credit for that.

The stranger stopped next to the woman, who appeared to be unconscious. He was tall, and his back was very broad. Stealthily the bounty hunter approached him and jumped onto his back. Immediately the stranger rose to his feet and threw punches wildly at the man on his back, while the smaller man attempted to pound the fighter's head, boxing his ears furiously. He screamed for his confederate to join the fray, but the other only sat on the ground, wiping blood from his mouth and wanting no more of the contest.

"The reward!" he yelled. "Help!"

But the fighter soon found some purchase upon the man's body and raised him kicking and screaming above his head. The fighter nearly lost his footing, and the vigilante who was borne above the fighter's shoulders rotated a couple of full circles, screaming, and glimpsed his associate recoil away on his back, and then find his feet and scamper off into the brush. Then he was thrown from this height and landed in a heap on the ground.

An odd surge of energy overtook the fighter. Suddenly the shouts of a raucous crowd of spectators filled his ears. They clamored for a show, and for blood. He fell upon the remaining bounty hunter, upon whose bloodied and soot-covered face was superimposed the face of some vanquishing and taunting opponent from the fighter's past career.

"Taunt me, will you?" he screamed angrily. "I will show you!" His fist thudded against the inert body of the vigilante.

The fighter's insane screaming roused the woman, who ran toward him and grasped his shoulders.

"Stop!" she said. "Stop, you will kill him."

The fighter came to himself, wiping his bloody knuckles against his trousers, and rising wearily from the prostrate bounty hunter.

"I am sorry, Miss."

"You saved my life. I am grateful to you."

"It was nothing. You are bleeding, miss. I can help you."

"I must get out of this place." She looked around at the unconscious bounty hunter, the exploded rifle, and she saw and picked up her knife from the ground. She searched the prostrate man's clothes and found no weapon, only some currency, which she took. The fighter for his part saw among their things a long wooden handle with a plate of metal attached at one end. He lifted and tested the heft of the club-like instrument, and thought that it might be useful to bring along.

They moved along the narrow trail in silence. "Do you know the region here about?" the woman asked.

"A little. You must allow me to treat that wound, miss. You are losing blood."

"Alright, at the next clearing we will stop."

They reached a shallow stream where the woman stopped to wash her face. The water stung her. She rinsed out a shawl in the clear water and stood up, dabbing at her face with the shawl.

"If I may, Miss." Standing in front of her. "I have some spirits, which may prevent infection. And a salve of a certain kind. It will reduce the bleeding."

"I am most grateful."

"Why don't you sit and rest on this large rock. You see, Miss, I am a professional fighter."

"Well, I think I should not be surprised," she said, recalling the melee back at the clearing.

"And these are some of the tools of my trade, so to speak." He looked about in a leather valise.

The stranger stood a head taller than her, with broad, massive shoulders. His face carried many individual scars, and there was a general puffiness about his eyes as well, which gave to his face a sort of squinting and ironic expression.

"For some reason I am well disposed toward you, Miss."

"Indeed, I would not want you for an enemy."

"Oh, that is rich, Miss."

"And do they still allow you to fight?"

"I am not so old, Miss."

"Oh, I didn't mean that. You are a good one, I should say."

"The spirits will sting a little, Miss. May I use your shawl?" She wrung it out further and handed it to him. "I thank you for stopping me - before. Or I might have killed that no-good rascal."

"That would have been a loss, I am sure. Ow!"

"Indeed. Something comes over me sometimes. It is as though I am fighting up on the stage again."

"Well, I am very glad you are not my enemy, fighter."

"Never, Miss."

She saw the look of concern that came across his face. "What is it?"

It had struck the fighter that the recent wound had nearly joined with that much older one upon her face. But he had difficulty expressing himself. "Oh, it is only that - well, the wound has almost bridged - I mean-- Does that hurt you - pointing to the older scar - there, I mean?"

"Not now, it doesn't."

"It is something that sets you apart, yes?"

She was silent.

"That you cannot hide, if you wanted to."

"True."

"And that is why those devils were after you. Oh, it is a strange world."

"Fighter" - looking straight up at him - "why are you being so kind to me?"

"Oh, this is a harsh world, when someone needs to ask that. I am one of you, aren't I? Don't I have scars, too?"

"You do, at that. I will trust you because you helped me when you had no reason to."

"None at all, except to help another fellow-mortal."

The woman was touched by this remark in spite of herself, and turned her head away for a moment. Evasively, she said, looking away, "That stung for a moment, but I'm alright." Looking at him again she said, "You are a strange character. You speak like this, and yet you have spent all of your life on the planet of Ben-Ora?"

"I cannot say as I blame you for thinking bitterly, Miss. But where else would I be? We do not have the use of flying machines, after all, like those beings who occupied our planet in the time of trial. May I say, Miss, you were very brave before, in the clearing."

"I was only desperate. Also I do not like being groped and handled by strangers."

"I could see. But to challenge, to stand and fight, when someone has drawn a weapon on you--"

"I have a little more experience with these things. The rifle looked as though it was badly made--"

"I am happy to say that I was not close enough to notice."

"And this melting down of metal is not well understood yet. I have seen the same thing happen many times. So I gambled, and it turned out well. If they had taken me in I might never gain my freedom again. It seemed a fair bargain in the circumstances."

"Indeed. The salve is going to hurt a bit, but it will help to close the wound. You are going to have a scar--"

"Well, there is nothing to be done about that."

The fighter had never been this close to one of the Elohin. He had tended to believe all of the disparaging things that were said about them, not being a very discriminating thinker - but his behavior had been, he thought, no worse and perhaps showed a little more open-mindedness than that of many of his fellow citizens. But now he felt as one who has had the scales pulled away from his eyes. He did not find any fault in the woman. Looking at her face, he thought that that awful red patch looked more painful than the wound that she had just sustained.

His own face was illuminated with a range of emotions. "What are you thinking of?" she asked.

"Well-- That is, just now, I am thinking that those men, and others, they are going to come back for us."

"Did you say, for us?"

"Of course, Miss. And, I think I should like - to accompany you."

"What!?" Her response was half question and half shock. When she saw that he was quite serious, she said deliberately, "Fighter, this is not your battle."

"Perhaps I wish to make it mine."

"But why?"

He did not answer immediately, standing before her now with arms folded, while she inclined back on the rock. He began to pace somewhat. "I might say that in my commonplace life I have seen very little that is noble done by my fellow-mortals, and I myself have probably done even less that is praiseworthy. For my dear mother I make an exception, may Gemaal be good to her. We clutch at shadows, and cling to falsehoods, we believe mostly what we are told to believe. But there is something different about you. There is a spirit, and a determination. And I cannot believe the calumnies that are spoken against your kind, for that is what I now believe them to be."

"But, don't you realize, if you cast your lot with me--"

"What could happen, Miss?"

"Well, you could come to a bad end."

"Believe me, my beginnings was not so very promising, either, Miss. I am not worried of the outcome."

"If that is how you feel, then I am once again obliged to

you."

He looked in her face. "Yes, the wound is healing nicely. We had best make some distance, is that correct, Miss?"

The woman nodded, pleased that she and the fighter shared the same thought. They continued along the path, which eventually gave onto a dirt road on which they walked undisturbed for several miles.

CHAPTER 12 - AT A SPRING

"I should like to bathe here in this place," the woman said.

They had stopped at a small pond with clear greenish water, with large stones about it and close stands of trees rising all around. At its longest point the pond was no wider than one could throw a stone.

"Indeed, it is a good mild morning for it."

"I should like to wash my clothes as well. These small bushes seem made for drying them."

"With this breeze it should not take long at all, Miss."

Will you help me?

"Why, of course, I am at your service. What do you wish me to do?"

"To see that no strangers come about, mostly. I shall not be worried if you are here."

"And where would you like me to be, Miss?"

"Why, close enough that I can hear you holler if any should appear."

"Understand."

"And if I hand my breeches and shirt to you, will you lay them over some of those bushes, there on the path."

"Of course. I will leave you to your privacy and return when I have walked about for a little."

The fighter started walking the trail that wound around the pond. His eyes scanned the bushes and trees for any movement, while he listened for any unusual sounds. Before he had gone very far, there was just the sound of the rippling water as the woman scoured her clothes with a small cake of soap. She plunged the clothes in and out of the water, and there was only this sound and the drone of insects. Common sorts of dragonflies hovered in place, with long, greenish-blue, stick-like bodies that were nearly the span of the fighter's palm. Their wings beat and thrummed with a blur and a hum of steady purposefulness which somehow pleased the fighter. The morning, and nature itself, seemed flawless, and he was filled with gratitude to be alive.

When he was just passing a stand of tall shrubs, the fighter paused and, peeling a branch away, ventured a look back. The woman was standing in water to her waist, and lifting her clothes in and out of the water. He continued until he'd made a circuit of the little pond.

He called, "I am returned, Miss. Not wanting to shout or startle you."

The woman looked up to see the fighter making his way to one of the broad sloping rocks at the edge of the water. Either his glance was directed high above the tree line, discreetly, or when he checked his footing, he crooked a hand over his eyes as if he was blinded by sunlight. His perch on the broad rock looked anything but steady.

"Be careful, fighter. I am quite under the water now." The woman reclined back and fanned the water with her arms and fingers. Her clothes floated nearby.

"So you are, Miss."

"Stand right there and I will bring my clothes to you."

"Yes, Miss."

She waited.

"Of course, Miss." He turned around.

The woman stepped carefully up the rock, holding the damp clothes to her chest, and when she stood behind the fighter she placed a hand on his shoulder and with the other she placed the clothes onto his extended hand where he could grasp them.

When he had gone a few steps, the fighter ventured a discreet glance as the woman stepped carefully back into the shallow water. When it was nearly waist high she splashed forward, and her pert bottom floated on the surface of the water briefly. Then she kicked, her legs struck out of the water as her upper body submerged. The fighter turned and sought out the small shrubs, not yet leafy, that the woman had pointed to. He smiled to himself, marveling at his improbable adventure and his fortune - whether it was good or ill, he did not know yet, but on balance he felt contented. When he had settled the damp clothes over the bushes he resumed his patrol around the lake.

Concentrate, he told himself.

Later, while her hair, and clothes, dried in the balmy, early-afternoon air, the woman sat wrapped in a blanket, which was her thin bedroll, on one of the broad flat rocks at the shore. The fighter also sat, usually with his back to her for discretion, but turning sometimes during their conversation.

"I have prepared some of the things we have collected, Miss, but I thought it best not to light any fire to roast them. We cannot see a great deal from our position here, and there could be others in the area."

"You are right.

It is meager fare, I am afraid."

"It will do."

"We are seeing remarkably little of any life, Miss. It seems that the land is uninhabited."

"If scurvy bounty hunters are all that this region produces then I am happy not to see anyone else."

"I am happy too that none have come back."

"I think that that party had the shit scared out of them."

"I don't doubt. It served them right."

The woman reached in her satchel for some of the remaining fig-like fruits which the farmer's son had given to her, and offered some to the fighter.

"How did you come to be standing there when they set upon me?"

"It is only that I had been watching them myself, Miss. I suspected that they were bounty hunters. I am no great catch, but nowadays an individual may be sentenced to a stay at a work farm for no other offense than bumming around without any silver in his pocket. And I thought that while I watched them, they could not surprise and apprehend me."

The woman nodded. "What is your name, fighter?"

"I am called Nahal, Miss."

"Like the mighty tree of that name."

"Yes. And you, Miss?"

" My parents called me Amara."

The name in the Ben-Oran tongue connoted peace, and calmness. "May I say, Miss" - turning his head to study her face - "you have not had a peaceful life." He shifted his body to look at her. The broad patch of scar on her cheek glinted where the sun struck it.

When she didn't say anything he added, "That blow has healed, somewhat." He thought to himself how the one scar was fresh, the other one old and seemingly indelible. "We might use a bit of the salve, but--"

"No, best to save it," she said.

"You should have let me murder him."

She grimaced. "How did Gemaal create two such as that, and one like you?"

The compliment she had paid him caused the fighter to be silent.

When they had finished eating and relaxed in the sun a while longer, the woman said, "I suppose we had better make some distance." She seemed reluctant to say it, and her eyes took in the still, greenish water, the droning dragonflies and encircling green trees.

"If you say, Miss. I will see if your things are dry, then."

The woman stood up on the sloping rock and stretched,

with the blanket around her. The fighter came past the shrubs with her dried clothes in his hands, clambering up the initial rise of the rock. He placed all of her things in one large hand and discreetly turned his gaze opposite to her and the water. The woman arranged her blanket on the rock and took her clothes from him and set them on the blanket and began putting them on. Her eyes scanned the trees for any signs of movement, and the fighter also looked closely over the narrower range where he permitted his eyes to wander.

He asked, "Shall we resume traveling in the same direction, Miss?"

"I believe so. Do you think it best?"

"I wish I knew more of this area, but I am a stranger to it." He had a sense, from the land being blessedly uninhabited but for some small animals, and from the rising and setting of their sun, that they tended in the direction of the colder weather. "It is fortunate the warm season is starting," he said, looking about the budding trees, and only gradually glancing back at the woman.

"Right. Well I think I am ready." The woman took up her blanket and shook it and placed it folded in her rucksack. As she ventured down the sloping rock she was surprised to find the fighter extend his hand to support her under the elbow. This gallantry caught her a little by surprise, upsetting more than helping her balance, and she collided directly with the fighter where he stood with his feet planted on the level ground. He held her about her shoulders, and her free hand remained pressed against his chest after she had found her balance.

"Do you feel better now?" the fighter asked, a kindly expression on his face.

The woman nodded and smiled very slightly, and the fighter was aware of the force of her hand pressing on his chest, and then tapping lightly for release.

"Right, here you are then." Releasing her and smoothing

the black cape upon the woman's shoulder.

"Yes, I do feel better. Are you quite alright?"

"Of course, Miss. I have noticed, there are some of the heronel berries here about the pond. They seem to like the water, you know. Do you like them, and shall we pick and wash some, to bring with us?"

"An excellent idea. I had not noticed any."

When they had collected some of the large red berries in a cloth sack, they followed the narrow path away from the pond out to an open meadow and resumed walking.

CHAPTER 13 - A CASUALTY OF THE TEKERIN

They had been walking for a few days, rarely seeing anyone. The land was gently rolling meadows covered with short grass, and sometimes a broad plain. The grass and small bushes and trees were the verdant green of an early growing season. They found few roads here, and only occasionally could they discern small paths in the direction of their walking, or bearing into the woodlands to the sides of them.

They had nearly crested a small hill, which was pocked with shrubs in flower, when both of them suddenly saw, less than a stone's throw below in the vale, a camp with several individuals.

"Shit!" Amara whispered, dropping down and simultaneously yanking down on the fighter's arm. Crouching, they looked circumspectly over the rise.

"Do you think they saw us?" the fighter asked. He did not relish a fight at this moment.

"It does not appear so." She gestured with her hand, and the fighter followed her movements as she backed off several feet, staying low to the ground. Then she moved forward to a place behind a flowering bush, near the crest, where she was better concealed. She turned and gestured for the fighter to move up, and he dropped next to her.

"Your eyes are better than mine," he whispered. "Can you see what they are doing?"

"They look a scurvy group," she answered. "One of them appears to be tied up."

A tall male stood with his hands tied behind him. It

appeared that one of the group was questioning him.

"What do you suppose he has done?" the fighter asked.

"From his manner, I think he may be one of the former Tekerin guards."

"You can tell this?"

"You look at him and tell me." The restrained man looked at nothing in particular and did not speak.

The fighter had been looking away, only listening to her voice, but now he ventured a look through the low shrubbery. "If he is one of those, then maybe he will be well and truly paid off for his cruelty."

"You cannot mean that."

"I am no saint, Miss. From what I have been told, the guards were terrible brutes."

"They are only what they were made to be."

"The fighter only harrumphed."

They both watched as the male who appeared to be asking questions suddenly threw a punch into the restrained man's stomach which caused him to double up and fall forward. They could see four additional males standing in the clearing.

"That was unkind," Amara said.

The fighter turned his head away disgustedly. He gazed back in the direction they had come, and wondered if they might still return that way, without further incident.

"And is he one of your kind, Miss?" The fighter's voice was regretful.

"I cannot be sure. I believe so."

While she watched, the males in the camp crowded around the bound man who rested on one knee. The one who had been talking, the nominal leader of the group, kicked the bound man in the chest and he sprawled backward.

"Oh, this is not a fair fight," Amara said softly. "Fighter? What do you say?" Watching a moment longer, she added, "One of them has gotten a rope. I am afraid they mean to hang him."

Agitatedly, the fighter plucked at some grass and threw it. "Must I risk my neck every time someone is doing wrong?"

"We cannot just leave him." She paused. "Fighter?" But the fighter continued looking away. "Do you mean will not help me?"

"Oh, bother!"

"Very well." She stood up.

"Miss, they will see you," he hissed. "Do you even know if they have sidearms?"

"You may wait for me here - or leave, if you are afraid."

"Afraid!" She moved a few steps down the sloping grass. "Oh, double bother!" Standing up, he said, "I have not come this far to have you perish due to your own willfulness."

He could see that her expression was pleased. As they began walking down the small hill he muttered one more complaint: "Must we make everything our business?" She did not answer, however, only regarded the ragtag group of males in the camp calmly, and approached them in almost friendly fashion. The fighter for his part had a grim expression, as though expecting the worst.

When they reached them, the evident leader of the group asked in a gruff voice, "What do you want?" His face had a crabbed and unpleasant look. "And may I say," gesturing with his eyes toward the mark on her face, "You risk your life just walking about here."

"We are just traveling through," Amara said.

"So are you and thousands of others. Keep on, then."

"Have you anything to drink?"

"None that we can spare."

She frowned. "Is that your prisoner there?"

"You might say that. Why is it your business?"

"But what has he done to you?"

"To us - nothing. But he is an Elohin - and a guard."

"But the guards are only what the Tekerin made them to be. Have you no common sense?"

"I will thank you not to provoke me, Miss. I have sense enough to know a villain when I see one, and to recognize" - staring at her - "one whose kind are generally not at liberty to be wandering the roads at present."

"Do not make it your business," the fighter said.

"It is alright," she said calmingly. "Are you regular army?"

"You ask a lot of questions for one who came to our camp uninvited. Does this scurvy group look anything like regular army?" He guffawed, and the other males took his lead. "Call us soldiers of fortune. And come to think of it, you might well be more important quarry than our prisoner there, for I see you are also one of the Elohin."

"Do not think of it," the fighter said.

She made a subtle calming motion. "Although I count five of you, I am afraid you are over-manned. So do not make idle threats."

"I see."

"I will give you one piece of silver if you will peaceably release your prisoner to me."

Ironically, "An entire piece of silver, for him? It hardly seems fair."

"Two pieces, then."

"Make it ten pieces and we will consider."

"We are somewhat straitened at the moment." In fact she and the fighter might have had five pieces of silver between them.

"I thought you looked like a couple of beggars." He turned and spit on the ground.

"Here, here," the fighter interjected.

"It is alright," she said, motioning to the fighter to remain calm.

"How about this." And she stared directly into their spokesman's eyes. "I will fight the strongest of your party for his freedom."

Two of the others guffawed loudly at the suggestion, and the leader responded, "Fight a female? It would not be seemly. And what would be the gain for us?"

"If you are concerned that you would lose--"

"It is hardly that."

"Or you could attempt to fight my companion here. But that would not be fair."

One of the others spoke up belligerently, "Why not fair?"

"Well, just look at him. He is like two of you."

"That is no matter," the one who had just spoken said.

"Let me fight him," said another, also young.

The older male who seemed to be the spokesman for the group held his hand up. "You have rather provoked us, Miss, and you shall have your wish."

"First," she said, walking over to where the prisoner lay silent and immobile on his back, allow this male to stand up, at least. She stood behind and lifted him by his shoulders until he had righted himself. He continued to look primarily at the ground, and seemed to register very little of the transaction which the woman had negotiated. Dark hair fell partly over his eyes.

"And let none of you cowards strike one who cannot defend himself." She returned closer to where the fighter stood.

"No weapons are to be used in this contest," their leader said. "Make a space, then, and begin."

With clenched fists, the smaller and younger man from the camp crouched and began moving in a half circle in front of the fighter, who stood flat-footed. He looked over at Amara as if for instruction, and she said, "You must put your hands up in front of you. Like this."

While she was speaking to him, his head turned away, the fighter's opponent threw a jab that nearly caught him on the chin. He raised his hands as Amara had suggested, and his feet began to move very slowly in response to the other male's rapid movements from side to side. The younger male threw a wild punch which caused him to lose his balance, and the fighter, seeing his opening, landed a punch to his head. He had held a good deal back, and yet the punch caused his opponent to crash to the ground and stay there.

The leader came and looked down at him. "You must think that you are very clever, Miss. You did not tell me that your man is a ringer."

"A what?" Incredulously.

"I know a professional fighter when I see one. Look, this one is still unconscious."

"I don't know what you mean. You have made a bargain-_"

"You have tricked us. I will not release the prisoner to you."

Subtly, she had maneuvered the prisoner to where he now stood between her and the fighter. Still, the one who was referred to as the former guard demonstrated no understanding of what was being discussed, and only looked rather forlornly at the ground.

"He is my prisoner and we will carry out our judgment. Justice will be done for the years of suffering caused by the invaders, and by the likes of him. And by your sort generally, he added pointedly."

"I apologize to no one. Anyway - what will your so-called justice do to improve anything?"

"It will make me feel better."

"To hang someone who has done you no harm?" She saw that his face had hardened. "If you are going to be obstinate we will meet your price, if that is still agreeable."

"It is."

"Miss--" the fighter started to say.

"Come here, Nahal," she said. She moved off a step to her left, opposite another of the camp party, while the fighter moved opposite the group's leader. The prisoner now stood between and behind Amara and the fighter. "Pay him his ten pieces of silver," she said.

"But, Miss, I don't--

"You heard me. I want you to *pay him off*!"

"Ah, yes, Miss." The fighter reached into his pocket, but when his hand emerged it made swiftly for the fleshy side of the leader's face, and landed with an authority that pleased the fighter, after listening this long to the fellow's obstinacy and impertinence.

At the same moment Amara drew a knife and sliced through the rope holding the prisoner's hands behind him, and she leaped and caught the male opposite her with a kick straight to the stomach which doubled him over.

One of the remaining males drew a knife and began to charge toward her. The one all had called the prisoner, in what might be called the first act of volition that he showed, interposed between her and the charging man. The fighter saw that his hands were at his sides, however, and instinctively he pushed the guard roughly to the side, as Amara stepped back to retrieve her knife which had fallen when she sliced through the prisoner's bonds.

Furiously, the charging male lunged with his knife for the prisoner who was falling to the ground, missing him, and then his eye just had time to register the female still without a knife, and finally the strange club-like instrument, like the forward end of a shovel, that the fighter had pulled from his back and swung toward his head. The clanging sound resonated in the clearing, and seemed to decide the remaining male who was standing to flee, rather than continue an unequal fight. He backed away and then jumped into some brush.

"Will we be safe if we simply leave them here?" the fighter asked.

"We will have to hope so. I believe they are done with their mischief. Let us make haste from here, though."

She and the fighter started off at a jog. She paused, looked behind, and then ran back to fetch the guard who was standing immobile, and pulled him roughly along by the arm.

The three of them had traveled some distance away. When they encountered any fellow travelers they concealed themselves in woods, or at least kept their distance, the fighter nodding gruffly while Amara pulled the shawl over her face. Once, in sudden contact with a group of hunters, they improvised a story that the guard was a prisoner they were escorting, and the fighter asked for the location of a secure jail where they might deliver him. The hunters indicated a road that led to a village, and when the fighter thanked them and they had watched them move off, the three of them continued in a contrary direction.

A couple of days later, late on an afternoon, they made camp near a stream. The woman thought it safe enough to build a campfire here. Thus, instead of the dry cereal and berries which they had been consuming direct from a sack, they roasted the meal into a kind of bread at the fire. There was even a kind of green crayfish or small lobster to be found at the sandy river edge, and the fighter and Amara picked some of these up between their fingers and added them to their repast.

The guard had been watching them catch the shellfish, and they were surprised when he walked toward the campfire with one between each thumb and forefinger. Amara gestured for them and he placed them down where she had indicated. She gestured to the guard to go and sit down, which he did, not far from the campfire.

"Nature always provides, fighter."

"Indeed, you are right, Miss."

She thought for a moment. "But do you not have any wish to make your way back to some safer place?"

"Why would you ask, Miss? I am content."

"I am only saying, I would not blame you. You have done a good deal for me already."

"No, do not think of it, Miss."

"Well, I am grateful. Do you know, I wish that I could live in a more peaceful world."

"I fully agree, Miss. My body is sore, and I think it is fair to say that I did not fight more when it was my occupation to fight."

When the meal was ready the fighter began eating greedily. Then he became aware of the woman looking toward the guard who stared absently at the fire, and preparing a plate for him. The fighter carefully put down his own plate and took the one out of her hand and brought it toward the guard. But he did not accept the plate from the fighter's hands, and, looking somewhat put out, the fighter placed it on the ground next to him instead.

The fighter returned and ate with gusto, and drank plentifully from the water they had collected from the stream. Looking at the guard, who had as yet not picked up his plate from the ground, the fighter said, "He is a great bargain that you have gotten for us, Miss. And well worth ten pieces of silver."

"He can hear you, fighter," she said, and studied the guard's face for any sign of his apprehending anything at all. His face remained blank and averted, however.

"Yes, but does he understand anything," he fairly shouted at the guard.

"Anyway," she continued, "you know that the ten pieces of silver was only offered in jest."

"You may have jested about the silver, but I am afraid the risk to my neck was very real."

"Do you mean in fighting those whelps, back there?"

"I do. It was rather well done, how you brought me into the fray. *You must hold up your hands like this*, indeed."

"I was not worried at all. I had no doubt that you would beat him."

"Yes? Well..." The fighter appeared somewhat mollified at this.

When they looked over again they saw that the guard had begun eating his meal.

They had proceeded for a few days, in meadows along the tree-line, or sometimes venturing into the forest where pathways permitted. One morning the woman remarked, "I believe I smell a fire, and meat cooking. Do you notice it?"

"Perhaps it is only that you are hungry, Miss."

"Perhaps."

But towards afternoon the fighter noticed it, too.

"Let us get closer," the woman said. "We must discover if they are friendly - or otherwise." They treaded carefully through the forest. It was nearly dark when they discerned, still at a great distance, a gathering at a campfire.

"Can you see their faces?" the woman asked. But in the dusk, and at a distance of more than fifty yards, the fighter confessed that he could not.

"Whether they are hunters, or whether they are of your kind--"

"I dare not approach them," the woman said. "But you might. We could wait here. If they are Elohin you could signal to me. If they are not, they might let you have a bit of food, at least."

"They might," the fighter said doubtfully. He was quite hungry, in fact.

"But if they are Elohin they might be helpful to us. But if you do not feel safe--"

"No, Miss. I shall go, and discover their purpose." He turned his eyes from the campfire to look at her. "But if there is any danger, please, do not tarry here."

She considered. "I think that my feet are swift," she said, as convincingly as she could.

"Yes, and so is your perception, Miss. I only mean that if this should go badly--"

"Of course, I would leave."

The look of disquiet on the fighter's face told her plainly that he did not believe her. "Just be sensible, will you?"

She felt that she had been rather caught in a lie, and knew not what else to add. Without protesting further, she nodded once.

He stood up, and slowly made his way toward the camp which was ahead on level ground, but the figures there were shielded from his eyes by the trees and brush. When he had drawn to within about thirty paces, he still could not see who were gathered here in the dusk. Abandoning all stealth, he made his way to the open path and continued walking forward. He clasped his hands atop his head and tried to appear calm in spite of his apprehension.

Instantly there were shouts of alarm, and daggers and hatchets drawn by the males about the fire.

"I mean no harm," he said.

They had, all of them, the marks about their faces that identified them as Elohin, except for the very young, who withdrew in alarm behind the adults.

"What do you want here," the adult males demanded.

"Only a bit of food, perhaps? There is a knife under my cloak, on my right side. You may remove it if you wish."

One conferred with his eyes with the others, and an older male of evident authority nodded. One walked carefully up to the fighter and removed the knife from its sheath.

"Why are you out here in this wilderness? Are you lost?"

"Perhaps not exactly, sir. There are two with me--"

"More of you--?"

The fighter had started gesturing to the woman to advance, but without taking his eyes from the gathering who watched him with understandable suspicion.

"Just two," the fighter said. The others were not yet visible on the path, hidden as they were by the presence of the fighter. When they saw her face, and the gaunt-looking and expressionless guard following behind her they all studied the strangers with increased interest, and gradually opened a path toward the warming fire.

"We are here in peace," she said, standing now in front of the fighter's massive frame. "I am sorry for our strange approach. We had to know if it was safe for one like me to come near."

"We do not yet know your intentions, Miss." The older one stepped forward. "Whether you know it or not, some of our own have also betrayed us for silver."

"I am aware of that. But trust me that I am only trying to find a bit of food, and some place of safety."

Several of them regarded the fighter, not to mention the guard, with suspicion and perhaps a degree of fear.

"And what of them?" the man asked.

"This individual" - nodding toward the fighter - "has saved my life when I was set upon by bounty hunters. I don't know why he has chosen this course--"

"I do not think I should trust him, if I were you."

The fighter looked at the speaker sullenly, but said nothing.

"Nevertheless I trust him completely. The other we believe to be a former guard of the Tekerin, who we saved from hanging."

"Are you the one called Amara?" one of the younger

Elohin asked.

She considered. "What do you know of me?"

"Only that there is one female who escaped from a prison, and is thought to have drowned, or gone into hiding, after jumping from a bridge. Are you that individual?"

"Yes, I will not deny it."

All who were gathered about took an increased notice of the woman, drawing closer to her, as did the children.

A middle-aged female detached herself from the group and pressed forward, pausing in front of the guard who now stood next to Amara. She peered into his face, and turned and said, "This is my son. He became separated from us recently, I do not know how-- I did not know if I would ever see him again." Then she said directly to Amara, and with a glance at the fighter, "He was not always like this." She seemed unable to say more, adding only, with elaborate bows, "Gemaal bless you for helping him."

"Be careful," some of the adult men warned. "We do not yet know their purpose."

But the guard's mother said to the visitors, "We have trapped some small animals from near the river, and have roasted them, and some vegetables. I am sure you are welcome to share in what we have." She looked about the group, which gradually appeared to assent.

In this way the guests were allowed to partake of the meal, famished as they were. They remained in the camp that evening, and when the morning became light they were treated to breakfast of some bread and hot tea. Most of the adults then stood around the fighter and Amara, while the youngsters watched from a distance or stood behind the adults.

She asked them, "Are you traveling in a particular direction?"

"We are moving, yes," one of them said. "We are tending toward the colder weather. At least, while the season is mild. Where we may go after that, we do not know."

Amara considered.

"Do you not think it a good plan?"

"It is probably a good plan," she said. "Perhaps it will place you out of immediate danger. At present it is our wish to continue by ourselves." She looked toward the fighter, who indicated his approval. "And we ourselves will probably go in the same way. We thank you, and I hope we shall see you again." She was far from certain that they would.

One brought a large satchel of food, which the fighter hoisted to his shoulder.

The one whom all had called the guard stood somewhat between Amara and the fighter and his mother and the rest of the camp.

"Do you think," Amara asked the mother quietly, "that he recognizes you?"

"I think that he does," and she patted his shoulder. The guard's face was as expressionless as ever.

When Amara hoisted her pack upon her back, over the long black cape that had served her for several seasons, and backed off a half step, the guard appeared suddenly agitated, his upper body trembling, as though he was physically torn between his group and his recent protectors. Abruptly he fell to his knees next to Amara and clutched at the hem of her cape and brought it to his lips. The fighter looked on quizzically at the scene, while Amara herself appeared quite astonished.

"Now, now," she protested. She reached down and clasped the guard by the shoulders. "Please, stand with me." When he did, she stared hard into his eyes, clasping his shoulders. He looked back calmly at her, his face wet with tears. She thought she could see the hint of a smile in his face. She nudged him away from her, and then she and the fighter made their way out of the camp with gestures of thanks.

CHAPTER 14 - TOWARD THE COLDER REGIONS

The party of about twelve individuals, with which the woman and the fighter had joined forces, at least provisionally, became part of a more general migration of the Elohin toward some mostly uninhabited regions of Ben-Ora. Each day the movement was swelled with the addition of entire families, some leading small livestock, others with sacks of ground meal and clay water-pots; and some, families or individuals, traveled with very few provisions, depending upon their situations, or the haste with which they had had to leave their villages. The moving mass of individuals had no leader per se. Among Amara's particular group, to which a few others had attached themselves, she had argued for some limited sharing of what scant provisions the group possessed collectively. Her motion had carried with only a little argument, which was surprising in view of the many dangers still faced by the refugees. As a result, and for her capability generally, she had emerged as the nominal leader of her group which came to number two dozen individuals.

The larger group, which had grown to several thousand in number, moved without any particular destination, but only a general sense of their direction. The woman had begun to think in terms of a defensible position, among mountains perhaps, but for days the landscape had only offered these flat plains. And they were not verdant, as before, but covered with a red clay whose surface was veined with dry cracks, as if no rain had fallen in weeks. There were few trees along the route to offer shade, either.

Few among those traveling had ever explored these remote regions. Some fur trappers seemed to remember a broad lake in the vicinity, which also fed a substantial river, but they were vague as to their exact locations. The group had filled water jugs and refreshed themselves at a small pond, but after a few more days of travel the need for water was pressing once again. Before them was only the flat dry plain, and because the pale green sky was completely clear at this time, it was possible to see ahead for as much as a day's travel, and it was clear that no water shimmered upon the surface of the land before them. The woman herself had grown worried.

Her group had stopped to eat when the afternoon sun was very high. There had been no shade for all the morning's travel, and as there was no prospect of any, the group moved off a bit to the side and paused while the others pressed forward.

"There is not very much to drink," Amara said, taking a place on the ground while a meal of coarse bread was being baked in a lidded pot.

"Perhaps - our children?" the female of a couple traveling with children asked. Her eyes moved between Amara and the cloth satchel on the ground which contained the jug of water.

"Of course."

"We should have stayed near the pond that we passed," an older male grumbled, staring into the fire.

"We all did well to move on," Amara said. "It was in the middle of a plain, with no defenses. The government forces could have swept over us like a plague."

An elderly woman who was traveling alone, a large liver-shaped patch of scar extending over one cheek, asked, "And do you truly think they will pursue us all this way?"

"There is every indication that they will. And from those

who have joined us recently, they are not many days distant."

"Would they kill us, do you think?"

Amara did not answer immediately, nor did the fighter say anything, sitting back on his heels to her left.

"If I may," one of the other males offered, "It seems it is either that or to be put into a prison indefinitely. What is worse?"

They had resumed walking for a few hours, when Amara saw, directly in her path, an elderly female sitting on the ground. She cried so abjectly, in almost infantile fashion, that Amara wondered if she had taken leave of her senses. The others only walked around her.

Amara and the fighter slowed their steps at the same time. Amara stood near the female and then kneeled. "What is wrong?"

"I am tired from walking, and I am awfully thirsty, Miss."

"Is that all?"

The female looked at her incredulously, as though surprised that anyone could find her complaints not sufficiently grave in themselves.

"You are traveling by yourself?"

"I had no time to bring anything. A mob burned our house, Miss. My husband--"

Amara looked up at the fighter. "That is dreadful," she said. "He is not with you?"

"He was killed, Miss."

"You must try not to fear for your safety now, at least. I believe that there is water up ahead."

"Is there, Miss? Where?"

"Can you not tell from the sky?" She stared in the direction of their travel. "How it lightens, there?"

The female shielded her eyes and stared ahead. In a moment she said, "I cannot see, Miss. I am very fearful."

"There is nothing to worry about. Here, I will show

you." And she lifted her own canteen by its strap over her head and handed it to the female. "Help yourself."

The woman accepted the canteen in her hands, but hesitated. "Are you sure, Miss? There is but little left."

"Finish it."

The female drained the canteen and handed it to her. "I am very obliged."

"Are you able to walk?"

"Certainly, Miss. I am much better now."

Amara helped her to her feet.

"Go on ahead," she gestured. "I will see you again."

When the female had moved off a little way Amara resumed walking, with the fighter next to her.

In time, they noticed there was a gradual rise in the terrain, and the beginnings of a broad mountain range that began to take shape directly in front of them.

"I wonder what is on the other side of those mountains," she said.

"It seems there is no other course but to press forward. Those rocks seem a very defensible place, am I not right?"

"I think so. Perhaps we might make our stand there."

"And is there really water up ahead, Miss, as you said?" he asked.

She didn't turn, only looked at the parched soil, and then at the sky ahead. Her expression seemed untroubled. "I have no idea," she said.

CHAPTER 15 - THE LONESOME PALACE OF MEMORY: PART III

The district prison was located on one of the main roads that led from the village, nearly a morning's travel on foot. Or what took nearly as long, one could travel by private or public wagon or coach, which were generally pulled by the stolid water buffalo or team. To visit her father, Amara and her family generally used a public coach, or if available and cheaper, they would hire a ride in an open wagon. On this, their first visit, the mother had prepared a popular Ben-Oran concoction of sweet berries with a sour and slightly bitter dressing. This popular favorite was nominally a dessert, and had about it an air of celebration. The mother entrusted this lidded pot to Amara to carry. From force of habit, Amara and her brother walked after their mother through the village to the depot where they had hired a coach.

"Why do you walk like that, brother?" Amara pulled up and stopped, scrutinized her brother, and held the pot, in a rough cloth sack, fast against her stomach with two hands.

"Like what?" her brother said, seeming nervous and reluctant to stop. "What is wrong with how I walk?"

"Why, nothing at all, really, if it is your business to swing lanterns to guide passing coachmen at evening. But why do *you* do it? Really, you seem rather tense."

"It is only when I am worried."

"But why worry about anything? *I* never do." And she

looked directly at him for emphasis, thinking to herself that Gemaal would forgive her for one small and helpful exaggeration.

"You do not worry, truly?"

"What is the good of it?" she answered sensibly.

The nervousness that she had commented now showed itself in a rapid fluttering of his fingers, which struck his palms in succession, and a spasm that shook his upper body, until he brought one hand to the top of his head, and ran it straight back through his hair, as if in an effort to calm himself, while his eyes closed and his face tensed.

"I am alright," Nataal said.

Amara was on the point of saying that he worried her, and that she had never known him to act in this way, but she thought it best to keep these thoughts to herself. Her mother had paused, well ahead of them, and called and gestured impatiently for them to follow.

"Relax," she said. But it was difficult to gain his attention. One of the nervous spasms shook his body, his eyes closed, and he ran his hand over the top of his head in the calming motion again. When his eyes refocused on her she said, "Let us catch up," as calmly as she could, and quickened her pace until they were next to their mother, who had stopped and waited impatiently.

"Must you always be contrary?"

"I didn't know that I was being so. We were just playing. Right, Nataal?" She pushed him away playfully.

"Just be careful you do not spill our berries or there will be no treat for your father. Hold with both hands."

"Yes, Mother." With mock solemnity, which her mother took no notice of. "Mother - why has father been sent to prison?"

The mother was silent for a moment. "Nataal, will you go ahead a space."

"Where?"

"Just - ahead."

Nataal started to protest, then trudged ahead of them several paces.

"I suppose it is because - he is considered dangerous."

"*Is* he dangerous?"

"Of course he isn't. Except he is a danger to speak at times when he ought to remain quiet. Gemaal help me if I understand the laws that are being passed, and the changes which have taken place in this land. Your father must always speak his mind, as you well know, about the conditions in which our race live--"

"But we are Ben-Orans, we are not anything else."

"Should I say, the conditions in which the Elohin live."

"But that is only their term for us. We are not different--"

"You are right, daughter. Just so." She patted her affectionately upon the shoulder. "They have passed laws, one of which prohibits assembly of groups to plan political activities. Of this one they have convicted your father, and have detained him."

"It hardly seems like a crime to meet and talk. Do the citizens not meet in the town hall and plot against us?"

The mother looked around to assure that no others were close enough to hear. "Indeed."

"Might they 'detain' us some day, as well?"

"Let us hope to Gemaal that the citizens will come to their senses."

"I should hate awfully to lose my freedom."

"You are too young to worry about such things now. Let us hope for the best, rather."

"Can we manage, without father's salary?"

"I have got some little work that I can do, at others' houses and fields."

"The houses of the well-off, do you mean?"

"Some, and some of our class. A few. Gemaal does not

teach us to hate, daughter."

Amara wanted to ask, Then how has the public learnt it? She held the question inside, and instead drew her head briefly against her mother's shoulder.

"Nataal!" the mother yelled. "Why are you so far off?"

"You asked me to," he shouted back.

"Wait for us." They turned onto the main street and to the depot, and entered one of the enclosed coaches. A middle-aged couple entered and sat opposite them, wishing them good day. There was little conversation in the cramped carriage. Which was just as well, the mother thought - she preferred not to name their destination, and, if asked, probably would have supplied only the name of the small hamlet where the prison was.

Amara noticed that the woman's skin was light in color and flawless. The man's face was ruddy and unscarred.

The sky was a clear pale green, the landscape was verdant, and a little dust was kicked up by the hooves of the team and the turning of the coach wheels. From the road could be seen, at long intervals, a small wooden farmhouse, and tilled fields; the occasional crossing roads. For the most part they saw open country of meadows and forests. Once the coach started there was very little conversation at all.

The prison was a large, looming structure on level ground, built like many public structures of a quarried, reddish-purple stone. There were barred windows at each of the four stories, and the place had an imposing, militaristic character, an effect to which some turreted towers contributed. When the coach let the family off they approached a small gated outbuilding and explained their business to the two guards inside.

"But you may not bring any food inside."

Amara clutched the bowl to her. "It is only some berries for our father."

"He is not allowed anything at present."

"What does it mean?" the mother asked.

"It means that he has committed some infraction of the rules, and is not allowed to receive anything."

"Are you sure?"

"That is what is written."

"Oh... May we leave this here, then, while we visit?"

The guard turned sullenly on her. "*I* am not responsible for your things." The children looked at him thunder-struck, and a little reproachfully.

"Oh, you may leave it on the bench there. It is nothing to me."

"Thank you," the mother said, gathering the children and anxious to conclude the interview.

"Take this." The guard handed her a wooden sort of coupon which was dyed a bluish color, and with a hieroglyphic denoting a wing of the main building.

The father was one of several prisoners, all males in this building, who were seated at a wide table running nearly the width of a large room. At a glance, at least half of the prisoners appeared to be Elohin. The father rose from his seat as they were ushered into the room. There was just one chair, which the children allowed the mother to use. When she reached her hands across the table that separated them, the father kept his own hands at his sides, and indicated with his eyes and motion of his head that he was not allowed to reach across. Guards stood at either end of the table and at other places. The mother felt too disappointed to say anything about the dish of berries, but was pleased to see that the father looked alright, only a little tired. She told him so.

"I am outside working, which I do not mind now the weather is warming. How are you, children?"

Both looked up at him and smiled slightly, speaking almost inaudibly, and awed by the strange and severe surroundings. We are well, they seemed to say, but both mindful of the coldness of the place, and their father's changed circumstances.

"When can you be out of here?" Amara asked in a low voice.

"I am hoping it will be soon, daughter." The Ben-Oran approach to justice was somewhat casual in that very few convictions met with any fixed sentences. The outcome might depend upon the prisoner's behavior following his or her imprisonment. But something in his look conveyed to his wife that he was in fact far from optimistic. For his part, there was more that he might say, but little, he thought, that would be understandable to the children.

He would not mention that he had been required to attend regular meetings with an official who doubled as a sort of prison chaplain and medical doctor. This official seemed determined to present the father's views - which were really little more than to believe that the Elohin were fully the equal of all Ben-Orans, and entitled to equal rights under the laws - as a kind of apostasy. The father was convinced that this individual was either malevolent or incredibly stupid; either way, that his influence was inimical to the father's release. And it appeared that the opinion of one who was nominally in authority counted for more than that of twenty more reasonable opinions. To claim that the father was insane, that his ideas were dangerous to Ben-Oran society and, conceivably, to himself, might well lead to an open-ended incarceration in this hateful place. The father hated to think of it: to reside here unproductively, to be separated from his family and unable to help their precarious financial situation. It was intolerable. But he tried not to show any of his fears, not here or now.

The mother said, "We have brought a dish of berries in dressing, but the guard told us we may not bring you anything."

"Oh, do not be disappointed about it. You go and have them now, that is enough for me. In fact, there is a little grove of trees, it is across and just down the road from the guards' station, which I can see from my--" He was going to say, "cell," but decided on something closer in meaning to "my room." "There are some large stones there which might serve you for a table. Perhaps I will be able to see you there."

"Yes, of course," the mother said. "We shall do that."

"I am sorry I cannot embrace all of you," the father said, standing up. The mother stood to go, and all raised their hands in farewell.

Outside they found the spot which the father had mentioned. All looked up at the prison windows from time to time, but furtively, and not expecting to recognize their father's face. The bowl was placed on the square cloth, on a level section of rock, and with metal spoons they all reached in and ate the sweet and sour concoction of berries, family style, until it was nearly gone and Nataal was allowed to tip the bowl up and extract the last bit of red juice.

In fact the family soon found that there was a small shop which sold this delicacy nearby, and not very expensively. Having discovered the place, the mother found it easier to come here with the children on visiting days, instead of transporting the dessert from home. In this way they could avoid any unpleasantness with the prison guards. The shop was located less than a ten minute's walk along the same road, within a small cluster of stores. Inside was a small counter and a half-dozen round tables. So popular was the dish among the Ben-Orans, and so plentiful the berries that were its main ingredient, that none charged a great deal for it. So it happened, as the warm season gave way to winter, and another cycle of seasons passed, it became a regular feature of their visits to stop at this place, usually after visiting the father, when the coach schedule permitted, and when the shop was not closed for a holiday.

Amara could recognize, now more than she did then, something valiant in how her mother strove at these times to create an adventuresome and almost festive atmosphere, amid trying circumstances. In memory, she saw herself and her brother and mother seated at one of the tables, and remembered savoring the sweet and pungent flavor of the berries, which, like her memories, were compounded of sweetness and bitterness.

CHAPTER 16 - AT AN ARMY CAMP

To a field camp of government troops, the overall commander of the campaign against the Elohin traveled with a large retinue of staff and security. He met in a small canvas tent with the local field commander, known as Danegha. (The commander pronounced his name Dah-NAY-guh.) He was tall and muscular, with a shrewd and normally amused look in his eye. The two had known each other professionally for most of their careers, and were on good terms whenever they had served in common. Danegha could not fail to notice that the other officer's uniform looked a little smarter and shone a little brighter; embroidered epaulets identified his higher rank. They greeted each other and sat at angles in canvas chairs, while the visitor's aide remained standing a few paces off. Only rarely did he look directly at the two individuals as they spoke, staring off into space, rather, and occasionally responding to direct questions from his superior officer.

The goal of the military campaign, in which Danegha's company of about a thousand troops was the forward guard, was to engage with the massing Elohin and to reach terms for their surrender, or, if it proved necessary, to bring military action against them. They would be returned to population centers for processing. Some Elohin who were believed to have committed crimes would face imprisonment, many - at least, so they were to tell the Elohin - would be allowed to live freely, and still others would be confined to detention camps expressly for their "kind." The expressed purpose was two-fold: for their protection, and to remove at once any possibility of their communicating with the Ben-Orans' former adversaries the Tekerin, who were almost universally believed to be intensively reconnoitering the planet. But there had been frustratingly little contact of any kind with the Elohin, as the field commander told the visitor, owing to their dogged march toward the colder weather. Even with their complement of females and young children, the government forces had not closed upon them in many days of traveling.

"The Governor is not happy with the pace of progress," the visiting commander announced.

"I understand. We pursue, but they are not yet within our sights. We do not have any idea of their intentions."

"Well, I should say it is to preserve life, and to avoid conflict if possible."

"So you may surmise." Danegha was going to add, "Commander," but the honorific seemed spurious given their long association. Also the visitor's manner with him had put him somewhat at ease. "Would you like some spirits?" he asked.

"I would not mind."

Both of their aides declined, and Danegha poured two glasses of spirits and handed one to his visitor before sitting down again.

"I wish that I could report more progress. Except to follow their movements, and send the odd scouting party to near their camp, when it is not too dangerous, we seem to accomplish little."

"I suppose they must pause sometime."

"Undoubtedly."

"You must simply redouble your efforts. Have you tried to send emissaries? I mean, some very fleet soldiers with little pack, to reach them and discuss terms with them?"

"I am not sure such a delegation would be welcomed - or

safe."

"But you must take a chance, it seems. There are always dangers."

"From the little we have learned from our scouting parties, the Elohin seem very under-equipped to make war."

"That is not surprising. So it ought to be all the easier to convince them to end this ill-advised trek into the wilderness, where they risk starvation or death by exposure, and return instead to the population centers as the Governor wishes."

"Where they face certain imprisonment, instead."

"Well, that is their fate. Or at any rate that is our Government's policy, which I do not have to remind you that is a soldier's duty to enforce."

The field commander sipped his drink noncommittally.

"I may have an idea," the visitor continued. "Suppose it is possible to slip a couple of soldiers into the Elohin camp--"

Danegha looked at his visitor with a slightly ironic look, which suggested that such a first step was itself no little accomplishment.

"And, when they are there, suppose that they eliminate the Elohin leader."

With a feigned calmness, "Who do you have in mind?"

"Why I mean the female rebel leader, of course. She is their true leader now, is she not? The one known as Amara?"

"I know of her. And you are proposing that she be murdered?"

"Why, yes. Does that shock you?"

"Somewhat, I confess. And not only this, but sending a small party in this way, it is a suicide mission."

"But can it succeed, that is the point."

"It may, or it may not. Are you very certain that murdering the rebel leader will have the desired effect?"

"Well, it would demoralize the enemy, would it not?"

"It - could," Danegha owned. "I have not thought of it."

"Frankly, I am concerned there is some danger that the

Governor could make an unfavorable peace at this time."

"And this would be unfortunate?" The visitor did not answer, sipping his drink. "I believe there is a chance for peace."

"The Elohin have chosen war with their rebellious actions."

"I am not sure if they have not simply chosen freedom over confinement."

"Do not be naive. It matters not to me if our army destroy the Elohin by force, or if an accommodation is reached somehow. But If anyone is capable of reaching favorable terms for her race, it is probably this female. She is very capable, from all that I have heard about her. That is why she is dangerous to our goals."

"Which are?"

"The Elohin must be punished for their rebellion. Negotiation is not a soldier's way."

"I am not sure. This course - the mission, that you are suggesting - is it on behalf of the Governor, then? Is it by his directive?"

"The Governor is misinformed and naive, and cannot be trusted to deal effectively with the crisis. If the Elohin are not effectively contained, they may well for the second time come to the aid of our former persecutors, the Tekerin - whose arrival here is imminent, in the opinion of many."

"But is that any more than speculation? Has anyone actually seen their craft, except for impressionable children?"

"It might be speculation, as you suggest. But can we afford to wait and see? Even if there is no invasion, the unrest in our society is multiplying. Even without an invasion, we will descend into an ever greater chaos, and face dissolution - from within, as it were. War between the Elohin and the majority population will become general--"

"So it has been, in effect, for many years now."

"Regrettable. But let us return--"

"To this mission you spoke of, do you mean?"

"Yes. Look here, are you squeamish about seeing the campaign to its conclusion?"

"I will not refuse a direct order, if I know from where it is issued."

"Well, as to that... The Governor will leave the details to us. You will have acted in your best judgment, and done what is necessary, based upon the exigencies before you. The fact is that we have not had this conversation."

"That this directive is not from the Governor is just what I did not wish to hear."

"But that is how it is, and you must comply with the order, or else resign."

"It is evident that my ideas of how to conduct a military campaign are somewhat old-fashioned."

"Then such ideas no longer belong in our world."

Danegha chose this moment to rise and personally refill his visitor's glass, with something like conviviality. "But, Commander, do you ever imagine a world in which our race will someday train for peace, instead of only war?"

"Whether that can ever be, only Gemaal knows. I do not make it my business."

Danegha sat rather morosely, without speaking.

"Frankly, I no longer understand you, my friend. Is it because she is a female that you express this reluctance?"

"I am uncomfortable in striking at an unsuspecting one who cannot see her enemies. But it is not only that."

"Is she not one of the hated of Gemaal?" the visitor asked earnestly.

Danegha paused and studied his visitor, and saw that the statement was spoken without irony. But this did not make responding any easier. "For myself," he said after a pause, "I am not certain that I know the mind of our Creator. We are all not equally gifted with such insight. If Gemaal has spoken to me, I don't believe it was to suggest that I bring harm to one of my fellow mortals."

"Do not press me, Danegha. Or so help me--" In a milder tone, "You called it a suicide mission, before?"

"For all that, I don't doubt there are any number of young soldiers whose hatred of the Elohin is strong enough that they would feel honored to be chosen for it."

"No doubt of that. And remember there are many other officers, too, who will have no qualms. Hundreds of, if you wish, less principled officers who would be very contented to see this mission through. Do you understand? Now let us have an end of it."

"I will do as you say. Perhaps, though, commander, it is you whose ideas have lost their currency."

"Then it is well that you and I are not paid to moralize, Major, but to achieve results. Now, to details. Could - say - two of your men make their way into the enemy camp?"

"The Elohin are not stupid - they are not very different than you or me. If our soldiers arrived in secret, they might well be found out and captured. If openly, they will be disarmed and watched with a sharp eye. In any case, how would they recognize this leader of the Elohin?"

"We have thought of this. We have someone in their camp - one of their own."

"That would be an advantage. How do we find this individual?"

"You do not have to. He is here."

"Here!"

"Have Haraan brought in," the visitor said to his aide.

Stunned, Danegha rose from his canvas chair and began pacing over a small area. The Elohin was brought inside the tent, and approached slowly. He was a rather small male in a ragged cloak, and his curled and unkempt hair fell partially over a broad patch of scar across his forehead.

"You bring him *here*," Danegha said in an undertone to his visitor, as though it was incongruous, even unacceptable somehow, to have brought the enemy thus into his private quarters.

"Be civil, my friend," the superior officer said. Turning and gesturing to the new arrival, "Haraan is here to help us."

Turning, "Is that true," Danegha asked coldly.

"Indeed, sir, I will help you." Bowing slightly.

"And what is your interest in this?"

Danegha's superior officer spoke. "We do not have to question his motives, my friend. He will be paid in silver, and he has sworn his loyalty. He has not been coerced, but came to us. That is enough to know."

Danegha looked sharply at the Elohin, and from the look on his face it appeared there was a good deal more that he would like to know about the character of the double agent.

"You must be some days out of your camp. Do your confederates allow you to come and go as you please? Do they not wonder what you are doing away for days at a time?"

"I am three days from camp - sir. I am a scout, and fleet of foot, and my peers do not wonder that I am sometimes absent for several days."

"So you say. And so, you would lead two of my soldiers to your camp - in cover of darkness, of course - and they would conceal themselves somehow. And how would they know your leader?"

"Well, I shall strive to be near her, sir. For I am a trusted member of her circle, as it were."

"Indeed." Danegha frowned with distaste.

"I will strive to be near her, and show with signs that she is our leader, so that there is no doubt of it. I shall clutch her hand--" bringing his hands together.

"Alright, then. You will leave with two of my soldiers tomorrow morning." He turned abruptly away, the Elohin bowing deeply with a look to the supreme commander.

Danegha's thoughts were troubled, and his sleep difficult that evening. Strange, he thought, or perhaps it was not so strange, how the superior person could arouse on the one hand the admiration of some, and the hatred - or was it envy, perhaps? - of another.

CHAPTER 17 - GEMAAL BE WITH YOU

The three of them, Haraan and the two assassins, made their way over a wide plain. Sometimes, at first sight of strangers, they would veer into the forests for concealment. From the instructions the two soldiers had been given, and the movements of the sun and moons, they knew that they were bearing in the right direction. The Elohin traitor would become more useful to them as they drew nearer to the rebel stronghold in the mountains.

None of the three spoke very much. If the two soldiers had any second thoughts about volunteering for the mission, they did not express them. Neither of them had known the other until the morning that they were brought into Captain Danegha's tent. Haraan's face was a stoic mask; sometimes, as they walked or rested, the soldiers in their turn would stare at him as though a question was forming in their minds. But they would become distracted by other thoughts, or Haraan would turn and face them and the questions would go unasked. To the soldiers at the moment, the Elohin's motives were not very much to the point, anyway, so long as the mission was successful.

They encountered almost no one in their travels. The local forces of the Ben-Oran army, such as it was constituted, were in a waiting mode behind them, while still more soldiers were brought in from the regional capitol and countryside to reinforce those massed at the camps of Captain Danegha and other officers. Between those areas and the Elohin camp was a peculiar stillness, that was due partly to the remoteness of the region, and partly to the battle that appeared to be looming. The screech of the occasional large flying bird sounded jarring to the solitary travelers, and then the landscape was silent again except for their footfalls in the short grass.

Of the government's forces, it might have been an exaggeration to call such a varied and loosely organized body of soldiers an army. It consisted of conscripts, some of them approaching middle age, as well as impoverished volunteers drawn by the small but, so far, dependable pay that was offered. Some of the soldiers saw in the campaign against the Elohin a government initiative that was reasonable and necessary. And there were many whose hatred of the Elohin was something more visceral and personal, even if some had never lived among them - even if their home villages were located many weeks of travel away from the principal sites formerly cultivated by the Tekerin, where the majority of the Elohin lived and remained.

The army, besides, was largely undisciplined, and poorly and variously armed with knives and hatchets, and bow and arrow. Firearms were very much rarer, and where they were found, they were usually neither very accurate nor reliable, unless the gunsmith had some particular capability. A class of weapon which was available to some, and which did function in a more repeatable fashion was the cannon; its more predictable results were due to its relatively greater mass, which allowed the barrel to hold together during firing. Smaller guns which were fashioned from the available and mostly unrefined base metals of Ben-Ora tended to behave unpredictably, and so they were used only in combination with simpler and more traditional weapons.

The party encountered a few bands of Elohin who were tending in the same direction. But usually they saw them at such a distance that it was possible to evade them. Just once this was not possible, when a half-dozen males, females and one small child surprised them at their campfire. Then the two soldiers improvised a pantomime in which Haraan was their prisoner, who they were determined to bring to the Government camp. Their prisoner remained speechless, while the two soldiers swore that they must fight to their deaths if the Elohin opposed them. There was a brief standoff, and when Haraan said to them, "Save yourselves," and, "Do not worry about me," the Elohin moved off, presumably toward the mountains. The three were obliged to wait for a morning until the group of Elohin were well out of their range, before resuming.

They broke for camp the same night, at a clearing in some woods, without encountering anyone else. They had traveled for four days. Their dinner was some preserved foods. They did not light a fire due to their closeness to the Elohin camp. It was nearly dusk, and the air was turning cool. They sat more or less facing each other.

"When will we reach them?" one of the soldiers asked.

"We can be there tomorrow," Haraan said.

"How do we approach their camp?"

"I suggest, any time after the sun has set. But we will not approach from the plain straight into the foothills, but in the cover of trees off to the side. When you are nearly in position I will break away from you, then you must follow me at a distance, and I will lead you straight to her. When she sees me I will endeavor to take her hands in greeting, and you will know it is her."

"Alright," the soldier said. "It sounds fine. I wish to be off of the main-traveled ways, lest we be seen and arouse suspicion. I suggest we begin moving that way very early in the morning, before the sun has risen."

Haraan nodded without saying anything.

The other soldier asked him, drawing his bedroll about his shoulders, "How much have they paid you to betray your leader?"

A look of warning came into the other soldier's face, but

he did not say anything. He reclined on his bedroll, with a hand propping his chin.

Haraan told him.

"It does not sound like a good deal of silver. Still, it is more than a common soldier receives in a quarter of the year."

"Do you mean to kill me for it?" Haraan asked.

"No," the soldier replied easily. "I could not do that while you are in our charge."

"I am glad to hear that."

The soldier shrugged, waved this off. "And have they paid you in full?"

"Only half. The other half is when the mission is successful."

"If it is successful, you mean."

Haraan did not say anything, but absently pushed his curling hair back from his forehead. The broad patch of scar there was just visible in the growing darkness. Then he seemed to remember himself, and pushed his hair with a more deliberate movement back where it had been over his forehead.

The other soldier noticed the movement of Haraan's hand. "You sure talk a lot," he said to the one who was asking all the questions.

"There is just one other question in my mind," he said, looking at Haraan, whose eyes were averted. "But - I suppose you have your reasons."

"You are going to talk me to death," Haraan said. He turned onto his side, minus any bedroll, but with his head upon his forearm, and faced away from the soldiers.

When it was not yet light, the party rejoined the plain and proceeded to their left into what became dense forest broken by occasional trails. Here their movement was more difficult. The soldiers could only trust in their accomplice's direction. Sometimes they could see the mountains rising off to their right. Occasionally small bands of Elohin could be seen moving in the open plain straight for the mountains - presumably, that remnant who had somehow escaped apprehension, and were adding, still, to the number gathered here in the mountains. How many there were, and how well armed, the soldiers thought they might be able to report with some accuracy when their mission was concluded, if they made it successfully back to the camp.

The light was fading when Haraan gestured to the two soldiers to pause. Their only sign that they might be near the enemy camp was a smell of wood smoke that had lingered in the air for some time.

"I believe we are close," Haraan said. He peered through the trees to what might have been the lights of assorted campfires. The soldiers could not hear any voices as yet.

"My friends, it all rests with you and Gemaal now. I will go ahead. You must keep me within your sight, and avoid being seen by anyone else. Whether successful or not, you see by the largest moon which is rising the direction back to your camp."

Haraan pointed back through the forest in the direction they had come. Neither was very clear about the way back to camp. But assuming that they could place some distance between themselves and the Elohin there was a possibility of regaining it, eventually.

"Gemaal be with you."

The soldiers nodded with grim expressions, and felt their bows for tautness, and reached under their shoulders where each had a sheath containing several arrows. Both suspected there would be opportunity for only one shot each, possibly two.

Haraan continued forward slowly. The soldiers allowed him a head start and then followed. They must keep him within their sight while watching their footing, and trying not to snap any branches below their feet. They were still some distance from any obvious activity, although they imagined they could hear voices, perhaps from scattered campfires. Sounds of small bells being struck, of finger cymbals being dashed together, rose upon the night air.

It looked as though Haraan had gained a small trail ahead, which the soldiers dared not use themselves. He looked back in their direction, and proceeded rather slowly in deference to their slower progress through the brush.

Suddenly a booming voice rang out, of someone hailing their accomplice by name. Instinctively the soldiers dropped to the ground, watching and listening.

A much larger male clasped his shoulders. "Is it you?!" he cried. "We were about to give you up for dead! Were you detained?"

"No. And I am quite well," Haraan replied.

"Well. Amara and the others will be pleased to see you back. Come."

They made their way upon the path while the soldiers followed some distance off, screened by trees and brush. The other male slowed down for Haraan, who pleaded some soreness in his foot, which allowed the soldiers to keep up.

They were approaching a clearing of about forty feet in diameter. At the back there was a blazing campfire which dispelled the cold, and where some game was evidently being roasted. Battered metal pots and kettles of tea hung near the fire or rested upon small heated stones. There were, in all, about ten individuals seated around the fire, and sitting or walking elsewhere within the clearing were a few small children and their caretakers, as well.

The male who was leading Haraan along the path whistled two notes, a lower and then a higher one, before emerging into the clearing, from where a few rose to greet him. There was a female with black hair at the very back of the circle, or rather a horseshoe, for none had their back to the path, and another female three places to her left. The first to step forward, however was a large and burly male - Amara's fighter - who stared at the newcomers without expression.

The male who had first greeted Haraan said to the group, "Why, look who is here!"

There was a general silence, and then the fighter spoke.

"Where are you all this time, Haraan? We were sure the government forces had killed you."

"You see I am very well," Haraan said reassuringly.

"Have you been detained by them?"

"If I had been detained by them I should certainly not be here now, would I?"

"I don't know at all," the fighter said.

Around the campfire only a few had risen. All looked curiously at Haraan.

"I have only been scouting. The government forces are but four days' travel from here. There are many thousand of them. That is why I was so long away, because they are some distance yet."

"This is nothing we did not already know," the fighter said.

There was silence within the clearing. Even the children had stopped moving and stared curiously at the new arrival. The two soldiers crept closer to the edges of the trees, their bows resting vertically upon the ground, while each removed two arrows and lay them on the ground in front of them. They were close to the central path, about ten feet apart, and as such they had a clear line to the center of the circle. It was still not clear to them which female was the leader of the rebels.

The black-haired woman at the back stood up, and walking to her left around the circle she walked directly up to the new arrival and extended her hands before her.

"We are happy to see you, Haraan," she said.

Haraan clasped her hands and bowed very low and

elaborately before her.

"You do not have to be so formal with me," the woman said to Haraan.

The fighter looked at him sullenly.

"Sit with us. You must be very tired."

"I am awfully so, and would prefer to rest."

"Oh, nonsense. Have some tea with us, and tell us what else you have learned."

"Well - alright." Haraan sat near the front of the fire, to the right, where there was a clear space. He looked at the ground, trying not to lift his eyes in the direction of the archers.

One of the inner circle, a male elder kneeling close to the campfire, lifted a steaming kettle of tea from its platform of rocks, gripping the heated metal strap on the top with a small piece of cloth. The male to his left tipped a metal cup upside down and then held it out to him. But the elder's pouring arm shook with some nervous disorder, to such an extent that many seated around the fire looked on with concern, none more than the younger male who held the cup in his hand beneath the kettle. When some of the hot tea dripped onto his hand he remonstrated,

"Here - Ow - Why not let me pour it?"

The younger male took the kettle in his hand, and looking much relieved he filled the cup and then stood suddenly and extended his left hand with the cup toward Haraan.

What happened next transpired very quickly. The first arrow struck against the kettle and deflected very slightly, but with undiminished velocity to the left and downward, and struck hard into the ground between Amara, who sat in front of a broad tree, and the male seated to her right.

The male holding the kettle barely had time to say, "What the devil--?" before there was a general commotion of shouts, and individuals rising to their feet. Amara herself saw, or perhaps only sensed, some movement in the brush at the edge of the clearing, some thirty feet away, and she pushed the male to her left to the ground, and rolled onto the ground in that direction, just before the second arrow thudded into the great tree before which she had been sitting, landing there a couple of feet above the ground.

"There!" voices yelled. Pointing, charging toward the edge of the clearing just right of the path.

"We are dead men," one of the archers said to the other. Both crashed from the brush onto the path, running away at full speed from their pursuers.

"Do not let them escape!" the fighter yelled. He rushed over to where Amara crouched to the side of the tree.

"Be careful," she said, and pulled upon his arm so that he crouched as well. "We must be certain there are no others."

"I cannot see," the fighter said.

Of the others only Haraan remained, standing in the middle of the clearing.

"Haraan," the woman shouted. "Do you see any others?"

He looked around cursorily. "Indeed, I do not."

The fighter and Amara moved to the edges of the clearing and peered among the trees and brush. Haraan appeared to join them in this effort, and then, Amara and the fighter somewhat reassured, they all stood near the center.

The fighter exhaled a long breath and said, "I wonder you do not join the chase, Haraan. Is it because you are too tired from all of your travels away from camp?"

"I think that is it. I am happy that you are safe, Miss."

"Is it not strange," the fighter continued, "that we have no sooner welcomed you back to camp, and these devils appeared and set upon us?"

"I do not know what you mean. I am sure it is very regrettable."

The fighter stood between Haraan and the woman, who studied Haraan without speaking.

"It is regrettable when trust is repaid with treachery."

"I cannot follow you." But Haraan's features were strained to the breaking point with an odd excitement, and his denials failed to ring true.

"When you were away, Haraan, did you visit at the enemy's camp?"

"Why would I--" Haraan began, and stopped. "You cannot believe--"

"Well, I am sure they are going to tell us when we catch them, those devils," the fighter said. He was bluffing somewhat.

Haraan grew more agitated and shifted away from them slightly. The other two did not see him fingering the hatchet that was held in a sling inside his jacket. When he turned around, the hatchet held low in his hand, he attempted to sprint around the fighter and make straight for Amara, but the fighter blocked his path. Haraan swung the hatchet forward and it caught the fighter on the top of his shoulder, very near to his neck.

The fighter winced in pain, and wrestling for the hatchet he was able to pull it away and hold it against his chest, but felt consciousness fading as he turned toward the woman and gasped, "You must stop him."

Haraan had backed off a couple of steps. As the fighter fell to one knee, his hand pawing the ground for support, the woman now saw Haraan turn and run from her in the direction of the path that led out of the clearing. She called his name once as she pulled a large hunting knife from a sheath at her waist.

"Stay down, Fighter," she called. The other male heard and quickened his steps, and as he did not stop she hurled the knife at his retreating back. The knife struck hard between his shoulder blades, and he stopped instantly, as though he was held momentarily by an invisible cord. She did not see the look of shock that formed on his face, only his hands reaching futilely behind him, and he fell forward a moment later.

She went over to the fighter who was sitting on the ground and, crouching, peered at his bloodied shoulder. "Are you alright?"

"I will be."

"Exert some pressure on it, until we can dress the wound properly."

"Certainly, Miss." He saw her looking over at Haraan, lying flat on his stomach.

"You had no choice but to stop him, Miss. He only would have done more harm."

"I have never killed anyone, and it grieves me."

She went over to Haraan, and, stooping, withdrew her knife with a quick movement. She reached and turned him onto his back, and saw that his eyes opened. He looked at her, his eyes dull and shining.

"Why, Haraan?" she asked him.

"Oh," he answered softly, "for the silver, of course." His eyes moved momentarily toward his chest, and she saw there was a cloth satchel tied about his neck. His eyes had a dismissive and ironic look as they inclined toward the satchel.

He looked into her eyes again while intensity faded from his face. "And because ... you are so many things that I could never be - loved by all of your kind, and admired for your character." A spasm of pain caused him to pause. "I did not love you for these things. I hated you."

Amara looked at him coolly.

"There is one other thing. More are coming after."

"I believe you."

"There will be a small advance party. If you can overwhelm them in these mountains - surprise them - and take their weapons - you will have a better chance when the assault comes."

She nodded. "I understand."

It appeared that he wanted to raise his hand to touch her, and raised his upper body slightly, but gave it up because of the pain it caused. She looked at him warily.

"Can you forgive--" he started to say. His eyes went completely still, and lifeless, but remained open, and with the inquisitive look that remained on his face, it was as though he still expected an answer. She closed his eyes with her fingertips, and then brutally ripped the satchel away from his neck and held it, and stood up.

"Someone will bury this traitor," she said to the fighter.

CHAPTER 18 - THE MOUNTAIN PASS

"This attack seems to have greatly altered the spirit of our people." The male called Zareth was sitting with legs crossed near the fire. He held a cup of warm tea in his hands. The early evening was comfortable, with a light breeze. They were, still, in the middle of the mild season. From a distance, some melodies played on the bells reached them.

"How altered?" Amara asked. "For the better, do you mean?"

There were no others about the small campfire. The fighter had gone off to the privy, or to one of the two areas alongside the river where, with sheets of cloth suspended from tree branches, the camp residents bathed. The two were within sight of the small lake of fresh green water which they had found, about which they had settled their makeshift camp. The lake, which was an hour's walk to circle, rested within a broad plateau in the upper reaches of the mountains.

"I was not thinking for the better. They appear to be more worried than before."

"What you call worry may only be vigilance, which we will all need in order to survive. It has shown us, at least, what our enemies are capable of."

"I am sure their action did not surprise any of us. The stories which I have heard told here are very troubling, indeed. And before I arrived here I myself passed through the village of Tinnar, where many of us had lived, and found that it had become a smoking ruin."

"Terrible. And had you any news of my village?"

"I heard that your mother is no longer there. No one knew where she lives."

"I think she decided that I was completely ungovernable when I was young - and she was probably right."

He laughed.

"And my brother?"

"No news, I am afraid."

"Perhaps I will see him here one day. I should like that." She hesitated for a moment. "And do you know anything of my daughter?"

"She has been brought up in a rather well to do family, in a different province. As I am sure you know. There is talk that she will make a match with a young man whose father is a mayor, or some such thing."

"Do you think - she knows who her mother is?"

"I am pretty certain she does not, Miss."

"It is just as well. I am happy that she can lead a better life than I could provide for her. Thank you." She smiled at the recent arrival at the camp, and looked over the dwindling campfire into the dusk.

He reached and touched her shoulder lightly, and held his hand there when she did not object. "May I ask if there is any male in your life?"

She looked obliquely at him. "You know that a female never tells or explains more than is necessary."

"Oh, bah!" he said, making a face.

"But that is what they say about us, is it not?"

"But you are not like anyone else, surely."

She would not tell him anything about the farmer's son, although he was still a good deal on her mind. Perhaps, if there were some female that she could talk to, she might. She wished, but hardly dared to hope, that she and the farmer's son might meet again in different circumstances. Logically, she thought that their affair was something now fixed in the past, and not to be renewed.

"What about you, Zareth?" she asked briskly, and the visitor felt obliged to take his hand away from her shoulder. "Have you any family of your own?"

"I do not. Years ago I cared very much for a female who was not of our kind. I think that she loved me, too. In spite--"

He stared at the fire. The skin about his jaw, on the side facing Amara, was raw red, the surface mottled. "It was impossible, of course," he said. He made a dismissive movement with his hand, as though tossing something into the fire.

Changing the subject, he said, "The musicians keep playing a tune, but I cannot recall its name."

"Do you not know this one? It is called, 'See, The Emerald Evening Closes Fast.'"

"I had forgotten it, I confess."

"I remember, we used to sing it at school assemblies sometimes."

"That could not have been much pleasure for you."

"Oh, but it was. Though you sound rather skeptical of it."

"No, I do not mean to be."

"Music was one of the only things that made life tolerable when I was growing up."

"I do not doubt it."

"I still enjoy music, though for much of the time I have had little chance to hear it, unless I sing to myself."

"Will you teach it to me?"

"I am a little out of practice now, to sing. Another time."

Amara leaned back, resting on an elbow with her legs stretched before her. The male assumed the same posture.

She returned to their prior conversation. "At least the attack did not harm any of us. And with the sentries that we have installed, I think we shall not be caught unawares again."

"You have become one of the natural leaders of our race."

"I did not seek to be. But if it what the others want then I shall do my best."

"Do you think that the enemy will attack soon?"

"Perhaps. I have heard that they will send a small scouting party into the mountains. If they approach through the same pass by which we came - and I do not see another approach - I believe we shall be able to surprise them, and take their weapons for our use. It will improve our means of defense, if there is to be a general attack upon us."

When, before a week passed, one of the teams of sentries spotted the approach of a small party of government forces, the news was swiftly relayed to the Elohin leaders, and a plan put in place. Their noncombatants - children, and the majority of females - removed to the rear of the camp with a protective force, while a sufficient force concealed themselves above the rocks through which the advancing army was thought likely to pass. The Elohin in this group were armed with several bows and arrows, some javelins, and all had daggers or short swords. The advancing party numbered only about thirty, and for speed they traveled without wagons but with some pack animals with saddlebags over their backs.

Amara, the fighter and a few others crouched on the top of a large rock from which they could look directly down into the defile, some thirty feet below, that wound irregularly through the rocks. To either side of the defile, which was about forty feet across in this area, Elohin crouched or lay flat on the upper reaches of the rocks, visible to Amara but out of sight of any on the path below. One who was situated at the front of the mountains made his way back to report on the strength of the enemy's force, and said that he thought they could not fail to pass directly below them. She was confirmed that their own forces were about twice those of the government army. Even if they were, in fact, inadequately armed, the enemy was unlikely to recognize this immediately, and the element of surprise, and their superior position, she thought, boded well for the outcome. She hoped that the enemy, once they understood their position, would agree to surrender their arms to them, and leave without casualties on either side. If it came to a fight, the government's forces must not in any circumstances be allowed to penetrate beyond this pass, which would place all inhabitants of the camp at risk. This, all of her council had emphasized, was an unacceptable outcome which must be prevented at all costs, by close fighting if necessary. But hopefully it would not come to this.

It was early in the afternoon. Some of the large grey birds who were native to the mountains floated serenely overhead with a rattling sound. Everything else was silence. Amara's small group could not yet hear the approach of the government's forces, only perceive, from the gesturing of the other Elohin arrayed along the tops of the rocks to either side of the pass, that the enemy forces were proceeding as expected.

She gestured to the few behind her to remain low and to stay back, and herself lay flattened upon the rock so that she could just see the winding path below. Her heart surged as the first of the government soldiers appeared in the defile and trudged forward. Soon there was a regular line of them, and a few water buffaloes brought laboriously through the pass and onto level ground, the attendant soldiers pulling upon their bridles. When the soldiers had proceeded about halfway through the pass, and the last of them had entered the defile, Amara stood up and extended one hand before her.

Before she said anything, some soldiers among the party were instantly aware of her, and some dropped to a crouch and turned their heads to see if any others were there. Amara herself was not armed except with a side-dagger, and with her dark hair and clothing she appeared very distinct against the clear sky. The army had stopped in its tracks, well aware of its vulnerable position in the defile. When she saw some panicked movement among the soldiers below she called out, "Stop. Go no further."

"Who do we speak to?" One of the soldiers, an officer by the cut and color of his uniform, disengaged himself from the group and moved to the front.

"It doesn't matter who I am. You have found those you came to seek." With this, she raised both of her arms in the air, and the archers stood up with their bows drawn and aimed below. The fighter, behind her, and a few others stood and gripped javelins resting upon their shoulders. At the show of force, the army's soldiers below drew into a tighter circle.

"And now that you have found us," she continued, "you will be invited to leave. You need not be harmed, but you will leave your weapons with us."

"Leave our weapons?" the commander asked. "That cannot be."

"That is how it will be," Amara insisted. "Or you will not leave here with your lives."

One of the soldiers bolted, running back in the direction they had come, but a single arrow landing just ahead in his path, he stopped and crouched, arms covering his head.

"We will not waste another warning shot. Now place your weapons in a pile in the center there, and step away. We will have need of them."

"A moment, Miss."

"Yes?"

"I believe you misunderstand our purpose here. We should like to speak with you, and see if we might come to some understanding."

Her understanding of the Ben-Oran character told her, even at this distance, that the commander was improvising some falsehood.

"Really. If so it is very strange. Your last delegation came here not to talk of peace but to commit murder."

"I am sure I do not know anything about that."

"Perhaps not. As for talk, understand that we cannot surrender our freedom for promises which may prove empty. Now, do as I have said or you and your soldiers will not leave this mountain alive."

The commander stared hard into her face, but she felt that his gaze took in as well the precarious situation of his small force trapped in the defile. For her part, she felt a long-ingrained and almost instinctual distrust of the soldier and all he stood for. She felt also a steely resolve, mingled with, to her surprise, a degree of sympathy. Another moment passed, and then the commander nodded once in the direction of his forces, and unhitched a sword from his waist and placed it on the ground. The other soldiers followed.

"I am going down there," she said to her group. She gestured to the Elohin stationed upon the rocks to maintain their positions.

"I shall come with you, Miss," the fighter said, and the two other males in her party accompanied her as well.

When they had climbed down and stood in the defile, the fighter stood next to her and gripped the javelin in both hands and pointed it in front of him. A handful of Elohin, with knives drawn, made their way among the soldiers to see that all were disarmed.

"I am glad that you are a reasonable individual, commander."

"You have left me little choice, Miss."

She made her way to the large pack animals which stood some distance from the small pile of weapons. She patted one on the neck and then peered into the saddlebags which were fastened about the animal. One contained some metal shot, which must have been for the pair of firearms, long and short, with barrels as wide as a male's thumb, that she had seen among the pile of weapons. She took the saddlebag and handed it to one of her circle. The others contained cereal, and one a small leather journal and some other personal items, and these she left.

The fighter, staring about him apprehensively, thought to say "Miss," but no sound came from his dry mouth. He touched her arm, and then started slightly as one of the large birds above him rose and clattered off. "It is alright," Amara said.

When she returned to the commander and stood before him, she said, "You stare at me very intently, commander." In fact he appeared very intent, and stone-faced. "I might almost say that you are impertinent."

"I do not mean to be."

"Perhaps it is that you have rarely seen your enemy this close." And she appeared almost to smile, staring back at him. Only the broad liver-colored patch of scar that extended across her cheek did not move, but seemed rigid, and impervious to any outward expression of feeling. "Or is it," she asked, "rather that you are not used to seeing him in these circumstances?"

"You seem to have triumphed," he said. "I only ask that you honor your promise that we may leave safely."

Those in her circle looked warily at the group of government soldiers, and looked up as if to assure themselves that the archers and others were still in place.

"You will not be harmed," she said. "You will find that we are not vindictive."

With a very slight nod, she backed off a few steps, as did the others. Silently, and with many backward glances, the government soldiers made their way back in the direction they had come, until their commander himself disappeared along the winding path.

CHAPTER 19 - FINALE: APOTHEOSIS

The woman stood at the summit of a gentle and gradual incline. The land was mostly clear and covered with grass, except for some shrubs and short trees, and except for a few level areas, the land rose evenly over several hundred yards up to where the woman stood. There was a sheer stone wall of rock directly behind her, rising several times her height, with outcroppings of green shoots and vines, and which was curved somewhat like a clamshell. Around and behind her were some of the other principal leaders of the Elohin, all of them either kneeling or with their legs drawn up under them, and listening. When the woman spoke her voice echoed slightly, and carried forward somewhat due to the curved rock behind her. Her glance took in all of the many thousands of Elohin standing below in a vast crowd on the gently sloping hill.

"My friends," she said, looking into the clear skies, "Gemaal has given us a beautiful day today..."

Her words seemed quite unexpected, when almost all of the recent talk was of war, of what might happen in what appeared to be the decisive conflict that was looming, and of what possible future lives the Elohin could expect to live when the conflict was over. Her simple words reassured the sprawling crowd, and a murmur of appreciation spread through the assembled and reached back to the top of the hill.

When she spoke she would pause frequently, while some in the front who could hear her plainly repeated her words to those further behind, and when the crowd murmurs ceased, she resumed.

"The future appears very uncertain. If this is war then we will defend ourselves as best we can. We know how we have suffered because of the falsehoods by which this society lives. But I am confident that, if it is Gemaal's will, there is a brighter future for us. We were not born to wander this world like outcasts."

Her words were repeated down the hill, and later the assembled voices surged up in approbation and continued for a good while.

"They say that we are the hated of Gemaal, but we know that this is a falsehood. This society has declared war upon even small children, who are physically unmarked by the years of occupation under the Tekerin. The children have done no wrong except to have been born to those which this society calls the Elohin. As they live with us, they share our hardships. Some of us have given up our children in the hope that, with their origins unknown to anyone, they might lead normal and peaceful lives. It is a painful and bitter choice, which none should have to make."

The crowd murmured as before, and then a low roar surged up the hill as the woman paused and collected her thoughts, before resuming.

"It seems that there is a battle to come now. We have not sought it out, but neither will we shrink from it. My friends, if this should be the end for some of us, let us not be in despair. Let us once more assert our pride and our faith in who we are. It is not Gemaal, or fate, that has decreed for us a life of hiding, of loneliness and separation from individuals and places that we loved. Inside ourselves, we know that the fault is not within us. If the battle cannot be avoided, we will stand proudly for ourselves. Let the Ben-Orans remember that we have resisted, and that we have fought valiantly against the tyranny of our age. If they do not understand this now, it may happen that the truth will be recognized in some more enlightened time in our future, which some of us may yet see. But that can matter little, just now. For now we must prepare to defend ourselves."

"When I am judged by the Creator, I would have preferred not to have anyone else's blood on my hands. But if, as the situation stands, all that awaits us is the ignominy of prison, then let us be prepared to take up arms, with whatever means that we have, to defend ourselves to the last."

The woman pauses. Her face is resolute. It is the face of someone who did not seek to be a leader, but whose circumstances have naturally led her to it. Nor is she, in her own mind at least, any natural public speaker, either by temperament, or by her circumstances until now; indeed, she feels that she has spent too much of her life in solitude - by necessity and circumstances, rather than choice. The crowd, in any case, is rapt, and the other Elohin behind her listen respectfully also.

Now the cheers of the assembled crowd have grown silent, as have her words. Her face is seen very clearly - magnified, perhaps - even to some wisps of black hair that are blown about her forehead by a breeze that swoops around the rock formation. Our view is clear. Yet it appears that the woman's face freezes from time to time, and her expression changes abruptly, as though there are gaps in the image that is presented to us. The perspective grows in clarity as Amara's face is seen on a large screen, while, below her image, pairs of hands with preternaturally long fingers move over lighted consoles and display panels. The hands and arms connect to a pair of creatures seated there, gazing raptly at the silent image on the screen, and examining and pressing with their delicate long fingers the lighted display before them. The sky that is visible away from the central viewing panels is a pale green without clouds, a typical Ben-Oran sky of a late afternoon.

Other panels are visible as well, and the scenes displayed

change regularly: for example, the view of Amara staring in three-quarters profile now gives way to a crowd scene on the broad sloping hill, and now to a close-up of a male Elohin of middle age who is wiping a tear away from his face, and gazing upward with a look of admiration as well as pride. The creatures look on dispassionately, or so it seems. Both are dressed in single-color jerseys and trousers. They are completely hairless, but except for the extraordinary smoothness of their heads, which resemble somewhat an egg with the smaller end pointing upwards, they do not seem vastly different from humans. Although the creatures are hairless, and hardly dissimilar, it is possible to speculate at a glance that one of them is female, based upon an extra degree of delicacy in her face. There is no one else in the observation cabin. The console tables extend far in either direction, and there is some slight lateral curvature to the mostly transparent walls that run the length of the cabin. The clear material appears to be glass or something similar. There are closed doors behind the two figures, which evidently give to inner rooms of the spacecraft.

The one who is evidently male appeared to be extremely curious as well as perplexed by the scene which was unfolding below. That was the appearance that he gave, although it must be admitted that the faces of the observers conveyed only a very narrow range of expressiveness. He rested his oversized head upon one hand and appeared to sigh. He felt somewhat unequal to the team's mission, which was to observe and to give an account of the Ben-Orans: their behavior, their values, their prospects for survival, even their potential usefulness to the visiting species. But what he had witnessed was a scene of chronic conflict, whose origins he was left only to guess at in some degree. The team was unaided by even a rudimentary knowledge of the Ben-Orans' language. If their language had been at all comparable to others that his species had explored, a speech recognition program using a visual scan of the subjects' mouths could have approximated the sounds that this primitive race enunciated, and then instantly translated their meaning to something he could understand, without actually having to hear their speech.

This degree of understanding, however, was not possible because of his species' unfamiliarity with the Ben-Orans, occupying as they did their small and remote corner of the known universe. So it was no matter that the visual feed came without sound, because neither he or his partner could have constructed any meaning from the speech of the inhabitants below. Sound would have been a distraction, in fact, and so it had been turned off.

"It appears that something is not correct with you," the female one said - more or less, anyway. The speech of the visitors had a grating sound, which was almost like the workings of a clock, though not as regular; and magnified, of course, augmented by squeaks and squeals. It is only possible to express the general import of the speakers' meaning.

"Do you believe that we will be able to complete our report?" the female creature continued.

"Oh, we can, in some fashion. But I am confused about the causes of the planet's many conflicts."

"You did not expect the inhabitants to be as logical as us, did you? Or that they could be like us? Why, they move only along the ground, drawn by brute animals."

"Yes, yes, I do understand, of course." But he didn't understand all that he had observed, in pantomime as it were, since the crew of the spacecraft had begun their observations here above the planet. Two groups were in conflict: one with numerical superiority, another, numerically smaller group which suffered persecution, clearly, with - in most instances - distinguishing physical markings. Except that progeny of the latter group, if they were not surrendered to the majority and raised among them, led a harsh and constrained existence much like the adults. The library histories provided some information about the genesis of the conflict, and the resulting fragmentation of Ben-Oran society, but the materials seemed inadequate to explain the planet's strange destiny. Or to predict its future, either.

In the course of their investigation, the team had been able to make only two clandestine visits to the planet. One was a night-time visit to the offices of a newspaper, or penny-dreadful; they could not understand anything of the Ben-Oran hieroglyphics, but some crudely rendered etchings and caricatures in recent issues had given evidence, at least, of a profound and persistent bias against the Elohin.

The main display panel directly above where the pair was sitting changed from a crowd scene to show the face of the woman again. A breeze blew her dark hair straight back and she spoke in words that the visitors could not hear and could not have understood. She paused, staring directly ahead with a peaceful expression, the beginnings of a smile on her face.

"You seem very intent," the female crew member said.

"N-n-n-n-n." Not really hearing, and staring up at the screen. In the black and white image, the broad patch of scar below the woman's left eye looked like a deep and recently incurred bruise.

This sound, "n-n-n-n-n," seemed to accompany deep reflection, before any thought was uttered by one of the creatures. The sound emerged out of the whirring and faintly clacking apparatus of their speech, from the drone of electro-mechanical sounds that were heard when two or more creatures interacted. In this instance, though, the sound seemed frankly born of inattention to what had just been said to him.

This nettled the female crew member to such an extent that her hand suddenly reached out and pushed away his arm that was supporting his chin. Predictably, his head fell forward until he righted himself, then he cradled his large head carefully between his hands before shooting a cross look at his teammate.

"What was that for? That can be dangerous, you know. I was thinking."

"Yes. Thinking about her, no doubt."

"Well, of course I was." Rubbing one hand over the top of his faintly pointed head, and then gingerly returning his hands to the console. "Isn't that part of our mission here, to study and to think about these individuals?"

"Since you have studied her so much, what have you decided about her?"

Staring at his teammate incredulously, "Why, I am not sure yet. Why ever are you talking like this?"

The female crew member had her jaw set firmly.

"You cannot be feeling jealous of her? I think you are." His mouth remained open in disbelief.

"Oh, be serious. The way you were staring at that female."

"At her? Well, if I was - a bit - does it violate any of the ship's rules?"

"Yes, a very important one: *I don't like it.*"

"What! First of all, that is not a ship's rule." She glared at him. "Alright, that is only a technical point. But, don't be angry with me. Why, from what I have gathered, we could not even mate with those creatures down there."

"Perhaps you want to."

A ratcheting sound purred, seemingly from deep within the male's chest, as though echoing some mental confusion.

"Don't be like that, he said. Look" - gesturing toward the screen - "she has none of your delicacy."

"Well. I suppose she hasn't." Preening herself, rubbing the top of her faintly shiny head.

"You see? And then there is all that *hair*." A very subtle look of distaste appeared in the rather stoical mask that was the creature's face. On the screen at that moment, the woman tilted her head upwards, and the wind swept her black hair from her face back to the tops of her shoulders.

"I really must agree with you on that point," the female said.

"Don't let us be angry then. There is work to be done in describing what we have seen here. And do not be jealous of her." Gesturing toward the screen again. "Don't you see, for example, that at this moment, for her and for her kind, their very survival is at stake? While we only have to look and observe here, and have no stake in the outcome." He examined and pressed some switches, and the display panel switched to a crowd scene, but it was not the crowd that was spread over the hillside.

This crowd was on the move, although their movement was not immediately apparent in the first, large-perspective view. Long columns of infantry moved through a terrain that was growing hillier, and when the view changed to a close-up, teams of water buffalo could be seen pulling wagons on which small cannons rested, some of them partially covered by canvas cloths.

"They are not very far away." The male peered at some numbers and figures upon the screen with the crawling army, and then at a screen showing the stationary Elohin in their redoubt among the mountains.

"Their enemy is only distant by, n-n-n-n-n--"

"They will meet before this day is over, barring accidents," the female crew member said, after studying the on-screen data herself.

"Yes. Just so. And with all that is going on," looking at his teammate "how can you view matters so narrowly? Thinking that I could prefer her to you!"

"N-n-n-n-n-- I suppose, I am just a female creature."

"Just a - what?" he repeated, a trace of astonishment appearing on his features. "Did I hear correctly? Don't give me that line!" he said sternly. "You know as well as I that you are in fact supremely logical. May I point out that you graduated at the top of your class in deep space navigation? Yes!" he insisted. "Think I don't know all about you? But you must - you must, try to see things from her point of view."

The woman was absent from any of the screens at the moment.

"You are right. I actually feel rather kindly toward her, and am very sympathetic to the plight of the minority group. Such a cruel fate is not deserved. I am afraid that they lack the resources to hold off the army that approaches, and that it will prove an unequal battle."

"Unless the ship's leaders decide to intervene."

"And what makes you think that would happen?"

"I agree, it is most unlikely," the male said gloomily.

"I wish there was more that we could do. Should we speak to the captain about it?"

"Perhaps we could."

"And I am sorry that I jostled your arm before. If you were not held together so well, I might have caused you to lose some data, which I would have regretted."

"No fear of that. And you are held together very well also."

"Thank you," she said. She was not quite sure what he meant, but took the remark as a compliment.

They sat very close together. The male looked at her. She brought her hands together on her chest, and tilted her head downward, in what must have been a gesture of trust, or of regard, and the male saw her and did likewise. The female leaned closer toward him, and still closer, and when the smooth domes of their heads were nearly in contact, and blissful expressions (at least, within the limits of the creatures' expressive range) appeared on their faces, then it seemed that an electrical energy passed between their heads, and a crackling, faint blue arc was visible there.

From within the male's chest, the mechanical-sounding whirring and purring noises grew more insistent, sounding almost vaguely alarming, like a cry that was pulled involuntarily from his chest. The sounds grew in volume, and then abruptly stopped. The female, who had seemed in a trance, came to herself and looked anxiously behind her to see if anyone had heard and might be even now approaching the cabin door to investigate.

"What are you doing?" the male hissed at her. "Were you trying to - conjoin our intellectual auras? Now?"

"Something like that," the female said, a little abashed, now the moment of bliss was passed. "But don't blame only me." It was fortunate that the pair was assigned a private observation cabin. This degree of privacy was to facilitate concentration upon the work that was before them and not upon each other, however, as they both well knew. With each moment that passed the female felt more confident that none had heard or would report their impropriety. It could be damaging if made public, for junior crew members such as themselves.

"I'm sorry. I want you to like me."

"I do like you. But we must concentrate."

"Yes. You are right."

But concentration was increasingly difficult for the male crew member. He recognized a resigned and wistful expression on the female's face, which endeared her to him, while the festive lights of the control panel - red, green, and blue - were reflected on her bald pate, and seemed to glisten on the smooth and as it were polished surface of her skin there.

"Oh, it is useless to try and resist you," he said suddenly, with something like passion, and he inclined his head closer, ever closer, to hers.

"Do not stop," she entreated.

As he drew nearer, the blue arc that joined their heads glittered and crackled more brilliantly than before. Their abandon - everything about this moment - indicated that the mingling of their mental energies could only result in an explosion. When he made contact with her a small spasm of pleasure altered the features of his face. His chest purred, but not alarmingly as before. Instead, the female, with closed eyes, trance-like, suddenly articulated a long-held note, in a keening, operatic voice - not *fortissimo*, but not *piano*, either - that sounded like:

"N-y-e-e-h--"

In a moment her voice was joined by the male's, whose face had a similar enraptured expression. His voice was deeper, and reedy like a bass clarinet:

"W-a-a-a-h--"

Their duet was very loud in the cabin, but neither of them seemed aware of this. They both seemed to have lost their senses. In looking at the male or, alternately, the female, it seemed possible to distinguish the separate timbres of their voices, though they were joined in a common delirium. Now it seemed their auras were definitively conjoined, and bliss could be read plainly on their normally severe faces.

At that moment, the ship's second-in-command, who was also the chief resident philosopher and sometime ship's beadle, thought that he heard the noise, too. He happened to be making his circular round of the spaceship just as the team members' aria erupted within the cabin.

Frowning deeply, and without knocking, he pushed decisively upon the cabin door and pressed briskly into the room. He fully expected to find a scene of complete abandon here. However, the recovery of the two team members was remarkable for its swiftness. At the sound of the door opening, their attention turned immediately to the instrument panels in front of them. It was as though they had experienced such an interruption one or more times before and were used to it. They turned rather casually from the consoles and viewing screens to view the new arrival, nodding slightly and maintaining silence.

A whirring noise came from within the second-in-command's chest, and when he had their attention, he asked in a severe voice, "Is there a problem here?" He remained very still while his eyes searched the team member's faces.

The female found her voice first. "Problem, sir?"

"I thought I heard - shouting."

"Oh, no sir. We are discussing our report, captain, and what we would like to say about the Ben-Orans. At least, what we have learned about them, from up here, mostly." A small but very ingratiating smile appeared upon her face.

"Indeed." The captain looked unconvinced, remaining stock-still and casting his eyes about the large cabin. On one of the screens was a close-up of the female inhabitant - Amara - whose image he had seen a great deal of since the ship arrived.

"It is somewhat confusing," the male offered, regaining his composure. "Especially, being way up here, and not understanding what anyone is saying."

"Well, it is not likely that you could hide among them and observe them directly, do you think?" As he spoke, the long, delicate fingers of the individual they called "captain" drummed against his chest, which was covered with a blue jersey. His body was bent slightly forward at the waist, so that some of the features of his large head were cast into shadow; also his feet stood somewhat forward of his middle, so that in profile his body resembled a crescent moon. Like the other two, his normally severe face allowed for a limited range of expressiveness.

"And so, what are your impressions?"

"They are fascinating, sir," the male said. "But very --" he looked to the female.

"Very unsatisfactory, I think we would say," the female

finished.

"Indeed?" Looking at both of them. "Unsatisfactory how?"

The male said, "They seem to have some capacity for logical analysis. But this faculty seems undeveloped, or attenuated. As a result they are highly susceptible to unexamined and unsupported beliefs. The most powerful of what we would call their emotional stimuli is hatred, typically of whatever is different from themselves. And many will forego correct behavior for silver, which is their form of currency. This is all highly illogical, and confusing to us."

"It is not surprising that you would find them so. I confess I have been rather appalled, myself. They are not so far advanced technically, or, perhaps more importantly, in cultivating positive mental states. If they seem 'unsatisfactory,' then I suppose that it hardly matters, because there is nothing that we need of them."

The video screen before them showed the woman speaking, and another the government's forces, massed and moving inexorably forward. A team of water buffalo strained in front of a cart that was mired in the soggy ground, and one of the government's soldiers bawled and lashed at the animals furiously.

"No," the captain continued, "we shall not make any use of them. Oh, I should hate to see these individuals used for any mere mercenary purpose - as they were before, I mean. That is not correct, and it is against *our* policy, at any rate."

"With respect, sir," the female began, "it is a dangerous situation below. Can their situation be improved?"

"It is entirely up to them."

"Isn't there something that we can do, sir?"

"Us? Why, to interact with them at all would violate several protocols."

"I think that I understand why," the male one said tentatively.

"It is very simple. Contacting them is simply not within our charter. And it could have unintended consequences."

"Such as what?" the female asked.

"Well" - very deliberately, his long fingers meeting in front of his chest - "you see their stage of development. If they were to become aware of our existence, what would it do their image of themselves? Why, it could alter their history.""

The male said, "With all respect, sir. You see the situation now."

One of the screens showed a group of Elohin looking up and listening with obvious concentration. The fingers of some played restlessly about their faces, and some looked at one another and spoke briefly.

The second-in-command said, "Do you mean this battle that is to come? Well, it is a shame if those individuals have been misjudged. Some say that they were not really to blame."

"Sir," the female said, there is no evidence that the minority group is responsible for any of what happened. The Tekerin invaded and they took what they wanted for as long as they were able. There might have been some Ben-Orans who benefited from the occupation, but clearly it was not the Elohin, who seem rather to have placed themselves closest to the danger."

"I believe you are right. The tragedy is that the majority population believe otherwise. I wonder if any of them pause to look rationally at the situation. No, the conflict is based rather on a kind of received wisdom which is nothing of the sort, which is by now impressed upon them as solemn truth. It is a conflict that has gradually rent their society. The god that they worship inflames rather than moderates their reckless behavior. Where will it end? I would like to know."

The captain was indulging a philosophical streak which was well known to the entire ship's crew. "I would be glad," he continued, "if the Ben-Orans could solve their problems. But as for our contacting them, do not think about it."

This did not appear to satisfy the two crew members, whose gazes shifted between the monitoring screens and the captain's face. "This female," he continued, nodding toward one of the monitors, is she a leader of the minority group?"

"I believe she is," the female crew member said. "What her experiences were I do not know. She seems to have drifted to this mountain stronghold among thousands of others. My impression is that the minority group has asked her to lead, and that she did not strive to be so. From the way that the others regard her it is evident that she has acquired some particular status. It may be due to her innate qualities, which many seem to find irresistible" - she looked meaningfully at her male colleague, whose face remained a mask, however - "or it may be that the experiences she has survived, about which we do not know anything, have given her a special status among her kind. I confess that I rather admire her myself."

She glanced at her male colleague again; this time she did draw a response from him, a look of mild surprise.

On a monitor which depicted the scene which was only a few hours of travel from the mountains where the Elohin were massed, the Government's army moved from the left to right over what appeared to be the first foothills of the mountains. The soldiers looked quite derelict. Some had firearms strapped across their chests or in side holsters, others carried short swords or bows-and-arrows or the like. At intervals were individual water buffalo, or teams, drawing variously sized carts filled with provisions. Some of the carts were open platforms with primitive cannon mounted upon them. The heavier vehicles bogged down in the fields or rutted roadways that the army traveled, and needed frequently to be shoved and lifted by nearby troops. Faces of squadron leaders barked furiously upon the screens. Among troops which had paused momentarily, there would appear individuals who from their actions and the fury of their speech evidently shouted invective against their enemies, the Elohin.

"It is extraordinary," the captain said. "They profess love for that which they call the creator of their world, but it is hatred which rules their minds."

The junior crew members watched the scene closely, and, sensing their apprehension, the captain directed their view back to the woman, who looked over the assembled crowd and waited to speak again. The look on her face was determined, almost smiling, and she began to speak.

The captain asked, "What do you think she is saying to them?"

The female crew member, her thoughts a little gloomy, replied, "Sir, I would not have any idea, not understanding her language."

"I know that, but--" The captain moved closer to the seated female crew member and placed a hand on her shoulder. "Can you imagine what she might be saying to her peers? No?"

A proverbial warm glow - a happiness almost sufficient to dispel the gloom of her thoughts - suffused her as a result of this collegial hand placed upon her shoulder, and something made her turn to look at her male colleague, to be sure he noticed that one had not been given to him.

"I am afraid," she said, "that I do not have what you would call the imagination to try and guess."

"No? And yet I have been told that there are some species who can freely imagine what they cannot see or hear. And in writing their histories, when a leader addresses his, or her, forces before a battle, the author attributes all manner of inspiring speeches to the leader, and creates a very entertaining narrative, indeed."

The female crew member was silent, and the male

(speaking for both of them, perhaps) said, "With all respect, sir, what is the point of speculating, since it is not helping anything?"

The captain could only respond with something like, "Well, well."

"Sir," the female said. "There is something that puzzles me about the Ben-Orans. I cannot describe it well, and I cannot come to terms with it. Perhaps you can explain it for me. It is as though - they choose to believe, the things they wish to be so."

The captain looked at her and thought for a moment. "I think I will agree with you. The inhabitants allow rash judgments to take the place of truths. And yet, you will find that such tendencies are not so uncommon."

"Really, sir? I find it surprising."

The captain continued, soberly, but with a certain sparkle in his eye which was stimulated by this young female's insights. "In many particulars, they remind me of a species that I observed on another planet, a long time ago. The inhabitants called their home, Earth."

The male crew member said, "Indeed, I have never heard of it. And do those individuals still exist?"

"It is a long time ago now. I have not thought to check in some time," the captain said.

The images on the monitors alternated, small scripts on the bottom giving the vicinities of the various scenes. Captain and crew members watched the images. It felt to them that they had reached what conclusions they could, and that there was nothing more to be done. This occasioned some regrets for the two team members, and for the captain, a certain wistfulness.

But as they watched one of the monitors, a direct down-scan of the advancing government forces, they all saw at once that a certain disarray had overcome the solid file of soldiers. What was more, most of them were now staring directly up into the sky. Some stopped in their tracks, some appeared to crouch in fear, and some ran wildly back in the direction from which they had come.

The three crew members looked among themselves in wonder. A close-up revealed looks of terror on the faces of the government forces, and panicked stares up into the sky. In several places, the troops attempted laboriously to change the direction of the carts and teams of water buffalo, hampered by what was becoming a full-scale retreat of the soldiers on the ground. They seemed at the moment to lack any clear leadership. The up-turned, panicked faces stared wildly in the direction of the great ship, in fact.

On the ground below, the faint whirr of the hovering craft sounded like a ghostly and otherworldly chorus of treble voices.

Slowly, carefully, as though he felt himself to be under direct scrutiny, the captain moved toward the console and then with one long and delicate finger he pressed down and a voice was heard in response, "Navigation," followed by the identifying name of the assigned crew member.

The captain introduced himself, and in a controlled voice he asked, "Lieutenant, what is our approximate altitude?"

"Our altitude, ah--"

"Lieutenant, I have rather remarkable news: our subjects down there can see us."

"See us, sir? Is that poss-- Oh. Correct, sir. We are at--" And the navigation officer provided the ship's approximate altitude, in the units that were understood by the crew.

"Are we stable?" the captain asked.

In a moment, "Yes. Shall I increase altitude, sir? Sir?"

"Maintain altitude." The captain studied a screen which showed a large wagon and team being laboriously turned around in the confusion, while other forces ran past pell-mell to either side of the cart and the straining, lumbering animals. The screen blanked and was replaced with a panoramic view, in which the reverse flight of the soldiers resembled more a swarm of insects, creating steady movement to the right, away from the mountains and the Elohin.

The Elohin appeared as yet unchanged, and uninformed of the precipitate flight of the government's forces. Nor, evidently, was the presence of the visitors' ship known to them, due perhaps to their placement on the side of the mountain.

The junior crew members looked at each other in consternation.

The captain said to them, coolly, "You were asking before if there was anything that we could do. It is possible that in our rather careless way we have done enough - or more than enough. But whether we have helped in the long term, I cannot guess."

The three of them continued watching the scene below as represented on the shifting monitors. Time passed, and with it the distance grew between the opposed forces. Amara's face seemed, still, amid the chaos, the picture of calm and determination. She spoke a short sentence, it seemed, and then waited as its meaning was murmured down through the Elohin assembled on the hillside.

The captain judged that the other army's retreat was now irreversible. As they all watched, the woman's face turned to the side as other leaders crowded near her with what must have been news of the government army's retreat. A special light suffused her face as she looked over the crowd. The Elohin were seen elsewhere, embracing and celebrating the unexpected development. Tears of gratefulness shone upon many of their faces.

"My crew," the captain said, and pressing on the console he added, "Lieutenant, I believe that our adventure here is complete."

"Awaiting orders, sir," the lieutenant said.

The captain left the intercom on, and pressing with his

long fingers upon the console, he blanked and then retracted many of the screens above, except for the one view that was still centered on Amara's face. Away from the screen, through the panoramic windows of the cabin could now be seen brown soil, rock and verdant hills, the pale green of the sky, and a distant prospect of a blue lake.

The captain said wistfully, "We are done here." Then in a brighter voice, and as though speaking to himself, "So hail and farewell, bright blue planet!" He raised up and extended his hands almost tenderly, greatly surprising his crew members, saying:

"In wisdom may you find peace."

Within the limited expressiveness of the captain's face, looks of profound doubt alternated with a stubborn optimism as to the outcome. On the screen, the woman's face froze, and then faded from view.

"You may bring us up, Lieutenant!"

AUTHOR'S AFTERWORD

"I Know Her So Well" -
A Heroine in a World on the Edge of Chaos

When I drive by the East Williston train station on Long Island on my way to work each morning - it is a stop on the Oyster Bay line to and from Manhattan - I sometimes see the 7:26 am train for the city already waiting on the platform. It takes my mind back to an autumn of some years ago, when I was developing the chapters and story ideas that would become the novel I would call <u>Pastoral of a Far Land</u>. This city-bound train sits on the "wrong" side of the track, and by some combination of scheduling and track-switching of long standing, none of the Oyster Bay-bound trains arrive in the interval. The 7:26 is sometimes there before seven at East Williston, while a couple of Manhattan-bound trains arrive and leave on the "correct" side of the track.

When I must travel to the city on a weekday, I prefer to take the 7:26 if possible, because it is one of the few ones that doesn't require the rider to change trains at the Jamaica (Queens) station. If you must transfer, you may be lucky to find a free seat, or you may stand near the doors until you arrive at Penn Station. I generally took this train for a period during that autumn, when I made several visits to a Midtown periodontist. This was when I was first developing ideas for my story, and I would record some of them in a small notebook, or if I did not have that, on scraps of paper - either when I was standing on the train platform and waiting, or else while sitting on the train, while it waited on the platform or after it started moving. These were excellent moments for thinking about the story and writing down notes for dialogue or action scenes and the like.

I can remember for example taking notes for what would become the first of the novel's memory chapters, the one showing my heroine Amara as a girl in the schoolyard: the snow on the ground, the flakes of soot in the air from the school furnace, the intense purple-red color of the quarried stone of the school building, and the antagonistic and scurrilous remarks of the girl's fellow students, who share all of the prejudicial and hateful beliefs of the majority against the minority Elohin. These scenes describing the girl's surroundings, and the schoolyard skirmishes, I lived very intensely in my mind, while I watched the autumn leaves falling onto the platform, or the passing scene from the train window of the trees turning red and gold. To be sure, from my train window many of these trees were ailanthus or "weed trees" sprung up around metal-salvage yards or railroad yards, but others were attractive oaks and maples in suburban communities near the Queens-Nassau County line. As I imagined my heroine persevering in her harsh and lonely surroundings, I suppose that I began to fall in love with her on some level.

And I think it's true, returning to my head-note, that I do understand the heroine very well: her ironic humor, which never seems to desert her except maybe in a few scenes of peril, and the flash of anger when she encounters injustice. Her idealism, her spirituality, her store of bittersweet memories. I was going to say her burden of memories, but that wouldn't be fair, because there is both good and bad in those memories, and, taken together, they are a part of who she is. So I think it is fair to say that I have understood at least one female, and whether she is made of flesh and blood, or is assembled (as here) from imaginary artifacts, either way that is an accomplishment of some kind.

Those times when I was waiting for or riding on the train were very fruitful, and physical details about how my mysterious planet of Ben-Ora looked, and scraps of dialogue, all came to my mind in a real profusion. I suppose that at these times I was very much to myself, in a sort of zone, and not much good for conversation with strangers. But in greater New York City that is of very little concern, as the casual conversation with a stranger is a rare thing. New Yorkers will always allow a person plenty of space, and it is even possible for many people here to fall into a labyrinth of solitude (in Mario Vargas Llosa's memorable phrase) - but that is the subject of a different essay.

Another day, while listening to the radio in a quiet, reflective moment, I heard the Simon and Garfunkel song, "The Boxer" - "In the clearing stands a boxer" - and an entire scene appeared before me ready-made. In fifteen minutes of note-taking I had the principal events and dialogue - the fighter's role in aiding the heroine in a situation where she was clearly overmatched - completely described in outline. I had a new and memorable character - The Fighter - to share the woman's adventures, and with his appearance the possibility of more varied and colorful dialogue, along with someone who is the embodiment of loyalty and decency in a corner of the universe that is hard-pressed for both. There is nothing of "The Boxer" in this chapter, the song supplied only a feeling, rather. The idea for that chapter was completely serendipitous. There really were times when as a prospective author I felt that I had only to listen and transcribe some extraordinary melodies that I could hear in the air. To some it might appear far-fetched to suggest that the story, and the means to express it, were providential gifts from God. Whether very many can believe such a thing today is an interesting question. Certainly *I* felt blessed, and still do, to have been given, from out of nowhere, a story to tell that engaged my mind completely.

As I view things now, it was the strangeness of my premise that really proved liberating to the writing of the story. Previously I had been thinking about a story of human prejudices, and the superficial judgments which all too often pass for truths among people in all societies. I had in mind, too, a story of heroism, which is a rare quality to find in our world today, which is so rife with self-interest and dishonesty. I suppose that is one of the reasons that I began to think about a very different setting, somewhere among the stars, but which might allow me to express a truth about human life and human destiny. On the simplest level, this setting meant that the story was no longer earth-bound, while the similar-but-different attitudes of the Ben-Orans toward their deity seemed to open up still another avenue for commenting upon the application and use and abuse of comparative religions on our planet Earth.

My characters, whether there is something strange about their appearance (the Elohin), or whether there is something awfully ugly about their thoughts - speaking about the overly impressionable majority population (but who are perhaps not so very different from Earth humans) - occupy a stage that is full of conflict. Extreme as the situation may appear, some readers have told me that the everyday hostility that is faced by the minority Elohin, and their turbulent lives of flight, danger and loneliness, are not so very different, historically, from the hardships that are faced by families whose lives have been scored by racial prejudice, or by an illness - mental illness, for example, or drug or alcohol dependency or other problems - and who have learned a defensiveness and separateness in response to a judging and sometimes hostile society, and who, like my minority, must also persevere in their own ways. Or at least, I think they mean to say, the relation of the Elohin, or the families I have mentioned, to their respective worlds differ only in a degree. And if the impressions of these readers are correct, there is a good deal of significance that lies below the surface of the story, which is as it should be. Who is to say if some may read this tale of adventure and conflict and challenge, and hear a sympathetic chord and think: It has been this way with me?

But if there are challenges faced by the minority on my mysterious planet, including a seemingly overwhelming tide of rote and backward thinking with its many harmful consequences, the story has also a kind of triumph and shows an indomitable will to persevere for what is right. Because I don't agree with many of those eggheads or members of the intelligentsia so-called, who seem to feel that if a story is not steeped in vice, hopelessness and degradation then it must not be significant. That is a paradigm that does no one any good.

I wrote the novel, rather quickly and very unexpectedly, mostly during a fall and winter. It was a case of writing under extreme necessity, and of theme meeting form in a most opportune way. Writing the novel, as I said, was something like hearing a song of joy, that I only had to listen for and transcribe. And at hours when I was not busy with other things like earning a living, and I found myself undistracted, the music would start up again when I listened for it. As a result there was very little of wasted time, or false starts. If there had been, I could not have finished the story in several months, when I was also working full-time, and relied for writing time primarily on the weekends, a few vacation days, and a couple of snow days when I would alternately write and shovel snow.

So I have often thought that no story was ever kinder to its author. I had ideas in plenty to sustain an effort of several months - chapter ideas, passages of dialogue or action sequences - and I recorded them and filled up about half of a legal-sized pad with notes. (I believe that an author's best ideas for a scene or other passage are his first ones, probably because the ideas are new to him and are presented most vividly and with greatest force; in no case should the author allow these ideas to simmer, but should write them down immediately as his first and best statement of the matter.) This pad, with a matching vinyl cover, I had bought impulsively while shopping at a five-and ten-cent store (or are they called dollar stores now) over the prior Labor Day weekend. I think now that I bought those materials on faith, thinking that some sort of story might come to my mind - but what kind of story, I had no idea. I had not written any new fiction in years.

Then in the months when I was at work on the book, sometimes I would look up at the sky, at the shifting formations of clouds, which have always struck me as ever unique, miraculous, and completely taken for granted by ninety-nine percent of human beings. I would think about my minority population also staring up into the sky, but finding a different and unearthly hue, as well as any number of the several moons that are visible at different times of the day or night upon the planet of Ben-Ora. I would imagine my hard-pressed minority as they struggled for survival amid the everyday slights and threats that were endemic in their world, and their cruel mass-incarceration which is underway when the story begins. I would picture the heroine, Amara, and her "kind" looking into the same sky as us, but from a different corner of our universe, and how they would wonder, but without a great deal of hope, if there was a way out of the madness of hate and unconsidered judgments, which condemned the Elohin to their lives of flight, struggle, and loneliness.

Perhaps the essential question of my story is: Will humans ever outgrow their madness? Is there yet hope for a spiritual revolution among people that is uncorrupted by self-interest, by smugness and intolerance of other beliefs, and hatred of those who are different from us, and by hypocrisy and cruelty, which are rife in the history of human development? For that matter, it is difficult to put one's faith in "religion," per se, because, clearly, religion has caused harm as well as good throughout history. It really is a profound question, then: Where will the requisite wisdom come from, if man is to outgrow his madness?

I am not any professional writer, only someone who enjoys language - I suppose, a sort of quaintly formal language, compared to the mostly vernacular writing which seems to predominate in novels of today. And I don't mean to disparage vernacular writing - one of my favorite authors, Chandler Brossard, excelled at this style. I studied creative writing with Chandler, and got to know him a bit when I lived in New York City. But Chandler wrote with a kind of poetry - parts of The Bold Saboteurs mark him as a rollicking Shakespeare of the vernacular style - whereas, too often today, the popular, colloquial style is a vice that often masks a poverty of language. For this reason, the popular style is lacking in challenge or interest, for some classes of readers.

But I began to say that I am someone who writes stories and novels from time to time under a sort of compulsion. I don't think that there is anything wrong with this. There is nothing that is more foreign to me, as someone who has been blessed to work for a living in the manufacturing world, as someone who defines himself (or herself) as "author," and who turns out a succession of books - because, "An author must write books!" - even when, as we very often see, many of the books lack inspiration and really have no reason for being. Really the worst reason for being that a book can have is that its author has decided that he or she is a novelist. It often happens that he started by writing one very good novel, and went on to write a string of them that had nothing like the vigor of that first book. Every reader, if he is honest with himself, will remember several such disappointing books where the well of inspiration had clearly run dry for the moment. This yields a book with little reason for being, except that the author decided that he is a full-time novelist and that what novelists must do is write.

So it may happen that an author has one good novel in him, if that, and then produces only derivative and unsatisfactory echoes for the rest of a writing career. Personally, if it happens that I don't ever again feel such a compulsion to write a book - if the story, personal circumstances, and alignment of the stars are not just so again - I won't grieve about it. It's a great blessing to have heard all of the right notes at least one time, even if I have rendered them somewhat imperfectly, and if there is no sequel I don't think I will be sad about it.

William Faulkner, having written <u>The Sound and the Fury</u>, did not owe the world anything more in an artistic sense. If he had written nothing else besides that masterpiece, and simply retired to his farm to raise racehorses and drink bourbon or whatever he pleased, only a few college professors should have found anything regrettable about it. This will sound like heresy to many, and not only to those hypothetical college professors. If a Harper Lee is remembered only or primarily for one book, I think it is more than enough. For one book, or short story or essay, or even a paragraph, may reveal the essence of one person's relation to the world.

Anyone who is fortunate enough to have spent any time away from cities - which have many attractions but may lead to a feeling of dislocation from nature - may have observed that annual southward migration of the tiger-colored butterflies of black and intense orange. (I think they may be called monarchs?) In New England you may see a profusion of these butterflies on a day in September, tending in a south-westerly direction toward Mexico, in which general area they (or those which complete the trek, anyway) will spend the winter. I remember seeing a long procession of them one day in coastal Rhode Island - imagine small groups, a few single stragglers, or large clutches of these delicate beasts passing all day long- all tending along the shore line where the land meets the relatively placid salt-ponds, a few miles inland from the ocean itself. And I remarked to myself then that following the shore line in southern Rhode Island and Connecticut, if that is what these delicate creatures were doing "by design" (or should I say "consciously?"), would certainly take them toward the sunnier climes that were their destination.

The naturalist writes about the many predators which the butterflies will face in their journey between the New England shore and Mexico, the unpredictable changes of weather and the danger of gusting winds near the surf. The poet describes the brilliance of the colors and the pathos of early autumn. The philosopher describes the arduousness of the three-thousand mile journey, the many dangers to be negotiated, and the odds of arriving at the destination, and reflects that the butterfly, driven as he is by instinct and seeing before him only his immediate goals and not his long-term chances of survival, presses on in his journey. Everyone brings his own special qualities and insights to the scene in question, which are all implicit in his account.

And if an author bring only one such scene to life, his or her insights are all implicit in the scene - his values, ironies, and perhaps, wisdom - and only the greedy or idle reader should clamor for more words, more essays, more books from him. We have all observed those really prolific novelists for whom writing has become a vice. They write just as naturally and predictably as certain organisms will ooze a substance. But you wish that instead of writing ten merely characteristic novels in as many years, they gave us instead one really essential one. This is a kind of pathology, and for those readers who clamor for still more works by these incessant scribblers, it is also a kind of vice, and a slavish devotion.

I read an article about one of those really indefatigable authors of fantasy novels, the kind with flying dragons, avuncular gnomes (which are endemic in the genre since the Star Wars movies), and maybe a Guinevere type of female astride a horse, with perhaps a kind of maul or battle-axe in her hands, or maybe just a new-style ray-gun. In these stories, the hero or heroine vanquishes enemies on almost every other page with a magical silver sword. I am not a fan of the genre. I don't think these can be called science-fiction novels, which are at least organized around some kernel of an idea, whether a good one or a bad one. You can guess from the covers, with their flying unicorns and things, just about what you would be in for as a reader.

Those authors are indefatigable, it seems, writing series after series, and still their devoted readers can never have enough of the stories. But I think that all of these stories and movies of "thrones," and dungeons-and-dragons fantasies which are so rife today, with their excessive gore, and their mock-portentousness, must be a colossal waste of time, not to mention a royal pain in the ass. They are ubiquitous, and they probably do not add measurably to the world's store of wisdom. And who can tell, for that matter, to what sorts of equally edifying characters the sword-wielding denizens of the genre will give way? No doubt there is an audience for such entertainments. But as my parents' generation liked to say, I would not go across the street to see them. And if any well-meaning person thought to buy me one of the recent tetralogies as a gift, for me they are so many nine-hundred page door-stops that I really do not need.

To speak more broadly about the august state of popular literature today. It appears that the vampires, like other dogs, have had their day (to paraphrase a remark of Lord Byron), and have been succeeded in the esteem of many by their close cousins, the zombies. Now there is a vogue in shape-shifters who change on a dime from human to snarling beasts, and back again, in many works inspired by a cabal of fabulist authors in recent years. "Private detective" crime-solvers of every stripe are in vogue, whether hard-boiled or warm and cuddly personalities. Like setters sniffing the air, they follow their leads in the single-minded pursuit of truth and justice – even, sometimes, on their own dimes. Of course they do.

I was surprised to have pointed out to me that one genre writer nowadays accounts for fully half of the books on the best-seller lists at any point in time. Reportedly he is a much more successful marketer than artist. Prolific, and slick as a harbor seal, he appears to be the current golden goose of the publishing world, a god of commerciality in its purest refined form. He is an established name, of course, a brand, and in this case familiarity breeds - well, not contempt, exactly, but perhaps a reassuring sense of a known quantity. And he has shrewdly realized that since his "brand" is so very marketable for the moment, it is not necessary to acquiesce to the limitations of what one author may humanly produce - even such a fecund imagination as that author's.

Instead (as I was surprised to learn in a magazine article), the author has set up a kind of "school" such as existed for Italian Renaissance painters, which allows him to partner with various genre-writers from around the world and so to produce multiple examples of these novels almost simultaneously, which become, in effect, like so many empty plates spinning in the air at once. One can only regret that Charles Dickens never thought of this expedient. I have only heard that the newer author is a bad and unimaginative writer, and also, reportedly, a rather kinky one. Life is short, and I have no wish to find out if these things are really true - no, not even in the interests of scientific inquiry.

This novel that I finished writing late one winter is the product of an occasional rather than a professional writer; as I have said, the work of someone who has worked for most of his life in the workaday world, and for whom writing is an avocation. This marks me immediately as an outsider to the game. Today in America (I can't speak for other societies), any would-be author who seeks to have his or her work reach the light of day faces tremendous odds. The work of creation must eventually confront the realities of the marketplace. And if creating his or her novel felt at all like the joy of transcribing a beautiful melody heard uniquely by the author, then it is at this point - when the prospective author asks only that "the media" read his work without prejudice, and without blinders, and comment intelligently upon it - then it is, that what began as a beautiful adventure may begin to feel more like (to quote a lyric of the late singer-songwriter Sandy Denny) a one-way donkey ride.

The problem may be, on the first level, that so many (shall we say) craftsmen are busily writing novels "to spec," that is to say in any one of the sixteen "flavors" or genres that are recognized within the publishing world - I should add, as of this month. But how much of it would be called good writing? In the arts today, everyone likes to say that they value originality, but this is almost never the case. Clearly it is fairer to say that within the cultural establishment what is perceived as most important is not the quality of the presentation, but rather does the work in question conform to a recognizable "type." If so, of course, then the work can then, conceivably, be marketed to a special "demographic." And this will appeal to that age-old faculty, devotion to the almighty dollar, which is no less strong in the publishing industry as in any other.

The problem with over-specialization, with writing by the numbers, is that trained monkeys can do it (or nearly so), and the results are generally insipid and have no savor for some classes of readers. With so many specialists plying their trades, is there a place for the sincere artist who thinks not of genre but only of his theme and the quality of the presentation? Who has told a story that is burned into his heart? It is an awfully depressing prospect. As if by pattern or conspiracy, the decline of America - as world power, as a society with values, as a place where Government exhibits some central planning instead of chaos, inaction and corruption - this decline goes hand in hand with a debased cultural life. How many original ideas have broken through the skeins of America's cultural establishment in recent years? If it has happened, was it by mistake? Instead of originality, one finds everywhere - in dime-store novels, in film and television and such - relentless attempts to piggy-back to some recent success.

In America it seems there is no shortage of published genre novels which feature formula-driven writing. What of the author who persists, through instinct or sheer stubbornness, in writing in some freely imagined vein of inspiration, and with evident sincerity, about something that he believes in? Will his or her work create an irremediable confusion and incomprehension among the minds of America's media insiders? Worse luck, if the treasure that he offers to the media may, even on a cursory review, be suspected of harboring an original idea - which is surely anathema in American cultural life today - then is the would-be author really shit out of luck?

In this universe, the artist who writes out of an inner compulsion and who chooses a form not because it is fashionable but only because it is congenial to him or her, and best suited to his materials – that author is rare, not to say endangered. Yet the sincere artist of today perseveres against the odds, and (to paraphrase the composer Edgar Varese) refuses to die. What the would-be author who is unpublished and without connections discovers, first of all, is that today the mainstream publishers will not even deign to read his or her work. Barred from direct contact, the would-be author is invited to partner with a type of intermediary, the literary agent. The notion seems to be that third-party agents act as proxies and intermediaries for America's cultural establishment, and may be trusted to know what submissions conform to this year's types and fashions, and might conceivably be saleable. This seems to be a new phenomenon of business practice in the publishing world, as it is now constituted. At least, insofar as an outsider can understand the process.

One publisher loftily writes on their website that they do not condescend to read just any would-be author's book (especially the outsider's, of course). They even say that if such people make the mistake of sending them any unsolicited material, they cannot guarantee that they will not make use of it somehow, without crediting the author. A neat trick! Now, chicanery and lack of ethics are not only accepted business practice in America, they are engraved on the company masthead! Much luck to them.

But from a business standpoint, is it a sound practice to leave the task of screening to third-party individuals? It seems a very odd state of affairs to anyone with any experience of working in American businesses. Would a restaurateur rely on a screening service to deliver the best available dinner rolls to his establishment, or would he prefer to investigate their quality for himself? The agents do not work for the publisher, and (except for a relative few) he does not know their tastes and prejudices.

Or in similar vein, imagine the case of an art gallery manager, who professes a love for contemporary art, and advises aspiring painters that he will not look at any images of original work that are sent to him, but that their work must be screened by third party individuals who do not work for the gallery owner and are not answerable to him, and who are basically of highly uncertain pulse and perceptiveness. A strange situation!

I have been sending extracts of my novel and trying

to establish an intelligent dialogue with representatives of the mass media, including third-party literary agents, but without receiving any constructive comments. Can the prospective author know what this third-party review actually entails? Is the person searching for literary merit, or the quality of ideas expressed? Perhaps. Can he know the values and capabilities of an agent? Their website may say that they care only about quality in writing, and only want to represent books that will add to the store of human happiness and society's advancement. How in the world do you know if this is true? It may be truer to say that some may actually be very comfortable with hackneyed novels that are not particularly well-written, but which in the person's view are of such a genre that they may stand a chance of piggy-backing to some other recent successes. The would-be author does not know if his or her work is being read without prejudice for the quality of the writing, or the significance of its themes, or if in fact this is a charade, merely a vetting process to identify work which may have commercial appeal, and which fits comfortably within a recognizable type or category, while rejecting work whose themes might, even on a cursory review, appear to be intellectually challenging - God forbid!

If the search criteria is the dropped name, or some hint that the author's work might be profitable, or that the would-be author has a certain academic pedigree, such as graduating a writing program that teaches a style of writing that is in vogue this year, then perhaps what is being screened out in this process is anything that is off of the commercial radar. But it would be very surprising if talent were the exclusive province of those with insider status, the well-connected, or holders of narrow academic pedigrees. If life were that simple then talent could be created by prescription and replicated at will by entrenched media insiders. But I don't think that talent, or the intrinsic interest of a work of art, correlate at all with secondary factors such as insider status, specialized training, or striving to write for a narrow audience.

The prospective author would like to receive constructive and intelligent comments about his work, and not a going-through-the-motions, pro-forma "response." If there even is a response. For that matter, given the general state of manners today, and with the adoption of new media like the e-mail, there is no longer a protocol for whether the author's queries will receive an answer. I say that no protocol exists - as for manners, one can forget about them in our age. Words like "manners," along with equally quaint terms like "loyalty," are found today only in dictionaries and books of Victorian poetry. That unfortunately is the world that we live in.

I sent extracts of the novel to many third-party agents, without receiving any indication that any among them engaged intellectually with the themes or the language of the book. When communication often appears to be a one-way street, some prospective authors may wonder if there is value in the process, and is it credible and as advertised. Does it makes sense to continue circulating his or her intellectual capital among individuals who seem unable to make any use of it? For me, what a waste of time that now seems! Yet my experiences were quite different in the more companionable venues of public libraries when I presented chapters of the novel, and in other venues; there, the material generally seemed to strike a chord with listeners.

But so went my communications with agents and such, one-sided as they were. Some kind of vetting process is going on here, presumably, but it seems to have little to do with quality. The current emphasis may be for a kind of casual "expressiveness" without a good deal of style, and perhaps not a great deal of what used to be called good writing. And for some readers, this could result in a lack of savor. One has the feeling sometimes that any required thinking has already been done for the reader - but is this a good thing? Some of the public avoid most of the effluvia of the mass media for these reasons. Anyway, such was my experience with reaching out to agents. I think if I had cadged a few passages from Shakespeare or the King James Bible and sent them, it probably would not have made any difference to that audience. The process does not feel credible. And after awhile, does it not appear that, in the Biblical phrase, one is only placing more pearls before swine?

Viewed in this light, the current practice seems to indicate a fundamental lack of sincerity on the part of publishers in finding an original voice, and to some degree it reflects a belief that what is needed above all is a shrewd judge of the saleability of a new work. Above all does the work conform to one of the distinct "types" or genres that the publishing world currently favors. One may well wonder, Does the mass media have any relevance to the flow of new and original ideas? Or is the main consideration rather, Is there that alluring and all-important smell of money about the work in question?

It is fair to say that we live in an age of specialization. It is also, in terms of the arts, very often an age of banality, and the observer of society can see for himself the kind of work that the caretakers of America's cultural establishment continue to present to the public. About literature per se, I have probably said enough. About films or television, it is probably best to say nothing at all. It feels as though a place of creative exhaustion has been reached, where a viewer looks with relief to find an honest and unscripted sporting event, as comparatively more entertaining than the other shows that fill most of the schedule.

One might make a singular exception for the sphere of classical music, where magazine editors are stalwart in upholding the old standards, and performers and musicologists continue to discover forgotten classics of the Baroque and other eras, and bring them gratifyingly to life for appreciative audiences. But in this classical music sphere we are speaking about the "two-to-three percent" of the record-buying public (to coin an old-fashioned term), which in itself may say something about the state of cultural life today.

As I write, prospects for my novel reaching many readers still remain uncertain. For me it ought to be a time of harvest, after the mingled work and exhilaration of producing the book. I want to remain positive, and some recognition would be preferable to anonymity. But in my mind, in some way, the possibility of reaching many readers is secondary to having produced the work. Rather than feel discouragement or bitterness, I would rather dwell in the atmosphere of courage, high spirits, humor and perseverance that, for me, also characterize the novel. Perhaps this means that I wrote it for the right reasons. I know that I was blessed to be able to write it, whatever interest it may attract.

If my fantasy does not please everyone - does not, in the minds of some, quite get to the heart of society's modern malaise - then I have done my best. One can't please everyone. More than ever today, original thinking seems to be dying on the vine, and the process is accelerated by widespread, almost constant exposure to the mass media which is made possible by the new technologies. Some have suggested that the long term goal of segments of the mass media is to further dumb down the public. This is an interesting idea. More than ever, there are many people who confuse wisdom with simply learning to think like their peer group (which is not wisdom at all), and critical acumen with simply liking what is in style. The lousy Philistines used to make fun of the Bible, too, and history has judged them as a scurvy lot of ultra-conformists who, like some others that I have been writing about, were impervious to any new ideas, and even boasted of the fact.

www.ingramcontent.com/pod-product-compliance
Lightning Source LLC
LaVergne TN
LVHW091537060526
838200LV00036B/640